Final Failure
Eyeball to Eyeball

Book 1 of an Alternate
Cuban Missile Crisis

by Douglas Niles

Contents

"Now the question really is what action we take which lessens the chance of a nuclear exchange, which obviously is the final failure."

President John Fitzgerald Kennedy
ExComm Meeting, 18 October 1962
White House, Washington D.C.

Final Failure is a five-book story of alternate history, set during a fictional Cuban Nuclear War of 1962. Some of the characters are actual historical figures, while others are the creations of the author. In each case, the narrative follows the conventions of historical fiction with regard to accurate portrayal of events...until a fictional incident on October 27, 1962, becomes the point of departure into alternate history.

In other words, this is a true tale of What Might Have Been.

For additional details, and updates regarding upcoming books in the *Final Failure* series, please visit <u>douglasniles.com</u> or <u>facebook.com/AuthorDouglasNiles</u>.

To Michael S. Dobson,

*In sincere remembrance of all the history, both actual and "alternate,"
we've shared over the years*

Prologue: P-Hour

"Let every nation know…that we shall pay any price, bear any burden, meet any hardship, support any friend, oppose any foe, to assure the survival and the success of liberty."

President John Fitzgerald Kennedy
Inaugural Address, 20 January 1961

22 October 1962
1852 hours EST (Monday Evening)
Oval Office, The White House
Washington D.C.

The Oval Office had been transformed into a reasonable approximation of a television studio. Sound and power cables snaked across the floor, which had been covered with a tarpaulin to protect the carpet. The massive wooden desk, constructed from timbers once part of the warship HMS *Resolute*, was now draped in black felt, with a backdrop of similar material, decorated only by the Presidential flag, hanging behind. Furniture was shunted aside to make room for multiple microphones, two cameras, recording equipment, and large banks of lights.

Now that all was ready, the technicians and publicity people withdrew. Attorney General Bobby Kennedy and the President's secretary, Evelyn Lincoln, were the only people in the Oval Office as the President entered from the side door, walking stiffly as he approached his chair. With one hand propped on the corner of the desk, John Fitzgerald Kennedy limped to the seat and collapsed, wincing in pain.

His younger brother offered no reaction. Jack Kennedy's back pain was a daily feature of his life, and the President

1

resented any attempts at sympathy or what he described as coddling. Eventually, he would accept a shot or two of pain medication, but as the clock approached the moment that the administration had designated as P-Hour—7:00 PM on this crucial evening—such steroid and narcotic relief would have to wait.

The television cameras were already focused, hulking robots with glass eyes trained on the massive desk and the man sitting behind it. Bobby adjusted a pillow behind his brother's back, helping him to sit straight in the chair.

"How's that, Jack?" he asked. "Do you want another pillow? Should I move the chair back a bit?"

"No, it's fine—thanks. Let's get going," the chief executive replied curtly.

Evelyn Lincoln reached a brush toward the President's slightly mussed brown hair, but he waved her away and straightened it using his hand.

With a glance at the clock, JFK nodded his readiness.

"Better send them in," he said.

Bobby went to the door and opened it, allowing Press Secretary Pierre Salinger to lead the cameramen and several sound and lighting technicians, all of them men dressed in suits, into the office. Each took up his station, the sound men kneeling before the black-draped platform as the bright lights came on one by one, washing the desk and its occupant in a bright arc of illumination. Bobby saw that Jack's face was already composed, free of any evidence of pain. Instead, he looked stern, serious…Presidential.

With an eye on the clock, Salinger nodded at the President. "Alright, Sir. We're on in ten seconds." He paused, hand upraised, and counted down with his fingers.

"Three, two, one."

John F. Kennedy stared squarely into the camera and began to speak, his familiar New England twang clipping each word with earnest intensity.

"Good evening, my fellow citizens.

"This government, as promised, has maintained the closest surveillance of the Soviet military buildup on the island of Cuba. Within the past week, unmistakable evidence has established the fact that a series of offensive missile sites is now in preparation on that imprisoned island. The purpose of these bases can be none other than to provide a nuclear strike capability against the Western Hemisphere.

"Upon receiving the first preliminary hard information of this nature last Tuesday morning at 9 A.M., I directed that our surveillance be stepped up. And having now confirmed and completed our evaluation of the evidence and our decision on a course of action, this government feels obliged to report this new crisis to you in fullest detail."

1901 hours EST (Monday Evening)
Harry S. Truman Annex
Key West Naval Air Station
Key West, Florida

Commander Alex Widener stood on the tarmac just outside of the pilots' ready room and watched the last of his F6A Skyrays, turbojet engine roaring as the afterburner spewed yellow flame, shoot down the runway. The powerful delta-wing fighter rose swiftly into the sunset shimmering over the Florida Strait.

At last: the base's entire fighter squadron, twelve aircraft, was aloft. The mission was combat air patrol, or CAP. The Skyray was a high-speed fighter capable of aerial combat at altitudes of 50,000 feet or more. Patrolling in pairs, the dozen planes of Widener's squadron already approached their stations, circling lazily, strung out along the Keys and ready to intercept any threat from the south.

And the commander knew that, for the first time in a long, long time, those pilots on the CAP mission faced the possibility of actual combat. Key West was the US territory closest to the island of Cuba, and Cuba had been the focus of an awful lot of American scrutiny over the last few months—scrutiny that had been immensely heightened in this past week. Widener, the base CO, was certain that the President's speech tonight, the television address announced only earlier in the day, would deal with the crisis.

Having seen the last of his charges into the sky, the commander looked at the hangars and the still-crowded assembly areas on the tarmac. Key West had never hosted so many planes, he knew: In addition to the fighter squadron, he'd been tasked with housing a squadron of RF8A Crusader low-range reconnaissance aircraft and a detachment of large, modern F4 Phantom fighters. He had just learned that a battery of Hawk antiaircraft missiles was on the way from Fort Meade, Maryland, and he been ordered to find space for a full Marine Air Group, fighters and ground-attack planes, that could be ordered here any day from California.

As he returned to the ready room, he was fully aware that something big was going on. Inside the steamy quonset hut, Chief Petty Officer Sullivan adjusted the rabbit ears on the little black-and-white television set, and by the time Widener had reached his desk, the picture was at least recognizable as the President. That Bostonian voice, flat and distinctive, was unmistakable even over the slight hiss of the feeble reception, and as he listened Widener immediately realized that things were every bit as serious as he had suspected.

"The characteristics of these new missile sites indicate two distinct types of installations," Kennedy said. "Several of them include medium-range ballistic missiles, capable of carrying a nuclear warhead for a distance of more than 1,000 nautical miles. Each of these missiles, in short, is capable of striking Washington, D.C., the Panama Canal, Cape Canaveral, Mexico City, or any other city in the southeastern part of the United States, in Central America, or in the Caribbean area."

The commander nodded his head in appreciation of the tactic. The President was making it clear that this was not just a problem for the United States, but a threat to the entire hemisphere. Widener had voted for Nixon in the '60 election, and had been vocally skeptical of the young Democratic Chief Executive following the debacle at the Bay of Pigs—when JFK had refused to authorize the air and naval support that might have given the anti-Castro Cubans of the invasion force a chance at survival. But he could only approve of Kennedy's resolute approach to the current situation.

He squinted as a picture, a photo reconnaissance shot with labels indicating various installations, replaced the President's face on the screen. The picture was too fuzzy to make out the details, but he knew he was looking at a missile base on the island nation just ninety miles to the south.

"Additional sites not yet completed appear to be designed for intermediate-range ballistic missiles—capable of traveling more than twice as far—and thus capable of striking most of the major cities in the Western Hemisphere, ranging as far north as Hudson Bay, Canada, and as far south as Lima, Peru," the President continued, ticking off facts like a prosecutor.

"In addition, jet bombers, capable of carrying nuclear weapons, are now being uncrated and assembled in Cuba, while the necessary air bases are being prepared...."

1902 hours EST (Monday evening)
Newsroom
NBC Washington Bureau
Washington, D.C.

The reporters clustered around the large TV monitor and watched the address in uncharacteristic silence. Each was aware of history in the making. Each knew that this was a major story, and each mentally ticked off every source that might provide a unique vantage. Each journalist planned phone calls, envisioned interviews, thought about hypothetical assignments.

And each of them, but one, was a man.

Stella Widener didn't take notes. The President's address to the nation was being recorded right here in the newsroom, and she would consult the film record—probably many times—before writing her story. In fact, she had written the story, had pieced together the situation before anyone else at her network. But when she'd presented it to her news director just this morning, he'd order her to kill it—because of pressure from the White House. Now, she could only stare at the screen, at that handsome, grim face. She listened to the chilling words in a room that was otherwise silent until, finally, her cynical and worldly colleagues could no longer restrain the need to comment.

"Damn, I thought for sure it was going to be Berlin again," one veteran newsman finally remarked, when JFK paused to take a breath.

"Nah, this year it's all about Castro," another replied knowingly. "And the Russians—this is some serious stuff."

"Hey, Stella," said a third. "Good thing you got out of Moscow when you did—they'd probably be sending you to a gulag if you hadn't finished filming two months ago!"

The gallows humor got a good laugh, heartened by the professional jealousy these men felt for the woman who had scooped them all with the first American film footage shot inside the Kremlin. Since her return to D.C. in late September, Stella had endured a constant barrage of suggestive remarks as veteran newshounds badgered her about how she had gotten Khrushchev to allow her to film the documentary. They wouldn't believe the truth—that it was good old-fashioned stubbornness and perseverance. She was a good reporter who relied on her skills and professional acumen to get the story.

But, she remembered, there was one dramatic exception. She flushed at a private memory: herself as a young reporter for the Boston Globe...a visit to a hotel suite to interview Massachusetts' young, handsome, and recently married senator...the interview that had propelled her career to undreamed of heights...the closeness of that familiar voice, and face, that filled the television screen before her now.

"Shh!" she said impatiently, trying to hear the speech—and to will herself away from the guilty memory. The men complied, no doubt because they, too, were fascinated by the portentous address. The President looked tired, Stella thought, as JFK continued. And kind of angry, as well.

"This urgent transformation of Cuba into an important strategic base—by the presence of these large, long-range, and clearly offensive weapons of sudden mass destruction—constitutes an explicit threat to the peace and security of all the Americas, in flagrant and deliberate defiance of the Rio Pact of 1947, the traditions of this nation and hemisphere, the joint resolution of the 87th Congress, the Charter of the United Nations, and my own public warnings to the Soviets on September 4 and 13. This action also contradicts the repeated assurances of Soviet spokesmen, both publicly and privately delivered, that the arms buildup in Cuba would retain its original defensive character, and that the Soviet Union had no need or desire to station strategic missiles on the territory of any other nation."

One reporter dashed to a typewriter at the back of the room, and seconds later the machine's keys chattered loudly, a frantic cadence underlying the urgency of the speech. No one else tore himself away, at least not yet.

"Do you suppose it's war?" someone mused rhetorically.

"No," Stella replied. "He wouldn't be announcing it like this if it was." She couldn't help thinking of her brother and father, and knew that if it came to war, they would both be on the front lines.

"The size of this undertaking makes clear that it has been planned for some months," the President accused. "Yet, only last month, after I had made clear the distinction between any introduction of ground-to-ground missiles and the existence of defensive antiaircraft missiles, the Soviet Government publicly stated on September 11 that, and I quote, 'the armaments and military equipment sent to Cuba are designed exclusively for defensive purposes,' that there is, and I quote the Soviet Government, 'there is no need for the Soviet Government to shift its weapons for a retaliatory blow to any other country, for instance Cuba,' and that, and I quote their government, 'the Soviet Union has so powerful rockets to carry these nuclear warheads that there is no need to search for sites for them beyond the boundaries of the Soviet Union.'

"That statement was false."

1905 hours EST (Monday Evening)
Bachelor Officers' Quarters
82nd Airborne Division
Fort Bragg, North Carolina

Second Lieutenant Greg Hartley was drunk, but not drunk enough. It seemed that the 82nd Airborne was going to war: all leaves cancelled for the entire unit, new orders coming down practically by the hour, a general stir of excitement permeating the ranks of officers and men. Still, the division's junior officers had been issued one last allotment of two beers apiece—just for today. Hartley had quickly consumed his own pair of Old Milwaukees, and since late afternoon had been buying bottles from his fellow officers. The going rate was $2.00 apiece.

In Hartley's somewhat fog-shrouded mind, it had been a good use of $14.00. Now, however, although he had money in his wallet and thirst in his throat, the supply seemed to have dried up. Having struck out on his last pass through the hall, he staggered slightly as he entered the BOQ's common room, standing behind a dozen or so other junior officers who all had their attention glued to the television set.

President Kennedy was talking. Hartley didn't want to watch, or listen, but like a moth drawn to some horrible, consuming flame, he found himself paying attention to his Commander in Chief's stark, frightening words.

"Only last Thursday, as evidence of this rapid offensive buildup was already in my hand, Soviet Foreign Minister Gromyko told me in my office that he was instructed to make it clear once again, as he said his government had already done, that Soviet assistance to Cuba, and I quote, 'pursued solely the purpose of contributing to the defense capabilities of Cuba,' that, and I quote him, 'training by Soviet specialists of Cuban nationals in handling defensive armaments was by no means offensive, and if it were otherwise,' Mr. Gromyko went on, 'the Soviet Government would never become involved in rendering such assistance.'

"That statement also was false."

1910 hours EST (Tuesday very early morning)
Chairman's Office, Kremlin
Moscow, Russian SSR
Union of Soviet Socialist Republics

Communist Party Chairman Nikita Khrushchev, his fist clenched so tightly that the paper crumpled in his hand, read a translated version of the speech as the actual broadcast—carried to Europe by America's imperial communications satellite, *Telstar*—droned from a radio speaker nearby. The translation had been delivered to him just during the last hour, courtesy of the American ambassador to the USSR.

In the large but Spartan office with the chairman was Foreign Minister Gromyko, recently returned from the United States, as well as Khrushchev's military adviser, Defense Minister Rodion Malinovsky. Gromyko's round face was beet red, his flabby jaw clenched as tightly as possible. Malinovsky's eyes remained downcast.

The other two men read from their own copies of the speech, and they understood the challenge that Kennedy was presenting them all. Both studiously avoided looking at the chairman.

"Acting, therefore, in the defense of our own security and of the entire Western Hemisphere, and under the authority entrusted to me by the Constitution as endorsed by the Resolution of the Congress, I have directed that the following initial steps be taken immediately," declared the American Commander in Chief.

"First: To halt this offensive buildup, a strict quarantine on all offensive military equipment under shipment to Cuba is being initiated. All ships of any kind bound for Cuba from whatever nation or port will, if found to contain cargoes of offensive weapons, be turned back. This quarantine will be extended, if needed, to other types of cargo and carriers. We are not at this time, however, denying the necessities of life as the Soviets attempted to do in their Berlin blockade of 1948."

"How dare he!" Khrushchev demanded hoarsely. "We will destroy him! He will not—he cannot—an impudent neophyte—a mere boy wearing man's pants!" But the bombast sounded hollow even in his own ears, and the familiar fears rose up.

Have I made a terrible mistake? If only they had discovered the missiles a week, two weeks, from now! All the launchers would be in place, ready to fire! What if...? His thoughts were jumbled, chaotic. He needed to think, to decide, to act! But all he could do was read, and listen, and feel a growing sickness in the pit of his stomach.

The President of the United States continued. "Second: I have directed the continued and increased close surveillance of Cuba and its military buildup. The foreign ministers of the Organization of American States, in their communiqué of October 6, rejected secrecy on such matters in this hemisphere. Should these offensive military preparations continue, thus increasing the threat to the hemisphere, further action will be justified. I have directed the Armed Forces to prepare for any eventualities; and I trust that in the interest of both the Cuban people and the Soviet technicians at the sites, the hazards to all concerned of continuing this threat will be recognized.

"Third: It shall be the policy of this nation to regard any nuclear missile launched from Cuba against any nation in the Western Hemisphere as an attack by the Soviet Union on the United States, requiring a full retaliatory response upon the Soviet Union."

1914 hours EST (Monday evening)
"The Tank:" Joint Chiefs of Staff Meeting Room
E-Ring, Pentagon, Washington D.C.

Air Force Chief of Staff General Curtis LeMay chomped down hard on his cigar, then eased the grip of his jaw so that he could furiously puff the faint coal back into fire. All the while he glowered at the man on the television screen. After a few minutes, he couldn't stand it any longer, pulling the cigar from his mouth and glaring at the Joint Chiefs of Staff seated around him at the table.

Clearly the chairman, General Maxwell Taylor, wasn't going to say anything. Taylor had parachuted into Normandy on D-Day, had finally risen to be the highest ranking office in the United States Armed Services. Yet now, at the whim of this piss-ant politician from New England, the Chairman of the Joint Chiefs of Staff seemed frozen and helpless.

It was too much for LeMay. "This is goddamn appeasement! That's what it is! Christ, we should have bombed the crap out of those sites last week, when we first found out they were there! Instead, we're pissing around with this 'quarantine' bullshit. We may never get another chance like this again!"

LeMay viewed the world from a soldier's perspective, and he was one hell of a soldier. A man of immense physical courage, he had led waves of bombers in dangerous, low-level raids during World War Two, until he was promoted to command the devastating strategic bombing campaign that finally brought Japan to her knees. He had famously declared "All war is immoral…if you let that bother you, you're not a good soldier." Now his job, one he viewed with intense and singular focus, was to see that if the next war came, the United States of America would prevail.

"And how a blockade is going to help, when the missiles are already there, is beyond me," Army Chief of Staff Earle Wheeler noted glumly.

"Doesn't he understand that we have ten times as many nukes as Khrushchev?" LeMay demanded in exasperation, realizing that Kennedy knew that fact very well. "That we have a bomber force that can hit the Russkis upside and down, without even launching our rockets? Hell, they don't have a single bomber that can reach our territory with enough fuel left to turn around and fly home again!"

An Air Force colonel entered the room without knocking. "Sorry to interrupt, Sir," he said, reporting to LeMay. "But you should know that all units have confirmed Secretary of Defense McNamara's order raising our readiness level to DEFCON 3."

"About goddamn time," the Air Force chief of staff replied, stuffing his cigar back into his mouth. DEFCON 3 was still two levels short of launching the nuclear strike that Strategic Air Command had been preparing for, but at least it was a step in the right direction. The President had ordered the increase in readiness about an hour before his speech. Now additional strategic bombers were being fueled and armed, leaves canceled for airmen and officers alike, and on each base some of the pilots went to their ready rooms, standing by for orders that might come through at any time.

But DEFCON 3 was too small of a step, for all that. Grimly, LeMay hunched forward, planting his elbows on the table as his eyes tried to bore a hole through the television screen. Kennedy had changed tacks now, directing his words—which, in Florida, were translated into Spanish and simultaneously broadcast southward from some dozen different television and radio towers—to the citizens of Fidel Castro's island nation.

"Finally, I want to say a few words to the captive people of Cuba, to whom this speech is being directly carried by special radio facilities. I speak to you as a friend, as one who knows of your deep attachment to your fatherland, as one who shares your aspirations for liberty and justice for all. And I have watched and the American people have watched with deep sorrow how your nationalist revolution was betrayed—and how your fatherland fell under foreign domination. Now your leaders are no longer Cuban leaders inspired by Cuban ideals. They are puppets and agents of an international conspiracy which has turned Cuba against your friends and neighbors in the Americas, and turned it into the first Latin American country to become a target for nuclear war—the first Latin American country to have these weapons on its soil.

"These new weapons are not in your interest. They contribute nothing to your peace and well-being. They can only undermine it. But this country has no wish to cause you to suffer or to impose any system upon you. We know that your lives and land are being used as pawns by those who deny your freedom. Many times in the past, the Cuban people have risen to throw out tyrants who destroyed their liberty. And I have no doubt that most Cubans today look forward to the time when they will be truly free—free from foreign domination, free to choose their own leaders, free to select their own system, free to own their own land, free to speak and write and worship without fear or degradation. And then shall Cuba be welcomed back to the society of free nations and to the associations of this hemisphere."

1915 hours EST (Monday night)
Casa Uno, Government Headquarters
El Chico, Cuba

The Spanish-language broadcast of the address had quite a few listeners across the "imprisoned island," with none paying more attention than a quartet of men seated around a bare wooden table on the second floor of this palatial villa. Cigar smoke clouded the air, much of it emanating from the tall, bearded figure at the head of the table.

Fidel Castro's eyes were narrowed and his lips compressed in an expression of unconcealed anger. To his right sat his brother, Raul, who listened with a somber air of resignation.

"Eso es basura!" snapped the Cuban leader. "What bullshit! He accuses us of aggression! And all the while his spyplanes fly back and forth above me!"

The third man at the table wore the uniform of a Soviet Army officer. He was Major General Issa Pliyev, commanding officer of Operation *Anadyr*, the Soviet project to install missiles in Cuba. In addition to the missile batteries, Pliyev commanded some 40,000 highly trained, well-equipped Red Army troops, some of them support units for the missles and supply chain. No less than 10,000 of those men were combat soldiers of the first class, organized into four motorized rifle regiments and deployed around Cuba. A squadron of IL-28 Ilyushin bombers—capable of carrying nuclear bombs—and MiG 21 fighters, the front-line Soviet interceptor, had also been delivered to the island.

Still, Pliyev was widely known to be skeptical of the mission and its prospects, and his dour expression indicated that nothing he was hearing now did anything to improve his outlook.

"And don't forget *la Bahia de Cochinas!*" snapped the fourth man, brooding and handsome, clad in an unmarked fatigue shirt and wearing a black beret on his head. Ernesto "Che" Guevara was widely known to be Castro's right hand man, and had been instrumental in bringing the Soviets and Cubans together for the breathtakingly ambitious Operation *Anadyr*. Now he inflamed *El Máximo Lider*'s mind as he invoked the abortive landing at the Bay of Pigs, a year and a half earlier.

"Yes!" Castro agreed with a shout. "This President has the audacity to send our own traitors against us—only to abandon them on our shores! We know he is a coward. But is he a madman as well?"

"Perhaps he is crazy like a fox, *mi lider*," Che suggested. "The Americans are ever striving to get their lackeys to do their fighting for them—in their war against the Nazis, and too at the Bay of Pigs."

Castro nodded, absorbing the famed guerilla's words, knowing of Che's long service to the socialist cause. Now, Guevera's eyes were bright, but he watched the Soviet general through narrowed eyes, as if wary of imminent betrayal. If Pliyev noticed the revolutionary's attention, he gave no sign, merely scowling as he strained to make out Kennedy's words.

"My fellow citizens, let no one doubt that this is a difficult and dangerous effort on which we have set out. No one can foresee precisely what course it will take or what costs or casualties will be incurred. Many months of sacrifice and self-discipline lie ahead—months in which both our patience and our will shall be tested, months in which many threats and denunciations will keep us aware of our dangers. But the greatest danger of all would be to do nothing."

Abruptly, Fidel pushed back his chair so hard that it toppled over. Standing up, waving his cigar like it was a weapon, he stalked around the room. *"Eso hijo de puta!"* he cursed. "That son of a bitch! This means war! I will mobilize my army tonight! Let the *yanquis* come! They have no idea of the hellstorm that will greet them on our beaches!"

1917 hours EST (Monday night)
Flight Deck
CVN-65 USS *Enterprise*
Caribbean Sea

A night landing on an aircraft carrier was never an easy task. Now, as Lieutenant Derek Widener maneuvered his F4 "Phantom" toward the stern of the massive ship, he felt the added complexity of martial tension. The tingling sense of alertness had permeated his two-hour flight, a combat air patrol over *Enterprise* and her supporting vessels.

Ensign King, in the second seat, fed him altitude and bearing information as the pilot kept his eyes on his airspeed indicator, and on that broad flight deck before and below him. The *Big E*'s landing lights burned low, a security precaution. The presence of the dark island of Cuba—the U.S. base at Guantanamo Bay lay 150 miles to the north—seemed to exert a dark gravitational pull far in excess of any natural physical force. Too, Soviet submarines were reported to be in nearby waters. Their torpedoes represented a lethal threat even to the mighty vessel.

Still, Widener was a gifted pilot, and his skills and training took over as the big jet settled and slowed, the flight deck growing gradually larger in his field of view. The world's first nuclear-powered aircraft carrier was a massive ship, the largest warship ever launched, and he should sure as hell be able to land on it! He watched the landing officer, and cut his engine at the man's throat-slash sign.

The Phantom, with its phenomenally powerful twin jet engines and ridiculously small, swept wings, thumped to the deck, and the tailhook snagged the arresting gear. With a sudden shock of deceleration, the lieutenant jerked forward, restrained by his safety harness as he felt the aircraft come to a sudden halt.

Quickly his crew chief approached, wheeling up a ladder as Widener popped the canopy and stiffly climbed out of the seat. Ensign King followed him out of the cockpit to step onto the platform atop the large, rolling ladder.

"Nice landing, LT," said Petty Officer Tuttle from below, with an enthusiastic thumbs up. "You might want to hurry into the briefing compartment. The President is still giving his speech, and the comm guys have managed to pull in a live feed."

"Thanks, Sam, I will," Widener replied, scooting down the ladder by sliding his hands along the twin railings. On the deck, he unstrapped his helmet as he jogged to the hatch leading into the pilots' compartment. Inside, several dozen fliers were gathered on the bench seats of the briefing room, watching a fuzzy signal on the television set up at the podium. Widener realized he'd arrived just in time to hear the conclusion of the address.

"The path we have chosen for the present is full of hazards, as all paths are; but it is the one most consistent with our character and courage as a nation and our commitments around the world," President Kennedy said. For the first time in Widener's memory, JFK look rather old and tired. His demeanor on the small screen remained stern and unwavering.

"The cost of freedom is always high, but Americans have always paid it. And one path we shall never choose, and that is the path of surrender or submission.

"Our goal is not the victory of might, but the vindication of right; not peace at the expense of freedom, but both peace and freedom, here in this hemisphere, and, we hope, around the world. God willing, that goal will be achieved.

"Thank you and good night."

1918 hours EST (Monday evening)
Oval Office, The White House
Washington D.C.

The bright klieg lights went out, and the President blinked, squinting into the sudden semi-darkness. He pulled out a handkerchief and wiped the sweat from his forehead as the technicians quickly began to gather up their equipment. Bobby stepped forward to offer a hand, but Jack curtly shook his head, pushing himself to his feet with only a small grimace.

"How do you think it went?" he asked, as the two brothers and Press Secretary Salinger started for the side door.

"It was perfect," Bobby said sincerely. "The right tone, tough and steady—a solid, measured response."

"You said exactly what needed to be said," Salinger chimed in.

"Well, that's it then, unless the son of a bitch fouls it up," JFK said, holding up a hand to brace himself against the frame as he passed through the office door.

Secret Service agent Bob Morris reached out to open the next door, and the President nodded his thanks as he passed through. Morris fell in behind the Chief Executive as he moved toward the elevator.

"I'm going to look in on Jackie and the kids," Jack announced, finally leaving his brother and his press secretary behind. The Secret Service agent followed him to the elevator but stopped outside the car.

"Good night, Mr. President," he said.

"Good night, Bob. And thanks," JFK said wearily, before the door closed and the elevator carried him up to the Residence, where his wife and two children were waiting.

* * *

The sound room resembled a closet, wedged into a small space between the Oval Office and the Cabinet Room. Though the speech had ended several minutes earlier, two reels of tape still rolled, steadily spooling duplicate copies of dead air. Finally, Ron Pickett reached out and turned the knobs, shutting the recorders down.

He was sweating, slightly. Even though the speech had been broadcast on all the networks and was recorded by countless agencies both official and private, he felt the burden of making sure that his recordings were perfect. The taping machines that almost filled this small room would provide the official documentation of the President's speech. Perhaps nobody would ever know about them, or hear them, but even so Rickett felt the pressure of that responsibility like a physical weight.

It was a weight he bore willingly, even eagerly, because he could do it so well. Now he checked the needles, reassured that they all rested at "0," accurately indicating that there was no sound reaching the microphones in the Presidential office. The needles monitoring the mics in the conference room flickered slightly, and Pickett knew that the cleaning crew was in there, quietly dusting, moving the chairs around. A vacuum cleaner suddenly started to whine, and the needles flickered upward.

Good. All was as it should be. Pickett boxed up the two duplicate tapes of the speech, labeled each in his precise, neatly blocked hand, and placed them on the shelf next to the tapes of all that month's eventful discussion. History had been made, was still being made, in this building, across the city, the nation, and the world—but that reality was far from his mind.

Instead, as he left the room, closed the door, and locked it under the watchful eyes of Secret Service agent Morris, Ron Pickett merely felt the calm satisfaction of a job well done.

2300 hours
Soviet Submarine *B-59*, Submerged
1300 miles NE of Cuba, Atlantic Ocean

The vast, rolling expanse of black ocean waters parted suddenly, churning into froth as a metallic prow and sleek, tapered sail emerged from the sea to glisten in the night air. Waves spilled to port and starboard as the rest of the boat broke the surface. Immediately the three diesel engines chugged into life, propelled the submarine even as they spun additional energy into the dynamos that began to reenergize the exhausted batteries.

Captain (2nd Rank) Valentin Savitsky, as usual, was the first one up through the hatch into the small observation platform atop the sail. He couldn't see stars through the overcast skies above, but at least the ocean surface was reasonably calm. The long, narrow deck below him remained above the waves, and he immediately opened the speaking tube and addressed his executive officer, in the command compartment directly below.

"Send the men up to the surface in shifts. Every man gets thirty minutes of fresh air. We will submerge as soon as the batteries are recharged."

"*Da*, captain," replied Commander Vasily Arkhipov, gratitude in his voice.

Indeed, that gratitude would soon permeate the entire boat, Savitsky knew. The submarine, a diesel-powered boat of the Foxtrot class, had been designed for the defense of the Soviet coasts and nearby ocean waters. It was a fairly reliable vessel, only four years old, but the design lacked several features of more modern submarines—in fact, except for the fact that it was larger, the Foxtrots were not very different from late WW2-era German U-boats.

And they had never been intended for a mission like this. Savitsky and his crew had been at sea for more than three weeks, running submerged except when they needed to surface to recharge the sub's powerful batteries by running the diesel engines—and then only in the dead of night. They had already crossed some ten thousand miles of ocean, venturing farther from Mother Russia than any Soviet submarine had ever done before. And for weeks, now, the problems had been mounting.

The submarine was one of four Foxtrots dispatched toward Cuba as part of Operation *Anadyr*, but Savitsky had no means of communicating directly with the other boats. Contact and orders from Soviet Naval headquarters, in Murmansk, was spotty, with a few long-range instructions reaching the submarine when it was on the surface. But those orders had contained precious little information, and absolutely nothing about the rest of the submarines, or anything else involving Cuba or the Americans. And constrained by the need for radio silence, Savitsky had been unable to send any reports back to the USSR, or to any other Soviet Bloc ships at sea. Secrecy in this mission was paramount: the Americans were not to have any clue that the Soviet navy was venturing into the western Atlantic Ocean.

He and his crew existed in their own little claustrophobic universe, and it was a universe growing more uninhabitable by the day. Forty-eight hours ago the boat's ventilation system had failed, and nothing the crew had done had been able to get the central fan unit to operate again. The captain suspected that the culprit was the high humidity, a corrosive effect of the steamy air caused by the warmth of these tropical waters. To compensate, they kept the hatches open between compartments, but even so the temperature in the boat was running at a steady 110 degrees Fahrenheit. In the engine room, where the diesel's were not cooling properly, it was even worse, ranging 20 or 30 degrees warmer than the rest of the boat—a virtual oven.

And the air quality was going from bad to worse. Carbon dioxide concentrations had risen to dangerous levels, and it was not uncommon for one or more of Savitsky's sailors to faint at his post. The diesel coolers had become completely inoperative, probably clogged with salt, so the overheating engines continued to raise the temperature in the hull. The only respite from the poisonous air were these precious minutes atop the water, concealed only by the cloak of darkness.

The previous night they had surfaced into stormy seas. The *B-59* had churned along, charging her batteries, but the thunderous waves sweeping over the deck had prevented the captain from allowing any of his crewmen to come up for a breath of fresh air. So they had sweltered and gasped through another day.

Wiping the spray from his forehead with an oily rag, the captain looked down to the foredeck, where sailors were already emerging from the forward hatch, stretching and breathing deeply as they escaped the stale air inside the hull.

"Captain?" Arkhipov's voice echoed in the speaking tube.

"What is it, Vasily Andreivich?"

"Feklisov, sir. He asks for permission to forego his deck time. He doesn't want to leave his baby."

Savitsky uttered a bark of laughter. "Permission granted," he said.

He thought of Lt. Commander Anatoly Feklisov and his charge, which was the one piece of modern equipment on this old-fashioned boat. The "baby" was a very special weapon, a type 53-58 torpedo. Like the other twenty-one torpedoes of *B-59*'s weapon complement, it was capable of running for more than six miles under the ocean while it sought the metal hull of an enemy ship. It could be pre-set before launch to curve through an arc, to climb or to dive, as it sought a target. Unlike the other torpedoes, however, it was not equipped with a standard TNT-explosive warhead. Instead, Feklisov's torpedo was capped by the RDS-9 warhead, a 10-kiloton nuclear bomb. The weapon was nearly as powerful as the one the Americans had dropped on Hiroshima during WW2. It was this torpedo that made the *B-59* a truly powerful ship of war. Feksilov would do well to keep a close eye on that device.

An hour later, again below decks, the captain made his way to the forward torpedo room, where he found the lieutenant commander, as usual, stationed right beside the nuclear-armed torpedo, encased as it was in its shiny gray tube. Eleven of the submarine's twelve torpedo tubes were loaded with conventional weapons, but the twelfth tube was empty, merely waiting for this lethal device to be activated and slipped into firing position. Once that had been done, a process that took only about five minutes, the *B-59* could unleash hell against any American warship, or even devastate a small fleet.

"How fares the boat, Comrade Captain?" asked the bookish younger officer. Lieutenant Commander Anatoly Feklisov was not so much a sailor as an engineer, in the captain's eyes. It was his job to tend the nuclear warhead, to maintain it, and to make sure that it would work if Savitsky ever ordered it to be fired. But the captain liked and trusted the young man, who sometimes seemed scarcely older than a boy.

"Not so good, Anatoly Yakovlivich," Savitsky replied glumly. "The air is shit, and getting shittier." He looked at the sleek gray container next to Feklisov, and thought about the power there. "But at least we can kick the Americans in the ass if they try to give us any trouble, eh?" he added, forcing a laugh.

"That we can, Captain. That we can," Feklisov agreed.

Meanwhile, the temperature in the engine room continued to climb, and the air grew even more stale, heavy with CO_2. The duty engineer, feeling dizzy, had to step forward for a moment, to get a few breaths of the comparably "fresh" air from the command compartment in the middle of the boat. He didn't hear the noise, only a small *snap* really, that emanated from the rear of the engine room.

There, in the very farthest aft part of the boat, a tired roller bearing had been turning relentlessly for more than three weeks, cradling the steady rotation of the starboard propeller shaft. Now, suddenly, a tiny fatigue crack broke the perfect seal where the shaft passed through the outer hull of the submarine. Unseen and unsensed by any crewmember, the crack was so small that only the tiniest trickle of water, at first, could force its way into the boat.

One: Operation Anadyr

"What if we throw a hedgehog down Uncle Sam's pants?"

Communist Party Chairman Nikita Khrushchev
Proposing Operation Anadyr, April 1962

15 September 1962
2340 hours (Saturday night)
Khrushchev Dacha, Lenin Hills
Outside of Moscow, Russia

The stately country home occupied a prominent bluff over the Moscow River. The great city, former capital of the czars and now the heart of the USSR, spread out in all its vastness below, yet here the countryside was wooded, rural, and private. The winding road rose from the river valley, past several checkpoints on the way to the sprawling compound on top of the hill. A tall, concrete barrier ringed the grounds of the manor, and alert KGB guards checked the credentials and faces of all who arrived. Other guards patrolled the outside and inside of the wall, some accompanied by dogs, all carrying their Kalishnikov assault rifles at the ready.

Yet past the wall, in and around the manor, the security teams and the paranoia might as well have been a distant illusion. The great house thrummed with lights and life. A string quartet played classical Russian music on a balcony while guests mingled, sampling from tables laden with exotic canapés centered around a mountain of glistening black caviar. Laughter rang out everywhere, growing louder and more deeply toned as the evening progressed and the wine and vodka flowed.

It was the kind of event that Nikita Khrushchev truly loved: a hundred people in attendance and having a good time, with himself as the center of attention. The evening was further enhanced by a unique opportunity: a chance for the de facto Premier of the Soviet empire to flirt with a beautiful American reporter.

For an hour Stella Widener had been working on him, making her case with every argument, expression, and wile she could bring to bear. She was trying to convince him to grant her permission to film a documentary, intended for American television broadcast, within the Kremlin itself. He had more or less decided to let her do it, but he enjoyed the power of his control, so he had not yet revealed the fact to her. Instead, the Chairman of the Communist Party of the Soviet Union had enjoyed every moment of the conversation.

"Did you know that Napoleon stood upon this very hill after his army occupied Moscow in 1821?" he asked her, veering the topic away from her job. "He saw the city in flames—we Russians burned it, you know—and he must have realized the end of all his dreams of conquest."

"That's a fascinating detail. Clearly you have a great insight into your nation's history," Stella said. "That's all the more reason to let me tell your story!"

"I don't see how I could let you bring your cameras into the Kremlin!" he objected in mock horror, gesturing vaguely toward the great city. "Why, you would be sure to capture many state secrets!"

He winked, even before the translator finished relaying his words to Widener, who flipped her blond hairdo with a shake of her head as she pressed forward with her cause.

"Really, Mister Chairman—it would be historic! Of course your security men would have final approval over everything I film. But think of the chance: you could show the West one of the most magnificent structures in the world! And you would have the opportunity to prove your peaceful intentions, to deny some of the terrible things that are said about you."

Though his official title was merely "Chairman," everyone at the reception understood that Nikita Khrushchev was no less than the supreme dictator of one of the two most powerful nations on the face of the earth. He was also a vain man, a volatile man, and a man who desperately wanted to be liked. The vodka buzzed in his system, but it didn't fog his brain, and he knew that the American woman was appealing to instincts that lay at his very core.

Still, he shook his head, showing a stern face. "I tell you, it is impossible. The hallowed halls of the Kremlin will not be displayed to the Western world like some gaudy drapery festooned about your imperial capitals!"

She shook her head, an expression of real regret on her face. "But now, when so much is at stake...when people worry about the tensions between our nations, about the possibility of war—" The translator kept up with her words so effectively that the Chairman cut her off in mid sentence with an abrupt chop of his right hand.

"The war you speak of is cold!" he declared. "Only the United States can make it hot! It is your President who always blusters, speaks of war and threats and bombs. We are a peaceful people, a peace-loving people." He remembered, he had seen, the price of that peace, at Stalingrad and Kharkov and Kiev, and he believed his own words.

"Then let me help you prove that," Stella Widener said, fixing her blue eyes on his face. She was a little taller than he was, but for some reason that didn't bother him. He sensed his stern facade weakening, and this he would not allow.

His excuse came as he saw Marshal Malinovsky looking at him from across the room. The Supreme Commander of the Armed Forces of the Soviet Union clearly needed a word with his Chairman.

"I tell you, I cannot allow it," Khrushchev said. "Now, if you will excuse me, I must attend to some state business."

For the first time, the reporter's professional mask cracked slightly, and she looked almost petulant. In the next second the Chairman turned away, satisfied, even pleased with the conversation. She really was a beautiful woman, so blond, so Western, and everything from her looks to her voice gave him a little thrill. He had something she wanted; that was nice. If only....

Then he spotted his wife, Raisa, in her straight black dress and sturdy shoes, talking to some generals' wives, and he felt a little sag of regret. He shook his head, reminding himself that he had won the encounter with Stella Widener, and that was perhaps the most important thing. He allowed himself to smile broadly as he approached Malinovsky, tall and resplendent in his uniform with the red stripes and gold epaulets.

"Comrade Marshal, it is good to see you," the Chairman said. "Do you bring me some news?"

"Indeed, Nikita Sergeiyevich. The latest dispatches from...the north," he concluded discreetly.

"Follow me." Khruschev led his senior military commander out of the ballroom, down a short hall and into his private office. The music, the laughter and conversation of the party reached them only as a muted background of sound. "What is your news...from the 'north'?" He laughed as he mimicked his subordinate's minor deception.

"I refer of course to the Cuban mission, Operation *Anadyr*," the general said stiffly. The name was the chairman's own brainchild: Anadyr was a river, city, and province in far northern Siberia, so it had appealed to Khrushchev to conceal the most tropical deployment in Soviet military history behind the name of an Arctic location. Some of the soldiers had even been equipped with skis, snowshoes, and winter clothing, all as part of the *maskirovka*—the cloak of strategic deception so cherished by Russian commanders.

"The surface-to-air missile batteries have all reached their positions, Comrade Chairman. The motorized rifle regiments and the personnel of all three divisions of the Strategic Rocket Forces have either debarked in Cuba or will be there within a matter of days. The rockets should arrive shortly, with the warheads about three or four weeks behind. Even as we speak, the troops on the ground are beginning to move out to their final positions—traveling by night, of course."

"And the Americans?"

"They have been watching, but they have seen nothing. They have an electronic surveillance ship patrolling back and forth off the north coast of the island. But our men are observing strict radio silence, so they have not been able to learn anything through radio intercepts. They overfly our ships on the open seas with their reconnaissance aircraft, but all our military personnel remain below decks during daylight. And the cargo—the military cargo, in any event—has been stored in holds for the most part. In the case of our Il-28 bombs, and the coastal gunboats, the items have been secured in crates carried on deck. And while the Americans fly and patrol over the waters surrounding the island, it has been more than a month since they have sent a reconnaissance aircraft over Cuba itself."

"Ah, perhaps they are afraid of our SAMs."

"Indeed, Comrade Chairman, it would seem so. Even the U2s cannot outfly our rockets. Comrade Castro has sent his own fighter aircraft up to make sure the Americans know they are being watched. Of course, he has older MiGs, though his pilots are well trained. Our own modern fighters, the MiG-21s, will be flown by Russian pilots. They are getting established on Cuban bases right now."

Khrushchev felt a little thrill again—the thrill of victory, of a gamble that paid off. Of course, the game wasn't over yet, but the dice were falling his way. Even before he had made the decision, last May, to send the nuclear rockets to Cuba, he had agreed to fortify the Caribbean nation's antiaircraft defenses with many batteries of the famed SA-2 missile, the same weapon that had brought down Francis Gary Powers' spy plane over the *rodina*, the motherland, three years earlier.

Malinovsky knew, all the members of the Presidium knew, that every piece of Operation *Anadyr* was Nikita Khrushchev's brainchild. And it was a brilliant, audacious plan indeed. It rankled them all to know that the Americans possessed almost complete mastery of the nuclear arms race. The United States had hundreds of medium- and intermediate-range missiles based in England, Italy, and Turkey, as well as an army of intercontinental ballistic missiles based in silos and on launchers throughout the plains of the United States. They had a fleet of long-range bombers capable of carrying thermonuclear bombs, and at least some of those bombers, with full weapon loads, remained in the air at all times.

The Soviets, in turn, had only a few dozen rockets that could fly around to the other side of the world to strike at American targets, and they were weapons of questionable reliability. Most of the ICBMs had to be stored outside on exposed launch platforms. They needed to be fueled directly before launching, a time-consuming process—and the corrosive nature of the liquid fuel meant that the rockets could remain fueled only a few days before suffering damage.

Most of the more effective Soviet strategic missiles were medium or intermediate range. From the *rodina*, they were able to threaten Western Europe, Japan, and Taiwan, but incapable of reaching the USA. And unlike the USA, the Soviet Union lacked client states in all corners of the world. While the Americans had allies almost completely surrounding the USSR, until 1960 Russia had not had a single reliable partner anywhere in the Western Hemisphere.

The Cuban Revolution, and Fidel Castro, had created the opportunity for Operation *Anadyr*, which would change all that strategic imbalance in one swift coup. It was the Soviet Chairman who had seen that opportunity, and seized it. In less than two months—right around November 1— Khrushchev would be able to announce to the world that the United States was now exposed to the full might of Soviet weaponry. Cuba would be safe, and the Americans would know the fear that their own nuclear might had imposed upon the rest of the world.

"Come, Rodion Yakovlivich—share a toast with me!" The Chairman felt ebullient enough to address his defense minister by his Russian familiar, tingling with that thrill of victory. He poured two tumblers of fine vodka, and he and his marshal shared a toast.

A few minutes later, Nikita Khrushchev was back at the party. He found Stella Widener, who looked very happy to see him. He smiled at her, opened his arms in a gesture of welcome and friendship.

"Miss Widener," he declared, beaming, tickled by the hopeful expression on her face. In his expansive mood, he decided to bring her suspense to an end.

"I have decided to let you make your film. You may bring your crews to the Kremlin tomorrow afternoon. I shall arrange for a security escort to meet you at the gate."

17 September 1962
0230 hours (Monday very early morning)
Battery 2, 539th Missile Regiment
San Marco del Fuego, Cuba

The dozens of vehicles in the Soviet convoy growled down the slope of the forested ridge, following the steep, rutted track into the valley. A column of motorcycles led the way, followed by a pair of armored cars, and then a file of massive, rumbling trucks hauling long trailers. The vehicles ran with dimmed headlights, moving very slowly on the narrow, only partially paved road.

Riding in the passenger seat of the second armored car, Lieutenant Colonel Nikolai Tukov leaned partially out of the open window, only to have the dense, humid air add another layer of sweat to his already sodden forehead and scalp. He heard the staccato crackle of the motorcycles at the head of the column, and as that sound fell back to a chorus of idles he knew they were looking at another delay.

Even before the armored car came to a stop, he'd opened the door, and as the air brakes hissed one last time, he dropped out of the cab and stalked up the shoulder of the narrow road, removing his brimmed military cap to wipe his head with a sticky handkerchief. A breeze teased him with a tiny waft before the atmosphere settled back to its normal, steamy stillness.

"What is it this time?" he demanded of the little knot of men gathered around their motorcycles. Some of these men were Cuban scouts assigned to lead the 79th regiment to San Cristobal, where Tukov's missiles would be installed. One of these men was speaking, in halting Russian, to a Red Army captain.

"The curve here, Comrade Colonel," reported the captain, who was in command of the motorcycle platoon. He gestured with a gloved hand, and Tulov had to wonder: *How could the man be wearing gloves in this heat?*

Even in the humid darkness, Tukov saw the problem immediately. The convoy—including the trucks hauling their long, tubular trailers—needed to make a hard left turn here. The advance crews had already come through and taken out a few telephone poles and, to judge from the gaping foundation and the cracked beer sign lying in the mud, a cantina that had once stood on the acute point of the intersection. There was almost enough room for the trucks to make the turn, but not quite: a ramshackle barn still stood in the way.

"Bring up the bulldozer, and don't waste any time!" Tukov barked. The barn would have to go before the trailers could continue on.

"No! No!" An elderly farmer emerged from a nearby house. He began to shout in rapid Spanish to one of the Cuban scouts, demanding to know why his barn was about to be bulldozed.

"For the good of the revolution," replied the Cuban militia captain calmly. "And so these Russian jackasses don't shoot you and me both, and bury us under the ruins of your barn."

"At least let me get my pigs out of there!"

"You have five minutes," the captain replied, which was about how long it would take the bulldozer to come up.

The distraught farmer hurried to the barn. Tukov looked at the Cuban captain. "You should know that even a Russian jackass might *comprende español,*" he said to the man in his own language.

"*Dios mío!*" the man declared, his face growing pale. "I did not mean to disrespect the great Soviet Union!"

Tukov shrugged. "If some foreigner was going to knock my barn down, I'd think he was a jackass too."

He sighed and trudged back to his car. Here they were in Cuba, to share in the glories of the next step of the global revolution. He was tired of this journey, tired of the stifling climate. He and his men, good comrades and well-trained soldiers all of them, had come to this new, foreign hemisphere, traveling farther from the *rodina,* than any other Soviet combat formations in that nation's brief, glorious history.

It might have been a voyage to hell, as far as Tukov and the other men aboard *Odessa* had been concerned. They'd departed from the Black Sea port of Sevastapol in late August, and for two interminable weeks had been tossed and turned by the waters of the Mediterranean Sea, and then the Atlantic Ocean. The officers, at least, slept in cabins—as a lieutenant colonel, Tukov had even had one to himself!—but the men had been crammed into open compartments below decks. Temperatures had soared to well over one hundred degrees, and the hatches had remained sealed during all daylight hours to screen the secret transport from the NATO patrol aircraft that managed to find them even in the middle of the great ocean. Seasickness had been rampant, and toilet facilities were hopelessly inadequate, so the conditions in the troop compartment had been almost intolerable.

Closer to Cuba, *Odessa* had been buzzed by US Navy attack planes based at Guantanamo. When it finally arrived at the busy port of Mariel, some 60 kilometers west of Havana, the Russians still had to wait until full darkness to debark. Here Tukov and his men had come upon the surreal sight of a previously debarked detachment in the process of building huge bonfires of the wooden skis and ski poles that had been sent along with several battalions. Tukov knew this deployment was called Operation *Anadyr*, after a Siberian region, as part of the *maskirovka*—the plan to deceive—the Americans, but he didn't know the guise had been extended to such ridiculous details.

Other details rankled as well. His men, well-trained and proud soldiers of the Strategic Rocket Forces, had been stripped of their uniforms and forced to wear gaudy sport shirts and casual slacks in an obviously vain attempt to disguise them as tourists.

For another week, the men of the regiment had waited, hiding in a stifling warehouse that had been designated as a "barracks" until the freighter *Poltava* arrived with the SS4 missiles, launchers, and concrete launching pads for Tukov's unit. They had everything they needed to become operational except the nuclear warheads themselves, which were to arrive in a few weeks on another ship.

But the regiment wouldn't wait for that. Instead, they'd loaded the missiles and launchers in trucks and trailers, and moved out of Mariel for their eventual base, near San Cristobal. The first night, the convoy had bypassed the town of Trinidad on a new road that had been bulldozed expressly for the purpose—the huge trucks couldn't fit through the narrow streets of the ancient colonial town. They'd hidden out in the forest during the day, and continued on tonight, rumbling over gravel and concrete bridges that had been erected over numerous streams.

Now, another delay. Tukov watched impatiently, smoking one cigarette after another, until the bulldozer had done its splintering, destructive work, cracking the weakened walls and flattening the pile of rubble so that the trailers, with their high ground clearance, would be able to maneuver past. Finally, the obstacle was removed, and the farmer and his pigs had disappeared. Tukov crushed out his last cigarette, climbed back into the armored car, and felt the lurch as the convoy started moving again into the hot, humid night.

27 September 1962
0730 hours (Thursday morning)
Tactical Air Command Headquarters
Langley AFB, Virginia

The burly chief of staff of the United States Air Force was not a young man, but he sprang down the three steps from his transport jet to the tarmac with surprising agility. Brusquely returning the salutes of the three officers who stood stiffly at attention before him, he pulled a fresh cigar from his tunic and started toward the command center with barely a pause.

General Walter Sweeney, head of the Air Force's Tactical Air Command, striding beside his boss, pulled out a lighter and touched the flame to LeMay's stogie. The two generals strode toward the unadorned brick building with the other officers—a pair of TAC colonels and Lemay's aide, who hastened off the plane after the Chief of Staff, almost trotting to keep up.

"Damn, it's good to be back on Air Force turf again," LeMay snapped, following a deep draught of his cigar. "Those tin hats in the Pentagon—not to mention the lily livers north of the river—really start to wear on me!"

"Welcome to Langley, General," Sweeney replied. "We might not be Omaha, but I think we can hold the civilians at bay for as long as you want to be here."

LeMay, well known as the founding father of the Strategic Air Command—based in the geographic heart of the nation in Nebraska—uttered a short bark of laughter. "Thanks, Walt. But we've got some business to take care of, and then I'll need to be back in D.C. by tonight."

General Sweeney cast a glance—a look that might have contained an element of relief—over his shoulder at his two colonels. "Everything ready for the conference?" he asked, already knowing the answer.

Indeed, less than five minutes later, the four officers were seated a large table in a wood-paneled, windowless room, secure on the second floor of the TAC headquarters. One long wall of the room was dominated by the map of an elongated island, a land mass that bore more than a passing resemblance to a crocodile, with a wedge-shaped head to the east and a winding, serpentine tail trailing out to the west. Just jutting into view at the top of the image, near the west end, was the very southern tip of Florida and the dotted line of the Florida Keys. A major from Air Force Intelligence stood next to the map, pointer in hand.

"Let's get started," LeMay said, with a flourish of his smoldering cigar.

"Yes Sir, General," the major replied curtly, raising the pointer.

"This map highlights our most up-to-date intelligence on the air defences of Cuba. Unfortunately, the data dates back more than a month, since the U2 flights were suspended on the order of the President—"

"Goddamn it!" snarled the Chief of Staff. "I've tried to get that notion through his pretty head—we need current pictures! Castro could have built a dozen installations in the time that we've been blinded!"

Recognizing the rhetorical nature of the objection, the major merely nodded. All of the men chafed at the restriction on aerial overflights, which JFK had ordered after a Nationalist Chinese U2 had been shot down over mainland China by a Russian-made surface-to-air missile—a SAM-2, like the one that had downed the CIA's Francis Gary Powers over Russia, in the last year of Eisenhower's presidency. Kennedy had been unwilling to risk another international incident, especially in the light of reports from sources on the ground that SAMs had been delivered to Cuba and could well be operational by now.

"Well, go on," LeMay said.

"Very good, Sir. As you know, OPLAN 314 and OPLAN 316 are already in place—representing quick reaction plans for attacks on Cuba with lead times of only four, or two, days, respectively. We have good reason to suspect that the Army and Navy would not be able to attain mission capability within that time frame, but based on the orders from yourself and General Sweeney, we are confident that the Air Force would be able to engage within as little as twenty-four hours of notification, for OPLAN 316. Given the wider range of targets and the greater number of assets required, OPLAN 314 would necessitate a lead time of thirty-six to forty hours, but could certainly commence in less than the forty-eight hours required by the plan."

"Are we going to be ready to install the plans on time?" the Chief of Staff demanded.

"Yes, sir. The target date—for hypothetical purposes—is 20 October of this year, and most of our deployments are already under way, or will commence in the next week or so. We'll use our bases in Florida for the strike aircraft, and bases throughout the southeastern U.S. for our medium-range bombers."

"I hope to hell we can get clearance for more photo recon by then!" the general declared, returning to worry that bone again. "The problem is, the CIA wants to keep complete control of the U2s. I've told Director McCone and the President that we need Air Force pilots in those planes. That way, if there's an incident, it will be a combat flier in danger, not some goddamn spook."

"Right, Sir." The major tried to keep up with the bullet train of conversation spit forth by his commanding general. "Of course, any intel we can get will enhance our target selection. But for now, we've marked out the known airfields and ground-force headquarters. The CIA has helped, breaking down eyewitness reports from the exiles that are still coming into Florida every day." He indicated a town called San Cristobal, southwest of Havana in the westernmost province of the island country. "We've heard about a lot of activity around here, even some reports of Russians. They're moving some big equipment around, including long trailers."

"That'll be a priority, if—when—we finally get permission to do some more photo recon," LeMay declared. "What about ports?"

"Of course, Castro doesn't have much of a navy to speak of, but we should be able to take out his gunships in the first wave of attacks," the briefing officer reported. "Most of his boats are based in the west, at Mariel and Havana, though he has a few in other parts of the country as well."

"What's the status of the MiGs?" LeMay asked.

"We know that the Cubans have about sixty Soviet-made fighters—a mix of MiG-15s, -17s, and -19s. Castro also has a cadre of fighter pilots trained in Czechoslovakia. The MiGs will obviously be priority targets—"

"My own fighter pilots have made no secret of it," General Sweeney interjected. "They hope Fidel dares to send those old jets into the sky. Wherever we find them, you can bet our own fighters will make short work of them."

"Um, yes Sir, of course," the major agreed. "We do have some reports—again from sources on the ground—that Khrushchev might have sent some MiG-21s, designated 'Fishbed,' to Cuba in recent months."

"Fishbed capabilities?" LeMay's two words came out as a question that the major didn't hesitate to address.

"Mach 2 speed, armed with air-to-air infrared missiles and a 30mm cannon. They're the enemy's most advanced fighter, probably nearly equal to our best. Avionics are known to include air-intercept radar. They can operate from rough fields and, like a lot of Russian equipment, they don't need a lot of maintenance. The Fishbeds would be a threat that we'd have to take seriously, Sir."

"And because we don't have current recon, we don't even know where they might be based!" LeMay barked to no one in particular. "What else do they have in terms of air assets?"

"This came in just last night, sir," said the major. He pulled down a screen while one of the colonels turned on a slide projector on the far side of the room. The device projected an image of a modern merchant ship on the high seas. She was traveling at a good clip, to judge from the foaming wakes churning along her hull and astern.

"This is the *Kasimov*," the briefing officer explained. He used the pointer to indicate a double row of large crates, apparently about the size of railroad boxcars, lined up on the ship's long foredeck. "These crates match the dimensions of the crates the Soviets use to transport the Ilyushin-28 light bomber—"

"The 'Beagles,'" LeMay snorted. "Not a lot of range, but they're not a defensive weapons system, that's for sure. Khrushchev might be sending some offensive weaponry to his Cuban pal." He paused, thinking and puffing.

"Get me some prints of that slide," he ordered. "They might help me change some minds up in Washington. If Castro has bombers capable of reaching even halfway into Florida, the President will have to take notice."

"And that's not all, Sir," the intelligence major added, continuing quickly as the Chief of Staff waved him to proceed. "The Beagle is a light bomber, short-ranged to be sure. But we've learned that they have the capacity to deliver nuclear weapons—one gravity bomb per aircraft."

"Now that should get somebody's attention, even in D.C.! Major," said LeMay, standing and turning toward the door. "Good brief. You just made my day."

05 October 1962
2030 hours (Friday night)
Oval Office, the White House
Washington D.C.

Five men occupied two chairs and a couch, facing the desk where sat the most powerful man in the Free World. Each man's face was earnest, voice level and determined. The first to speak was John McCone, Director of the CIA and one of the few Republicans in the Kennedy White House.

"Mister President, we need to get some more pictures! Right now they have a curtain pulled around that island, and God only knows what they're doing behind it! We haven't had an overflight since late summer, and the Reds have been sending tons of freight to Cuba—two ships arriving every day, on average."

The President listened carefully, elbows resting on the desk, his handsome features creased by a frown. Before he replied, however, his National Security Adviser argued the point.

"It's just too dangerous, Sir!" McGeorge Bundy declared. "Remember, when Powers got shot down over Russia, that knocked our relations with the Soviets to hell, for two years! We've at least got a dialogue going with them again—over Berlin—and that's too important to take a chance on messing it up."

"And we know they have SAM sites all over the island," Secretary of State Dean Rusk noted. The balding, mild-mannered diplomat spoke with a softer tone. "SA-2 missiles, the same one that shot down Powers. And just last week that pilot from Taiwan. It would be only too easy for them to shoot down another U2, and we'd have an international incident on our hands that would be hard to control."

"But we can't operate in the dark, without data. We need more intelligence," Secretary of Defense Robert McNamara noted, his delivery clipped and precise. "We need to take the chance and get those pictures. It's absolutely essential that we collect some more solid information."

The President leaned back in his chair and closed his eyes. Robert F. Kennedy, the President's younger brother, United States Attorney General and de facto prime minister, recognized the spasm of pain that Jack tried to hide. The younger Kennedy knew that his brother was always in pain, and always trying to hide it.

"Well, Bobby, that's two in favor, two against. We seem to have a deadlock. What's your vote?" JFK's voice was calm, almost as if he was asking for an opinion on what to have for dinner, or what movie to show in the White House screening room. Bobby knew the President would make the final decision, but he also knew that JFK liked to gather opinions, to listen to the arguments of men he respected—even those who disagreed with him—before he took action.

"I think we should send the spyplanes and take the pictures," Bobby declared. "Senator Keating is making noises again about our being soft on Communism, and he's using Cuba as his club. And Director McCone is right: we really don't know what's going on down there. But there have been enough reports from refugees—whole villages being dislocated, long convoys of trucks in the night—for us to believe that something is up. And we need to know what it is."

"All right," said the President decisively, sitting straight again and looked at the DCI. "Send a couple of U2s. See what kind of pictures they can get. And we'll decide where to go from there."

"Yes, Mr. President. I'll do that—this time of year we might have to wait for a week or two before we get clear weather, but at the first opportunity we'll get those pictures."

"Good," Jack said with a curt nod. He turned to look at his Secretary of Defense. "Now, what kind of strategic report are we getting from the JCS?"

"They didn't want to stray from SIOP 62, Sir," McNamara replied. "If it comes to any kind of an exchange, General LeMay maintains that anything less than a complete demolition of the Communist Bloc would leave us wide open for retaliation."

For the first time Kennedy revealed a flash of anger. "Goddamn it! They still say the only way we can use our nuclear arsenal is to hit every target they can find, all at the same time?"

"They were locked into the plan, Mr. President. I agree we need more flexibility, but it's been like pulling teeth to get that out of them. They're working on it, though: the new plan, SIOP 63, is ready for implementation. It includes five levels of escalating response. Levels one and two, at least, avoid direct strikes on cities."

"Thank God for that! I can't believe the way these guys are ready to talk about the obliteration of half the globe! It's not acceptable! Tell them to put the finishing touches on SIOP 63 and make it official. There's no reason that every kid in Bucharest and Budapest should get burned to death just because we can't get along with Moscow!"

"I'll go back and tell them to make it a priority, Sir," the secretary replied. "They'll have to finish it up. It's not like they haven't heard your point of view before."

Sensing a pause as the other men collected their thoughts, Bobby cleared his throat. "Now, about Mississippi," he began. "Things have settled down some, but the FBI has picked up reports of fresh KKK activity."

They all had fresh memories of the "Battle of Ole Miss," where, with the backing of the United States Army National Guard, James Meredith had been admitted as the first negro student in the university's history. The whole situation had become a sore point for JFK, and his explosive answer confirmed that fact.

"Jesus, Bobby—not today! I don't have time for it right now. Bring it back to me tomorrow!"

"Yessir, Mr. President," replied the attorney general.

The tension in the room lingered for a moment until a knock sounded from the door. "Come!" snapped JFK.

It was veteran Secret Service agent Bob Morris who stuck his head into the Oval Office.

"Excuse me, Mr. President," he said. "But your wife said to tell you that it's time to tuck the kids into bed."

Kennedy leaned his head back, his face creased with a shadow of a smile. "Thanks Bob," he said. "Tell Jackie I'll be right up." The door closed and the President looked at each man in turn. "And thanks, fellows," he said with obvious sincerity. "I couldn't do this without you."

* * *

Bob Morris was still on duty three hours later, as the clock neared midnight. Now he was stationed in the basement of the White House, where the elevator shaft terminated. The smell of chlorine lingered in the air, evidence of the private swimming pool. He was waiting for that elevator and wouldn't be able to go home until it had arrived.

A few minutes earlier he'd been handed a brief note, written by another agent. It read "2 Special Visitors, ETA 2345." He wondered, idly, if they'd be blond, brunette, or redhead. He tried not to think of the First Lady; he liked her, and he didn't like this part of his job

The chime sounded, indicating the arrival of the elevator. He was mildly surprised to see that the passengers were not only blond, but that they appeared to be twins. He recognized one of them from a previous visit, though, as usual, he'd not exchanged any conversation with the special visitor. He couldn't help overhearing, however, as the first girl pushed her way through the door into the pool.

"Don't worry," she said to her sister in a conspiratorial whisper. "You're not going to need your swimming suit."

2352 hours (Friday night)
Submarine *B-59*
North Atlantic Ocean

Captain Savitsky retired to his cabin shortly before midnight. The space was barely a closet, with a bunk just long enough for him to lie down on it. He had a tiny desk, safe, and cabinet crammed in there with the bed. Submarine *B-59* had been churning steadily into the ocean for five days now, passing around North Cape, the Faeroe Islands, then Scotland and Ireland as they'd made their way into the Atlantic Ocean.

The crew of the boat had fallen into an easy routine. The captain was pleased by their high morale, but worried because he knew so very little about their mission. They were far from their base on the Kola Peninsula near Murmansk, and neither he nor anyone else aboard knew their ultimate destination. Now, in the middle of the night, they ran on the surface, as fast as their three diesel engines could propel them. Those same diesels were recharging the batteries, which rapidly drained whenever *B-59* submerged below snorkel depth and had to run on electric power. The radio antenna was high in the air, ready to receive any signals from home, though the boat was under strict radio silence and couldn't send any kind of message.

He removed his boots in the tiny compartment and sat on the bunk, which allowed barely enough room for his legs to stretch toward the hatch—and of course, his were the roomiest quarters on the cramped, utilitarian boat. No wonder the men called the Foxtrots "Pig-Boats," he reflected. He had left the hatch open, so he looked up immediately as a sailor, one of the radiomen, drew up outside of the captain's quarters.

"Sir! A message from Moscow!" reported the crewman, handing the captain a sheet of filmy paper. Amid several lines of gibberish, Savitsky saw a phrase—"Long live the October Revolution!"—that set his heart to pumping.

"Send for Commander Arkhipov and Lieutenant Commander Maslennikov," he ordered the radioman. "And close the hatch behind you." As soon as the sailor had departed, the captain leaned over his bunk and dialed the combination to his small safe, from which he removed a thin envelope. He was holding the envelope in one hand, idly slapping it against the palm of the other, by the time the other two officers tapped against the metal hatch.

"Come!" he ordered. Arkhipov pulled the hatch open. "Squeeze yourselves in here and close it behind you," the captain ordered, stretching his legs onto his bunk so there would be room for the two men to stand. A moment later they stood over him, watching expectantly.

"We have received the message from headquarters indicated in our initial orders," Savitsky said. He extended the envelope to political officer Maslennikov. "Please confirm that the seal is intact."

"It is, Comrade Captain," the commissar replied, showing the envelope to Arkhipov for confirmation.

Without further ceremony, Savitsky used his pocket knife to slice through the seal. He pulled the single sheet of paper out, read it—making an effort to keep his face expressionless, despite his surprise—and then handed it to his executive officer.

Arkhipov could not maintain the poker face as he passed the note to the political officer. "Cuba!" he said. "That's an awfully long way from the *rodina*!"

"I believe no Soviet submarine has every journeyed so far from the motherland," Savitsky agreed with forced aplomb. "We have the honor of making history for our revolution, and our navy."

"Indeed, comrades," Maslennikov added, handing the sheet of orders back to the captain. "To Cuba!" The commissar officer, who was a good crewmate despite his somewhat unmilitary role, seemed shaken by the news, but determined to display enthusiasm. Savitsky admired him for that.

The captain summarized the rest of their orders: they were to escort merchant ships that carried important cargo to Cuba, and to defend those ships—and themselves—if they were attacked. They were not to allow the Americans to interfere with the movements of Soviet ships, and no restrictions were placed on the type of weaponry the submarine could employ in accomplishing the mission. They all understood what that meant: Even Feklisov's nuclear warhead was a legitimate asset in performing this task.

"So, Vasily Andreivich: In a few minutes you will go to the plotting compartment amd commence drawing a new course. We have an ocean to cross! But, before then, what can you both tell me about the concerns we will face on this rather unprecedented voyage?"

"I think the morale of the crew is high," Maslennikov answered after a moment's thought. "They will be proud of the assignment and make every effort to ensure that our orders are executed promptly and honorably."

The captain nodded in agreement. "We have sufficient fuel to reach Havana, I expect—though of course we will need to make detailed calculations, now that we have this knowledge. The crew will be able to maintain normal rations for at least another month, so food should not be an issue." He looked at Arkhipov. "Commander?"

"You are right, Comrade Captain. We will need to pay special attention to the water filters, of course. Our boats are not used to operating in warm waters."

"That's a good point. We'll issue orders to control water use even more tightly than normal—we'll need all the fresh water we can distill just to make sure the batteries keep functioning."

"Captain?" inquired the political officer. "Do you suppose the entire brigade will be joining us in Havana?" They all knew that *B-59* was one of four boats attached to the 69th Brigade, and it was common knowledge—at least among the officers—that the quartet of Foxtrots had all departed port on the same day.

"It would seem likely," Savitksy acknowledged, "though whether or not that is the case should make no difference to our mission."

"No Sir, of course, not," Maslennikov agreed hastily. Even as he spoke, the captain pulled three small glasses and a metal flask from a compartment on his sea desk. He poured a dram of vodka into each glass, and each officer lifted his in a brief toast.

"To the *rodina!*" Savitsky declared.

"To the motherland!" his senior officers repeated. All three men tossed back the clear, burning liquid in smooth swallows.

"Now, I'm going to get some sleep," the captain announced. He felt strangely calm and settled, now that he had the answer to his most burning question. He glanced at the chronometer on his bulkhead. "Stay on the surface for three more hours, then take her down. I want to be under water well before dawn."

06 October 1962
1123 hours (Saturday midday)
Battery 2, 539th Missile Regiment
San Cristobal, Cuba

Tukov looked up in annoyance from the blueprints on his mapping table. The steamy heat wore on him, and he was trying to establish the final layout for his rocket battery. He didn't need any interference from the aide who had just pushed open the tent flap.

"What?" he demanded in irritation.

"I am sorry, Comrade Colonel, but there is a visitor—a distinguished visitor—here to see you."

"Unless it's General Pliyev himself I don't have time—"

Tukov bit back the rest of the remark as a cloud of cigar smoke preceded a tall, bearded man, clad in worn fatigues, who strode boldly into the tent. Though he had never seen him in person, the Russian officer recognized Fidel Castro immediately—and found himself at a loss as to how to address the leader of the Cuban state, who was smiling broadly.

"Comrade Fidel!" Tukov finally exclaimed, standing abruptly and snapping to attention. Another man followed Castro into the tent, and he recognized, as everybody would recognize, the smoothly handsome features of Che Guevera.

"Greetings, Comrade Tukov!" Fidel said expansively, waving his cigar enthusiastically. "I hope you are finding everything you need as you and your men get settled in my country!" He spoke in rapid Spanish.

Tukov replied in the same language, albeit more slowly. "Very good, Sir. Your men have been most helpful." He gestured to the blueprints. "I am just making final decisions on the emplacements, and then we can begin excavating, clearing for the roads and the launch pads. The SAM batteries are already deployed around the perimeter, most satisfactorily."

"So it is true—you speak our language!" the Cuban leader declared, obviously pleased. "Tell me: how did this come to be?"

"I fought with the Loyalists against Franco, in Spain, Comrade," Tukov explained. "I was a young platoon leader there for more than two years, in command of two dozen brave men—all Spanish nationals," he added, feeling a surge of pride at the memory—even as the old bitterness came back. "We would have defeated the fascists, if not for the cowardice of the Western World."

"True." It was Che who answered, his voice surprisingly soft in contrast to Fidel's effusiveness. "You and your comrades heroically carried the torch of socialism beyond the borders of its birthplace. A noble cause, indeed. But have faith: the revolution will come to Spain within our lifetime."

"I believe that too, comrade," Tukov agreed, starting to relax. "Just as the two of you have brought the revolution home to the Western Hemisphere."

"And you and your comrades have augmented our revolution splendidly," Castro said, striding around the spacious tent—which suddenly seemed rather small—while Guevera stepped to the table and began to study the schematic diagrams. "Your battery—correct me if I'm wrong—is of the medium-range ballistic-missile type, is it not?"

"Indeed, Comrade Fidel," Tukov agreed, feeling more comfortable now that he was on familiar ground. "We have four launchers for the SS-4 rockets. We expect to have the launchers installed and ready for operations by the third week in October. We have a total of six rockets for those launchers."

"Splendid! The range of these missiles will allow a target as far as way as Washington D.C. to be destroyed, I understand. Could they be made to reach New York?"

"Washington is at about the limit of our range, Sir. I think New York is too far away for the SS-4 to reach, at least from here in western Cuba. I would need to do some more calculations to give you an answer with certainty—obviously, my current focus has been on readying my battery for operations. Target decisions and capability will be determined in the future." Tukov felt vaguely uneasy with the line of questioning. He well understood the horrific power of the weapons under his command, and it was his firm belief that they would never actually be employed. The whole idea of a deadly long-range rocket force was to deter the enemy from taking action that might cause those weapons to be used.

"Or New Orleans?" Castro continued, as if Tukov hadn't spoken. "Surely they will reach that far. Miami, Atlanta, without question. Let the *yanquis* tremble with that knowledge!"

"Indeed, *mi lider*," Guevera acknowledged, in that smooth, detached voice. He turned his attention to Tukov. "The warheads for these missiles—the thermonuclear devices? You will keep them here, with your battery?"

Tukov's stomach began to churn. "I'm afraid not, Comrade. The doctrine of the Strategic Rocket Forces requires that the actual...devices...must be secured in a separate and highly protected location. Of course, they will be close enough that we can bring them here and mate them to the missiles in a matter of hours."

"Hours? Not minutes?" Castro frowned, and it was a terrifying frown indeed. But he waved his cigar and seemed to clear away his displeasure with the gesture. "General Pliyev was describing this process to me, and we have located an underground bunker—already in existence—between here and Havana. Now tell me, Colonel, do you have time to give me a tour of your facility."

"Of course, Comrade," Tukov lied. He gestured to the aide who still stood by the tent door. "Cover these blueprints until I return."

Then he followed the two revolutionaries from the tent. He barely saw them walking ahead of him, as instead his mind focused on a stark and terrifying thought:

These men are actually talking about firing my rockets!

He wondered if either, or both, of them might actually be insane enough to try.

1630 hours (Saturday afternoon)
Approaching Key West Naval Air Station
Key West, Florida

"Geez—take it easy, Derek! What the hell are you trying to do?"

As her brother banked the little Piper Cub almost ninety degrees, Stella Widener squawked a protest in spite of her best efforts at self control. The coral blue waters of the Florida Strait sparkled below her window for a second, and then the little airplane soared over land—over concrete, more specifically. Her brother grinned as he leveled the plane and began to descend toward the landing strip.

"I wanted to check out the flight line," he explained, with no hint of apology. He pointed past her face, out the starboard window of the cockpit. "Look at those babies lined up there. I'd heard a rumor they sent some Phantoms down here. It's true."

Having grown up in a family of naval aviators, Stella was no stranger to aircraft types. She quickly spotted four large fighters hulking over the dozen delta-wing F6 Skyrays that she knew formed the permanent fighter detachment for the Key West NAS, the base where their father was currently the commanding officer.

"They're huge," she acknowledged. "Except for the wings, that is." Indeed, the F4s, which were America's newest and most capable aerial interceptor, looked like they had shorter, stubbier wings even than the much smaller, single-seat Skyrays.

Derek snorted. "With those turbojets, they almost don't need wings."

She heard the pride in his voice and understood his emotion. During the flight down from Washington, he told her that he'd not only qualified to pilot the Phantom, but had been assigned to the squadron that would fly from the USS *Enterprise*, the largest and most modern aircraft carrier in the world. This quick visit, the two of them seeing their father at Key West, was the end of his leave. He was due to report to the ship, already at sea in the Caribbean, in just two more days.

As Derek slowly brought the Cub down to land on the final short section of the long runway, Stella took a deep breath. She spotted her father, standing at ease in his summer white uniform, waiting for them beside the small hangar reserved for little piston-engine, propeller-driven planes like the Piper. His face, as usual, was a mask, and she wasn't sure she was ready for the effort that would be required to penetrate it.

This whole trip had come about in a whirlwind. She'd barely seen the last edits of her ground-breaking piece on the Kremlin, which had been broken into segments to run on the Nightly News for a week. As the work week neared an end, she'd wanted nothing more than to put up her heels, catch up on her rest, and maybe go see a movie with one of her girlfriends. That all changed when Derek called just before five p.m. on Friday with a plan for this excursion. After they met for breakfast Saturday morning, he'd driven them out to the small private airport, where he'd rented the Cub for the weekend. After a stop in Georgia to refuel, they were about to land on the last island in the Florida Keys for dinner with their father.

Commander Widener strode up to the plane before the propeller stopped turning. Derek popped out through the pilot's door, saluted, then clasped his father's hand as the glimmer of a smile cracked the elder officer's mask.

Stella came around the Cub and accepted her father's embrace, hugging him back with just a hint of reserve. "You're looking more beautiful than ever, Stel," Alex said.

"She just got back from Russia," Derek boasted. "She got the first American film ever shot inside the Kremlin!"

"Really?" the commander said. He sounded surprised, though Stella had told him the news in a letter as soon as she'd landed back in the U.S. Hadn't he read it? More likely, it hadn't made much of an impression on him. He still seemed to view his daughter's career as some sort of hobby. Now his head tilted to the side. "How'd you manage that?" he asked.

The young newswoman flushed. She was used to such jabs from her fellow newshounds, but it seemed strangely inappropriate coming from her father. She was a good reporter! Yet she couldn't suppress the vivid memory of the night in Boston—and she knew that she wasn't above using her looks, her sex appeal, in pursuit of a story.

"I keep telling you, Dad—she's damned good at what she does," Derek interjected. Stella was grateful as he gestured, turning the conversation to the hulking, modern fighters lined up on the tarmac a hundred yards away. "So it's true—you got some Phantoms in here now?"

From the ground they looked even larger than they had from the air. The short wings swept downward at a sharp angle. The canopy on one of the F4s was raised, revealing the two seats—one behind the other—for the pilot and weapons officer. The cockpits on the remaining fighters were closed, and looked like bulging glass eyes atop the solid mass of fuselage. An array of objects dangled from beneath the wings and fuselage of the nearest Phantom, and Stella guessed the torpedo-shaped pods might be additional fuel tanks. Stubby rockets with bristling tail fins clustered onto a weapons mount near the end of each wing.

"They're here for an unknown duration," Alex Widener explained, in his precise naval jargon. "Castro's been acting up—he's sent some MiGs over the strait, where they've harassed some of our recon flights. MiG-19s, not the best Russian stuff. Just a couple days ago I scrambled a pair of Skyrays to chase them back down to their island."

"They sound pretty bold," Derek noted. "Wouldn't you love to send a few rockets up their tails?"

The base CO nodded firmly. "That's what it'll take. But we don't have the will in Washington to do anything about it."

"Maybe the President isn't ready to start a war," Stella observed pointedly.

"It may not be his choice to make," Alex replied. "I wouldn't be surprised to find out that Khrushchev is putting in some nukes down there. Ninety miles away from our shores—while we sit here and do nothing!"

"Nuclear rockets?" she responded. "He wouldn't dare!"

Her father looked at her like he was trying to decide if she was trustworthy. She flushed under the scrutiny, but the commander merely shrugged and looked at his watch. "We'll have dinner at the O-Club in two hours," he announced. "Why don't you get cleaned up from the trip? I want to show Derek around."

"Derek is dirtier than I am," she replied, her tone sharpened by her father's apparent dismissal. "I'd like to join you on the tour. Unless you think I'm going to give something classified away to the Russians!"

Widener blinked in surprise, then nodded. "Okay," he said. "That's my jeep over there. I'm going to leave a message in the command center, and then we can get started."

* * *

A little less than two hours later, they entered the Officers' Club and stopped in the bar while their table was readied. Stella ordered a glass of wine, while her father had his usual, a scotch and soda. Derek—who would fly them back to D.C. in the morning—settled for a Coke. The bartender then flicked a lighter first to Stella's and then to the commander's and the lieutenant's cigarettes. Alex gave his daughter a slight glance of disapproval but didn't comment— the battle over her smoking had been settled with an uneasy truce several years ago.

"Those Crusaders on the far side of the field," Stella asked, exhaling a pleasurable plume of smoke as she remembered the F8 fighter jets they'd seen on the tour of the base. "I've seen them before, but these were different. They looked like they had glass windows under the fuselage. What's the reason for that?"

"Very observant of you," Derek said, obviously proud. He explained, before their father could reply. "That's the RF8 variant. It's a photo-reconnaissance ship, not a fighter." He turned to Alex. "I know they're specialized for low level recon, and you told me you think Castro has nuclear missiles down there. Don't tell me you've gotten pictures?"

"Nothing so straightforward," the commander replied. "The RF8s are on standby, awaiting authorization. As for those rockets, it's just a hunch of mine—and a few others. We've heard rumors based on eyewitness reports coming in to Navy intelligence. You know that there's a Pan Am flight every day from Havana to Miami? Well, each one of those flights is packed with people who are eager as hell to get out of Cuba, and to get back at Castro—they hate the son of a bitch. So it's an intelligence gold mine. I've heard that more than a few of them have reported on very long trailers being trucked out to remote locations in Cuba. I can put two and two together as well as anyone—except, apparently, our Commander in Chief!"

He tossed off his drink with the last remark and glared at Stella, ready for a challenge. She just sighed and shook her head. "You still can't get over the fact that Nixon lost, can you, Dad?"

A potential minefield of a conversation was aborted when a white-jacketed steward appeared to escort them to their table. Alex curtly gestured at his empty glass, which the bartender replaced immediately. Stella waved him away from her half-full wine glass.

The base commander naturally got the best table in the Officers' Club: a semi-private space in the corner of the dining room, with a westward view of the Florida Strait, a gorgeous sunset, and a fringe of palm trees lining the beach to the south.

"So, tell us about the Big K," Derek suggested, using the nickname that some press outlets had applied to Khrushchev over the past few years. "Did he pound his shoe on anything? Or blow his top?"

She laughed. "Actually, he's kind of a funny little man. He laughed a lot and flirted shamelessly. He's very proud of Russia, and the Kremlin—which really is a beautiful building, a palace really, as well as the seat of government. I think he let me do the story because he wanted to show it off. I got the impression he really wants to be liked."

"He's got an odd way of showing that," Alex declared.

"Well, he's full of bluster, that's for sure. He even made some threats about 'American imperialism' and so forth, though I'd swear he had a joking gleam in his eye when he made them. I think he's pretty insecure. Did you know that he never really went to school, that he really was raised from a peasant family? He was working inside metal boiler tanks, cleaning out coal scum, before he was a teenager. I think he's sincere about believing that Marxism is leading his people to a better life."

"What do you think about that?" Alex challenged. "You're not going Red, are you?"

"Of course not, Dad!" she snapped, offended. "And neither is our President, just because he's not willing to let you send bombers off to Cuba!"

"By the time he does, it will be too late," her father noted dourly, waving at the steward for another refill of his cocktail. "I tell you, Kennedy's just a pretty boy—too soft for the job!"

"He is rather handsome," Derek teased, as usual trying to ease the tension between his sister and their father. "You must have noticed that when you interviewed him, didn't you? Back in Boston, when he'd just been elected to the Senate?"

She flushed angrily at the thought that Derek might somehow know what had transpired in that hotel room interview six years earlier. But her brother's tone was light, gently mocking, and she exhaled as she realized he was just being himself.

"His looks have nothing to do with his strength as a leader," she retorted. "But he has a tremendous amount of charisma, and a rather unique ability to see problems from the other person's point of view. That might actually be a useful skill for a Commander in Chief!"

Their food—exquisitely grilled grouper fillets stuffed with stone-crab meat—arrived, with another refill for Alex and a second glass of wine for Stella. She felt just a little light-headed but recognized that her father seemed well on his way to getting drunk. They talked about happier times as they ate, sharing memories of their mother, avoiding mention of the cancer that had struck so cruelly and fatally just three years ago. The two siblings kept the conversation going as their father seemed to sink deeper into melancholy.

"You know, they've told me to find space for a Marine air group," Alex announced suddenly, while they started to nibble at slices of tart key lime pie. He shook his head. "Do they know how small this island is? We're a backwater, a half-assed way station on the road to nowhere!"

The outburst surprised Stella. "But all that you said about Cuba—surely Key West is a tremendous asset for keeping an eye on Castro?" Or attacking him, she added silently.

"No." Alex waved the remark away. His hand was unsteady, but his voice was firm. "It's going to be Berlin where the shit hits the fan. And hit the fan it will. I know our military will be ready. I just hope the man in Washington is up to the task. I'm afraid he's going to fuck it up…fuck up everything."

Stella winced. Her father rarely used profanity in front of her, and she knew it was an effect of his intoxication. She and

Derek escorted him from the club, and though her father walked steadily enough, she thought she felt the eyes of all the officers, their wives, and the club staff, boring into them as they went out to the porch and down the stairs. She hoped it was just her imagination.

Derek drove the jeep back to the base commanders' bungalow, leaving his father at his bedroom door with Alex brusquely brushing off any attempt at further assistance. The two siblings sat on the veranda, watching the moonlight reflect off the still ocean water.

"You can't report about what he said, you know," Derek said finally. "Those rumors maybe aren't classified, but he doesn't really know what's going on down there in Cuba. No American does."

"Of course!" she answered. "I know that."

And she was telling the truth: nothing her father had said would find its way into her reporting. But she couldn't help thinking that he had given her some valuable insight into the potential for trouble, just ninety miles south of this little island. She remembered his account of fighters scrambling to chase away patrolling MiGs, and she knew that in a matter of days her brother would be piloting an aircraft of his own, not too far from here. *Enterprise* was based in the Caribbean—it was a matter of public record.

"Derek, be careful," she said quietly, then kissed him goodnight before heading to her father's guestroom.

The pilot, who would sleep on the couch, tried to brush off her concern with an easy grin. But he stayed there on the porch, watching the waves, for a long time after his father and sister had gone to bed.

09 October 1962
0700 hours (Tuesday morning)
Headquarters, United States Air Force Command
Pentagon, Washington D.C.

"Goddammit! Don't tell me the weather is still socked in!" barked Air Force Chief of Staff Curtis LeMay.

"I'm sorry, General," replied the colonel on the other end of the telephone line, no doubt relieved that his angry commanding officer was hundreds of miles away. "We've had almost unbroken cloud cover over the whole island for the last ten days."

"Shit! Well, let me know if you see any sign of a break. We've got to get some pictures of that place!"

"I understand, Sir. Of course, I will let you know immediately if there's any change in the outlook."

The meteorology officer, based at MacDill AFB in Florida, signed off with, to his credit, no audible sigh of relief. LeMay slammed down the phone and puffed on his cigar, glaring at the phone as if it was personally responsible for his frustrations. After a moment he got up and stalked around the spacious office—one of the premium locations on the elite "E" ring of the Pentagon.

One entire wall was covered by a map of the globe, with a series of blue icons representing bomber and missile bases for the United States Air Force, notably the Strategic Air Command. Another series of icons, in red, marked missile sites, airbases, and industrial complexes within the vast swath, something like half the land mass of the earth, representing the communist countries. The map was an accurate depiction of an oft-quoted capsule of LeMay's view of the world: The planet earth was divided between SAC assets and SAC targets.

Though the United States Navy, with its nuclear submarines and their arsenals of Polaris missiles, comprised one element of the American nuclear strike force, to LeMay the next war was going to be an Air Force show. He had under his command some 3,000 nuclear warheads, nearly all of them fifty or a hundred times more powerful than the atomic bombs men under LeMay's command had dropped on Hiroshima and Nagasaki in August of 1945.

He had B-47 bombers based in Europe, capable of carrying multiple bombs directly to the USSR and the other Bloc nations west of Asia. Here in the United States, he had multiple wings of fast, modern B-52 bombers, planes that could fly over the North Pole and then spread out to hit hundreds of targets across the Soviet Union. He had whole fleets of refueling tankers, capable of keeping his bombers airborne for a theoretically unlimited amount of time and distance. And that didn't even account for the Minuteman, Titan, and Atlas missiles secure in their silos in Nebraska, Kansas, and much of the heartland of the United States. Many of these lethal weapons could be launched within ten minutes of a "fire" order and would carry their payloads to the other side of the planet in a mere half an hour or so.

At first, all of these weapons had been locked into a single, tightly planned, carefully coordinated scheme for a mass launch: SIOP 62. Under SIOP 62, SAC would have eliminated every communist nation in the world as a military threat, in one convulsive sweep of destruction. It would leave every major city, from East Germany and Yugoslavia in the west, to China and North Korea in the east, a smoldering, radioactive wasteland. Military airbases and missile installations would be turned to glass, seaports reduced to water craters, and the lethal threat of world communism would be eliminated forever.

LeMay took another furious puff as he remembered the political interference that had watered down his magnificent plan. Just this past summer, on President Kennedy's orders, SAC had been forced to refine the SIOP plan into a series of—in LeMay's opinion—half-assed staged attacks. Phase one was limited to Soviet missile sites, bomber bases, and submarine installations. Phase two authorized targets that were still removed from cities, such as army bases and antiaircraft centers. It was not until Phase five that the full annihilation attack could be launched. By then, of course, it might be too late.

Why did the politicians have so much trouble seeing the obvious truth: Right now the United States had a tremendous strategic advantage. In a year, or at most two, that advantage would seriously erode, as the Soviets introduced more and better ICBMs to their arsenal. America had a current advantage of at least ten to one, probably much more, in long-range nuclear strike capability. But the enemy was catching up.

LeMay turned from his world map to a smaller image, recently mounted on a second wall. This one displayed the island of Cuba, with major cities and geographical features highlighted. Known airfields and coastal ports were shown, but the vast center of the country was a cipher. In the general's mind, that blank area could be teeming with rocket and fighter bases, bomber airfields, and fortified military camps. If he found the targets, he could destroy them.

After a long political wrangle, he had finally gained control of the U2 spyplane program, ripping the machines from the CIA's clutching grasp. He had pilots trained to use the unique aircraft, and he knew each U2 had an array of cameras that could definitely unlock the secrets concealed on Castro's isle.

How dare, then, that a mere layer of cloud should have the audacity to interfere with his plans?

1850 hours (Tuesday evening)
Headquarters, Soviet Military Mission to Cuba
El Chico, Matanzas Province

The headquarters compound for all the Soviet troops of Operation *Anadyr* had once been a reform school for wayward boys. Now, the sprawling complex of buildings, with its dormitories, classrooms, and sports fields, had been turned into the headquarters for the vast array of Soviet military power that had secretly been shipped to Cuba under the guise of Operation *Anadyr*. One splendid building, the former headmaster's villa, served as a residence and headquarters for Fidel when he visited.

Colonel Tukov arrived at the compound just before sundown, his driver having made the two-hour trip from his missile base near San Cristobal at the maximum speed possible. Fortunately, they'd been able to follow one of the few good highways in Cuba for most of the way, since Tukov's missiles were the closest to Havana of any of the sites, and El Chico was only a dozen miles or so southwest of the Cuban capital.

The rocket officer had been surprised by the summons to headquarters and, no stranger to the workings of the USSR, a little worried. He had previously met General Pliyev, the commanding officer of Operation *Anadyr*, but did not know him well. Yet the venerable cavalryman had a reputation as a no-nonsense soldier of the old school. Earlier this year, he had commanded the troops that broke up a workers' strike in Novocherkassk, an intervention that had resulted in the deaths of many workers. He would brook no resistance, no foolishness.

Tukov wasted no time making his way to the headquarters, which was located in the administration building of the former school.

"Comrade General, Lieutenant Colonel Tukov reporting as ordered!" he barked, snapping a smart salute.

General Pliyev looked up from the map he'd been consulting, blinked a moment as if trying to remember Tukov. "Ah yes, Tukov—in command of the San Cristobal battery. Of the 539th Regiment. Come in."

Tukov saw that Pliyev had been studying a map of western Cuba. His own battery was clearly marked, as well as the six SAM sites surrounding it. Not too far north of him was the camp of one of the Motorized Rifle Regiments, a powerful unit of the Red Army equipped with tanks, artillery, and tactical nuclear weapons.

"I understand that Comrade Fidel has paid a visit to your battery. Is this correct?" the general asked bluntly.

"Yes it is, sir. He came with Comrade Guevera and asked for a tour of the site. I showed him around. I hope that is acceptable."

"Not that you could have stopped him" Pliyev said with the shrug. "But I wonder: Why did he select your unit for his only personal inspection?"

"I'm not sure I can say, Comrade General. Perhaps because we are the closest battery to Havana. It may be that he was informed that I speak Spanish. He seemed to want to confirm this fact for himself."

"Ah, yes. Those years in Madrid, fighting Franco. I understand you did some good work there."

"Thank you, General. We tried, but we lacked the strength to prevail."

"And now, Colonel, we have some strength here, do we not? In your battery alone you have enough power to destroy six large American cities. What do you think of that?" Pliyev sounded like he could barely believe that fact himself.

"I will follow my orders until death, Sir," Tukov replied, hoping that was an acceptable answer to the odd question.

"How is security?"

"We are very well guarded, and the local population has been moved out. Security, I think, is excellent, sir."

Pliyev scowled, and shook his head. "Maybe it is on the ground," he replied. "But what about the air? These missile batteries need too much space, have too much equipment, to stay hidden. Do you know that the initial reports of our advance team suggested that we'd be able to hide our batteries in coconut groves?"

"That would seem to be inaccurate, Comrade," Tukov replied diplomatically.

"And if our bases are spotted, that would blow the lid off this entire operation, this entire island."

"Can we use the SAMs to destroy American surveillance planes?" the battery officer asked.

"We have not been authorized to fire, as of yet," the general declared in frustration.

"Well, we've avoided discovery so far," Tukov suggested. "Perhaps the Americans will hesitate to fly over us merely out of fear of those SAMs."

Pliyev waved away the assurance. "Perhaps, but remember this: an American spy plane could fly overhead and take pictures any day. And those pictures could blow this whole crazy operation to pieces."

Two: Mission 3101

13 October 1962
2050 hours (Saturday night)
4080th Strategic Reconnaissance Wing
Edwards Air Force Base
California, USA

They called it by a name that seemed like it came from some science-fiction story: a "high-protein, low residue" meal. United States Air Force Major Richard Heyser preferred to describe it as "steak and eggs." For what it was worth, as he sat down at the private mess table to tuck in to the large plate of hot food, he would also call it "delicious."

An airman had awakened him only twenty minutes before, after Heyser had slept most of the day away in a darkened bunkroom. After a quick shower, he donned his fatigue uniform and ate the meal that the cooks had specially prepared for him. Not only did he like the food, but he appreciated the "low-residue" element. Once he got into his flight suit, it would be a very long time before he'd be able to get to a bathroom.

It was already dark here in the California desert as he was given a short jeep ride from the barracks to the ready room. Entering the small building a half mile from the hangar area, he donned the protective gear required to fly his unique airplane. The U2 would carry him up to 70,000 feet in the air, where the atmosphere was too thin to sustain life. As a result, the pilot's suit was more like astronaut's than an aircraft pilot's. Leaving his helmet off for now, he walked into a small airtight chamber and sat down in a comfortable chair. He spent the next hour breathing pure oxygen, slowly leeching all of the nitrogen from his blood. He didn't begrudge the time—he knew that, in the event of a suit failure at high altitude, condensed nitrogen would quickly inflate into bubbles in his veins and arteries, clogging his bloodstream, to cause the painful and possibly fatal condition deep sea divers had long known as "the bends." An hour of O_2 would make sure that didn't happen.

While he was breathing the cool, dry air, he took the time to go over his briefing sheets, which had been updated just the previous evening. He knew that his would be the first spyplane mission over Cuba in several months. Now he read that, according to classified sources, a Soviet-style air-defense system, which had been under construction all summer, had been activated just a couple of days before. This meant that he ran the risk of an attack by the lethal SA-2 antiaircraft missile, the same type of "SAM" that had shot down Francis Gary Powers' U2 over Russia in 1960. Just a few weeks earlier, another U2—one operated by the Nationalist Chinese out of Taiwan—had been shot down by a SAM while conducting an operation over Red China. He filed the information away without trepidation: he knew he was a great pilot, and that—in his opinion—would trump any threat from ground-based missiles.

He also read that the early weather reports from the Caribbean predicted skies would remain clear over the island of Cuba for at least the next few days. This mission had been authorized for more than a week now, but on each previous day, cloud cover over the island had forced a postponement—usually before he had even been awakened, and always before he'd made it to the oxygen chamber. This report of clear skies was the news that the 4080th SRW had been waiting for, and it meant that the mission today was probably a go. Heyser knew that other aircraft from a different USAF recon wing, RB-47 Stratojets, had already deployed to Florida. They would soon be in the air, standing off of the island but confirming the forecast as soon as dawn brightened the tropical skies.

After he'd spent a little more than an hour breathing the oxygen, another pair of airmen came to drive him out to the aircraft in an Air Force van. Heyser wore a mask attached to a portable O_2 tank in order to maintain the gas's saturation in his blood. As the vehicle approached and illuminated the U2 with its headlights, Heyser looked through the windshield and admired the sleek lines, the graceful and slender shape, of an airplane that was like no other machine in the world. He felt the usual thrill of pride in knowing that he was one of a very, very small group of men who could fly that plane. And of them all, he'd been selected for this, perhaps the most important aerial reconnaissance flight ever undertaken.

Heyser, and his Air Force colleague Major Rudy Anderson, had not been directly involved in the squabbling between the CIA and the USAF over the U2 program, but he knew the background. He's learned that the plane, a product of the Lockheed "Skunk Works," had initially been commissioned by the intelligence agency, after the Air Force had sought heavier, more military looking designs, in the early '50s. The intervening years had shown that none of the other recon planes had the flight characteristics, neither the range nor the ceiling, of the U2, so it wasn't long before the USAF had contracted for a U2 fleet of its own.

But in the meantime, the CIA's U2s had been upgraded with improved engines, which allowed them to attain the almost inconceivable altitude of nearly 14 miles above the ground. In the end, it had been politics that pushed the program into the USAF's eager hands: in some cases, such as this mission, the U2 would be required to intrude into the airspace of a potentially hostile state, and the powers-that-be had determined that the man who flew such a mission had better be a commissioned military officer, rather than a civilian spy. Further wrangling had resulted in the CIA grudgingly handing over some of its high-performance U2s to the Air Force.

As the clock entered the early hours of 14 October, Major Heyser prepared to take one of those planes into the sky. He was not a large man, but even so he had to squeeze himself into the very tight confines of the cockpit. He ran through the pre-flight checklist, and everything was a go. At 0230 hours, local time, he released the brake and allowed the single powerful engine to start him down the long runway.

For all of its tight cockpit space, the U2 was a fairly large airplane. The wings were long and gently tapered, a full one hundred feet in span, as opposed to the mere sixty-foot length of the fuselage. In order to save weight, many typical items of aircraft equipment had been omitted. Those wings, for example, would have scraped on the ground from their own weight, since the designers had been unwilling to install extra wheels. Instead, each wing was held off the runway by a strut, with a wheel on the bottom, that rested in a socket on the underside of the wing, midway to the end. The strut was not attached to the plane in any way except for the gravity that caused the wings to sag downward when the U2 stood at rest. When the aircraft lifted off the tarmac the struts and wheels would fall to the ground, where they would be collected for reuse by the ground crew.

The force of the jet engine pressed him back into his seat as the U2 gradually accelerated down the runway. Since the plane was designed for the thin air near the stratosphere—and power assists on the controls would have added unnecessary weight—Heyser had to use all of his considerable strength to pull back on the stick, forcing the balky machine into a very shallow climb. A minute later he felt the freedom of flight and banked very gently as he continued to gain altitude. He continued to gradually get higher and higher as he crossed southern California, Arizona, New Mexico, and Texas, until by the time he reached airspace over the Gulf of Mexico, he was more than ten miles above the placid, still-dark waters below.

14 October 1962
1150 hours (Sunday midday)
Chairman's office
Kremlin, Moscow

The Defense Minister and Foreign Minister arrived together, ready to brief their Chairman on the latest developments in Cuba and regarding Operation *Anadyr*. Nikita Khrushchev knew that just an hour ago Foreign Minister Gromyko had been in contact with Ambassador Aleksandr Alekseev, the Soviet Union's senior diplomat in Cuba. Following this meeting, Gromyko would be taken to the airport, where he would board a plane that would carry him to the United States for a diplomatic conference with President Kennedy—part of a series of meetings that had been scheduled for the latter part of this year, in an attempt to improve communication between the two superpowers.

Khrushchev gestured at Gromyko to go first. "What is the latest word from our revolutionary comrade in Havana?"

"Comrade Fidel has repeated his request that we announce the presence of the missiles, and of our mutual defense treaty, immediately, rather than waiting until the missiles are operational," Gromyko replied. "He is delighted with our deployment of strategic weapons to his country, but feels that knowledge of that deployment, and awareness of our mutual defense pact, will serve as additional deterrent to the imperialist enemy."

"Impossible! We have come so far already. The plan will work best as a *fait accompli*," the chairman insisted. "The Americans must know nothing about our missiles until those missiles are ready to fire."

"Comrade Alekseev has made Comrade Castro aware of your views, and the Cuban leader accepts your decision. But he did want his opinion made known to you," Gromyko replied apologetically. His reticence was understandable—there were not too many people willing to let Khrushchev know that they disagreed with him.

"And we are very close to readiness now, are we not, Rodion Yakovlivich?" the chairman asked, turning his attention to the Defense Minister. "Are any of the missiles ready to fire if the order was given today?"

"No, Comrade Chairman," Malinovsky replied, understanding that his leader was asking a rhetorical question—Khrushchev had been briefed on a Operation *Anadyr* on a daily basis and knew down to a matter of hours the progress made on each of the installations. "But the SS4 launch sites are well under way, and all of the equipment, launchers, missiles, and warheads have arrived in Cuba. The warheads are being transported to a secure storage facility, while the launch installations themselves are rapidly being made operational."

"Best estimate, then?"

"I believe I can assure you that within seven to nine days from now, the SS4 batteries will be ready to fire. Those in central Cuba are approaching completion slightly ahead of the batteries in the west, near San Cristobal in Pinar del Rio province."

"Splendid! Even those, mere medium-range ballistic missiles, will change the balance of power completely." The chairman leaned back far in his chair, lifting his short legs to rest his feet on his desk. "The Sandals, as I recall, will be able to reach Washington D.C. and even New York City, from Cuba. It will serve the Americans right to feel the threat of nuclear destruction from just beyond their borders—as we have known that threat from imperialist bases in Turkey, in Italy, in England."

Khrushchev nodded in satisfaction at his own reasoning before continuing. "And the SS5s, the intermediate-range Skean rockets? They will take a little longer, will they not?"

"Indeed, Comrade Chairman. Most of the SS5 equipment, and all of the warheads, are still at sea. Some of the initial preparations have been made, but the warheads— aboard *Alexandrovosk*—will not even arrive in a Cuban port until another ten days or more has passed."

"But when the IRBMs are ready, we will be able to strike at every corner of the United States. The Yankees will have nowhere to hide!"

"Almost completely," Malinovsky agreed, adding slyly: "Of course, Seattle and the northwest corner of their country, as well as Alaska and Hawaii, will remain beyond even the

SS5 range. But the bulk of the United States will be vulnerable to a fast strategic strike."

"There you have it," Khrushchev stated, as if the facts had made his case. "We will wait until both the medium-range and intermediate-range ballistic missiles are ready to fire before we announce their existence."

"Very well, Comrade Chairman. I will convey word to our ambassador," Gromyko replied.

"And I will encourage our troops to work even faster than they are right now, in support of the *rodina*," Malinovsky added, invoking the sacred cause of the Russian motherland.

"So, very soon the Americans will know what it is like to fear annihilation! They will be so surprised!" Nikita Khrushchev exclaimed, clapping his hands in giddy excitement.

Across the desk, Defense Minister Malinovsky and Foreign Minister Gromyko did not seem to share his glee.

0730 hours (Sunday morning)
Altitude: 70,000 feet
Approaching Cuban coastline from the south

So far, Photoreconnaissance Mission 3101 had gone off without a hitch, but Major Heyser knew that the truly risky stretch awaited him, a few miles in front of his nose—and some fourteen miles below. An hour earlier he'd been given the "all clear" by the crew of the RB47 on weather forecast duty, so he proceeded on the due-north course that would soon carry him directly over the communist-controlled island.

The details were encouraging: Cuba's skies were free of cloud cover. No defensive fighter patrols had been detected, though even if they had, Heyser would have proceeded with his mission. No other aircraft on earth could fly high enough to challenge a U2. As far as the surface-to-air missiles, the pilot was prepared to take his chances.

His target area lay in the westernmost province of Cuba, Pinar del Rio. He had been ordered to make a single pass, from south to north, which would leave him over the island for only about twelve minutes. Rumors from ground sources indicated suspicious activity there, especially around the town of San Cristobal. His job was to confirm or deny the suspicions of the various United States intelligence agencies.

Heyser doublechecked the camera controls as he crossed the line below, where the blue water turned to verdant greenery, and then he activated all systems. It was merely a transition of color from this altitude—he could only imagine that his eyes made out a strand of beach between the sea and the tree cover.

The main piece of equipment in the belly of the U2 was the monstrous, high resolution "B" camera, which exposed each frame on an eighteen-inch by eighteen-inch negative. The reel of film for the B camera was nearly a mile long, and so heavy—and the U2's flight characteristics so sensitive—that it was sliced down the middle so that it rolled in equal lengths onto drums to the port and starboard of the camera, in order to equalize the weight. The B camera shot straight down, while a smaller "tracking" camera captured images stretching from one horizon to the other on two-inch squares of film. Each could shoot multiple frames per second and would continue to record images until the pilot turned off the camera motors.

Heyser could make out little in the way of detail from his lofty height, though his chart showed him that, about halfway between the south and north coastlines, he flew over the town of San Cristobal. He kept his eyes and ears tuned to his controls. A buzzer would sound if the aircraft was picked up by SAM tracking radar, and the buzzing would accelerate to a staccato zat-zat-zat of noise if the airplane was hit by the more intense missile-targeting radar. His flight over Cuba lasted the expected dozen minutes, however, without either of his radar detectors giving any indication that the Communists knew he was there.

Even so, he breathed a little easier once he was over the Florida Strait. He gradually reduced his power, bringing the U2 almost to a glide as he lost altitude over several hundred miles, flying northward toward his destination of McCoy AFB, in central Florida.

0900 hours (Sunday morning)
Battery 2, 539th Missile Regiment
San Cristobal, Cuba

At dawn, Tukov made a walking tour of his installation, which—for all its incredible striking power—did not cover a terribly large amount of ground. His battery, one half of the 539th Strategic Rocket Regiment, consisted of four launchers and a total of six missiles, centered around the headquarters compound. Each launcher was supported by an array of trucks that carried equipment for fueling and servicing the rockets. Long tents had been erected, and the missiles had been moved into them for protection against both unwanted observation and potentially destructive elements of the weather.

The final stage of preparation was the laying of massive concrete pads, one for each launcher. These platforms had been cast in the Soviet Union and trucked, at great difficulty, to the battery site. Two of the pads were already here, while he'd been informed that two more were on their way and should arrive by tomorrow.

The Soviet colonel knew that elite infantry units of Castro's Revolutionary Armed Forces had cleared the residents from a fairly wide area around the battery, and that the Cuban soldiers constantly and aggressively patrolled the area to ensure that no unsuspecting hunter, herder, or sightseer—not to mention potential counterrevolutionary spy or saboteur—wandered too close. To further enhance the battery's security, Tukov assigned Russian troops to guard the perimeter of the installation, within the boundary of the fence that had been quickly installed.

He knew that, out of sight of his immediate area but close enough to support, a series of six SAM sites had already been created, surrounding him with a ring of powerful antiaircraft rockets. The SA-2 launchers were located in a Star of David pattern, with antiaircraft missiles based at each point of the star and the MRB launchers, Tukov's responsibility, in the middle.

Additional protection on the ground was provided by the presence of the 134th Motorized Rifle Regiment encamped between San Cristobal and the coastal cities of Mariel and Havana. Tukov hadn't visited his fellow countrymen's camp yet, but he had seen it marked on Pliyev's map and had approved. An MRR offered tremendous combat punch, as it was equipped with an armored battalion containing thirty of the USSR's most modern tank, the T-55. The armored formation was augmented by three battalions of well-trained infantrymen, all of whom could be transported in armored personnel carriers. A battery of artillery, antitank, and antiaircraft units, including several FKR "Frog" battlefield nuclear-rocket launchers, provided massive fire support.

If the Americans came, they would almost certainly come from the north, Tukov knew. Thus, after landing on fiercely contested beaches and battling through Cuban coastal-defense units, they would have to fight their way through the 134th MRR before they could reach the rocket battery. All in all, it was the best he could hope for.

His tour completed, he walked down the dirt road from the fourth launcher back to his headquarters compound, which was a cluster of tents enclosing his communications equipment and the unit's kitchen and infirmary, as well as sleeping and living quarters for the headquarters staff—the crews of the individual launchers camped near their weapons. Right now, his men lived in tents. Only after the equipment was fully operational would more permanent types of creature comforts be considered.

All these observations, procedures, and concerns—the area defense, the progress toward completion, the accommodations for his men—ran through his mind until he saw the Cuban army jeep, with a uniformed driver at the wheel, parked outside of his headquarters. He bit back his frustration as Che Guevera emerged through the tent flap.

Tukov's personal sentry, a loyal peasant lad named Gregori Smirnovich, looked at Tukov in mute apology, and the officer could hardly blame the young soldier for failing to stop the charismatic revolutionary from entering the colonel's headquarters in his absence. Though he had a thousand things demanding his attention, the officer forced a smile onto his face and saluted Guevera.

"Comrade Che. It is an honor to see you again at our humble unit position," he declared in Spanish.

The Argentinian flashed a sly smile. "There is nothing humble about your unit, Comrade Tukov. I think you have more destructive power at your fingertips than perhaps any general or emperor from any previous era throughout the long and violent history of man."

"You know, that's true," Tukov conceded. "Though matters of seeing that my men are housed and fed, that my equipment—however powerful—is operational, sometimes keep me from seeing that large picture."

"You must never lose sight of it. You, your men, your glorious revolutionary republic, are examples to all of us. I cannot overstate how much your presence means to Comrade Fidel and myself, to all of Cuba. You give us a chance to stand against the *yanqui* menace, a menace which has loomed over this country since it gained independence from Spain."

"Is there something I can help you with this morning?" Tukov asked, entering his tent as Che followed him.

"Perhaps it might be the other way around," said the Latino. "Perhaps you know that I have been entrusted with command of western Cuba—Pinar del Rio, in particular. When the Americans come, this will be their first target."

"You say 'when' as though it's a foregone conclusion. Do you have some new information on the American response?" Tukov asked.

Che merely shrugged. "I believe it is inevitable. The enemy finds our regime intolerable and will act to destroy it."

"Your revolution is doomed, then?" The Soviet colonel was surprised: Che did not seem depressed at the prospect he so casually presented.

"This is not my revolution, Comrade—it is a revolution of world socialism. Sacrifices must be made, and those sacrifices may have to include myself, Comrade Fidel, possibly this entire country. If, by sacrificing ourselves, we can bring about the transformation of the world, I would gladly lay down my life."

Tukov was appalled by the casual description "Surely it will not come that, comrade," he suggested. He continued gamely. "Of course, in the event your supposition is correct, I agree. The area from Havana west, including San Cristobal, will be the first target of an American invasion." It was not a great leap of logic, since anyone who looked at a map would reach the same conclusion.

"And I did know," Tukov added, "That San Cristobal, and all of this end of your country, has been placed under your command. Congratulations on an important assignment."

Che waved away the compliment. "My men have made me a headquarters bunker, less than an hour's ride from here. It is deep in a cave and should be proof against any kind of attack—not that I intend to spend much time there," Che added hastily. "But I have taken the liberty of writing down directions, and the necessary passwords, so that you and your officers can establish direct communication with me. In the event that something occurs which impairs our general strategic communications network, of course."

"I am honored, Comrade Che." Since the 'strategic communications network' of Cuba relied essentially on a web of antiquated telephone lines, such a contingency was not a bad idea, Tukov knew. Privately, however, he resolved to hold on vigorously to his place in the Soviet Armed Forces chain of command. Things would have to deteriorate very much indeed before he took orders from even the highest ranking of Cubans—especially when he had heard Che and Fidel both express their surprising willingness to employ Tukov's weapons of mass destruction, even when such use would inevitably result in the absolute obliteration of their cherished island.

For now, the famed revolutionary seemed content with Tukov's expression of gratitude. "I want you to think of me as an able assistant, ready to help you in any way I can," Che concluded, his handsome face creased into a cheery smile. "If you have need of anything, anything at all, please do not hesitate to ask.

"Thank you, Comrade Che," Tukov replied, happy to see his visitor heading back to his jeep.

"*Viva la Revolucion!*" Guevera declared as his driver fired up the engine.

"And long live your homeland, and mine," Tukov replied.

He said the last words in Russian.

0950 hours (Sunday morning)
McCoy Air Force Base
Central Florida

The most difficult part of a U2 flight was arguably the landing. Those long wings caught so much air beneath them that at the high-atmospheric pressure near the ground, they almost refused to relinquish their grip upon the sky. So the CIA pilots, and their Air Force colleagues, had come up with a unique tactic to overcome this last bit of resistance. A spotter on the ground would race along the runway behind the plane as it settled for a landing, radioing precise instructions to the pilot related to exactly how much distance remained between the U2's wheels and the tarmac.

Since no military ground vehicle was fast enough to perform this task, the various bases hosting U2s had resorted to a rather colorful variety of civilian cars. Heyser had never landed at McCoy, so he was curious as to what sort of vehicle his spotter would employ.

The major glided toward the runway at less than 100 feet of altitude, aligning his flight path with the long strip of concrete. Tuning his radio to the local frequency, he spoke into his helmet mike. "This is flight 3101, ready for landing. Do you read me?"

"Copy loud and clear, Major. Do you see me—off to port, gaining speed now?"

The pilot looked out through the clear canopy as the plane, still slowly descending, gliding on virtually no engine power but still at a ground speed of some 150 miles per hour, crossed over the end of the runway about a dozen feet above the ground. He saw his spotter at once. It would have been hard to miss the fire-engine red Corvette convertible, with the top down, accelerating from the side. One airman, no doubt an experienced sergeant, drove the car, while the landing officer perched on one knee in the passenger seat. His left hand clutched the top of the windshield while the other held a microphone to his mouth.

"I've got a visual," Heyser reported.

"Good, Major." Even through the crackling microphone, the pilot could hear the wind roaring around the speaker's face. "You've got eight feet of clearance under your gear, now seven. Hold her steady."

He flew over the car but knew it was racing to catch up as his speed dropped to 140, then 130 and on down, as he fought to bring the airplane down to the ground.

The fatigue of the long flight made itself known as Heyser kept a firm grip on this stick, trying to will the slender airplane onto the runway. He had to settle gently because, as another weight-saving measure, the U2 was not equipped with standard, very sturdy landing gear. Instead, a pair of lightweight wheels, not unlike those one would see on a bicycle, extended directly below the cockpit, while a smaller pair of similar wheels dropped from the tail. Since the wingtip support struts had been left on the field at Edwards, the wingtips themselves were protected by metal skids that were intended to prevent damage once they sagged to the tarmac. By then, of course, the airplane would be traveling fairly slowly.

Finally the pilot felt contact with solid ground, and he rolled along, gradually decelerating, for more than a mile. The wings, as expected, slowly settled until both tips touched ground at the same time, a perfectly balanced landing. A screech of noise accompanied by a shower of sparks exploded from each skid, but the additional friction quickly brought the U2 to a rest.

"Perfect, Sir—very well done!" exclaimed the landing officer as the Corvette rolled past at a gentle fifty miles per hour or so. "Welcome to McCoy, Major, and I will see you at the hangar."

"Thanks for the escort," Heyser replied, watching the flashy red sports car speed away.

An Air Force maintenance crew came roaring toward him in a "deuce and a half" truck. The vehicle skidded to a stop beside the aircraft, and three enlisted men hopped out. Two lifted the starboard wingtip while the third quickly installed the strut to hold the wing off the ground. Moments later, they repeated the process on the port wing. Thus supported, Heyser goosed his jet engine with a little more power and taxied the U2 toward the line of hangars.

When he finally scrambled from the cockpit, he was met by the landing officer, a first lieutenant who had jumped out of his Corvette to greet Heyser with a crisp salute. Behind him stood a USAF major and a captain, and a pair of men in civilian clothes. Enlisted men swarmed under the fuselage, hastily opened the camera bay doors, and wasted no time in extracting the canisters of film. The two senior Air Force officers picked up the small cans from the tracking camera and started off at a fast walk, while the pair of civilians wrestled the heavy rolls from the B camera onto a dolly.

"How was the mission, sir?" asked the landing officer.

"Easy. A milk run," Heyser replied honestly. He watched as the film was hurriedly readied for transport. The civilians started rolling the dolly toward a small transport jet at the next hangar.

"What gives?" the pilot asked his fellow officer, indicating the men in suits. "Aren't they taking all the film to Omaha?"

"Orders," said the lieutenant. "Part of the deal we made with the CIA. The tracking film goes to our boys at Offut. But the detailed stuff from the B camera, that's going straight to D.C."

2110 hours (Sunday night)
"The Press Club" Lounge
Washington, D.C.

Stella wasn't sure she should believe her eyes, but she felt pretty certain that she recognized the man in the black suit who had just walked into the bar. She excused herself from the group of reporters she'd been talking to and went over.

"Bob?" she said. "Bob Morris?"

He turned, holding the mug of beer the bartender had just drawn for him, and blinked in surprise. "Stella?" he replied in obvious recognition. She couldn't help noticing that he seemed very happy to see her. "Stella Widener. Wow, it's been…well, a really long time."

"Since our senior year at Alexandria," she said, remembering back to a high school period that seemed like it belonged to a different woman's life. "You took me to homecoming that year," she reminded him.

"Don't think I don't remember," he said. "We graduated together that spring—class of '50."

"Don't remind me!" she said with a laugh. "That was twelve years ago!"

"Sorry," he replied sheepishly. "It was a long time, but I remember it like yesterday. You were—you're still—that is, you look amazing. How are you? What are you doing?" A short hesitation, a glance at the bare fingers of her left hand. "Are you married?"

"That's a lot of questions, more like me than you, I think. Which I guess answers your middle question first: I'm a reporter. I started with the *Boston Globe,* now I work for NBC here at the Washington bureau." She tried to keep the pride out of her voice—in fact, she'd been the first female reporter hired by any of the national networks. "And I'm well, I guess, and no, I'm not married. What about you?"

"Not married!" he declared hastily. "And I'm working for the Secret Service. I got hired by Treasury out of college, and I've been there ever since."

Her reporter's senses tingled. "Are you in the anti-counterfeiting branch?" she asked disingenuously.

"No." Now it was his turn to be proud, she saw—and he was less adept at hiding the fact than she hoped that she had been. "I'm with the White House. Presidential Detail."

"Wow! Congratulations Bob—that's wonderful." She really was impressed. At the same time, she was keenly aware of an opportunity to add a source to her notebook, if she went about it carefully.

"And you—NBC, huh? I knew you'd make good, somehow. That must be fascinating work now. We live in interesting times." His tone turned wistful. "I never saw you after graduation, you know. What happened to you? I stopped by your house that summer, but your family had moved."

"The life of a Navy brat," she said, truthfully. "Dad got transferred to Pacific Fleet and moved the family to Pearl Harbor. Of course, I didn't stay there long—I went to Harvard in fall. You were destined for Georgetown, if I recollect, weren't you?"

"I've never strayed too far from home," he admitted. "But dang, I'm glad to see you. Listen, can I buy you a drink? Do you have plans for dinner?"

"Yes, and no," she said with a genuine laugh. "You always were quite the gentleman," she added. "That homecoming dance, that was my first kiss."

He chuckled, an easy, genial sound. "I think it was for me, too," he admitted. "So how about we go to this nice steak house I know, just around the corner. I'd love to get caught up with you."

"Me, too," Stella said. "Let's go."

She did remember that kiss, vividly. And she realized that she wouldn't mind picking up right where the two of them, twelve years earlier, had left off.

These were interesting times, indeed.

15 October 1962
0410 hours (Monday early morning)
National Photographic Interpretation Center
Washington, D.C.

The B camera film had been developed by the Navy's high-speed lab in Alexandria. Even so, the process took most of the night, so that the transparencies didn't arrive at NPIC until nearly dawn. The NPIC director, Arthur Lundahl, had been called at home around midnight with an alert to be ready, and he and several of his staff were already in the office, waiting, when the Navy courier with the sealed, heavy envelopes, arrived.

"Quite the neighborhood," the petty officer commented, after he'd climbed the stairs to the second-floor office.

"Makes good cover for a secret installation, doesn't it?" Lundahl said as he signed receipts for the images. Indeed, the NPIC location looked rather scary from the outside. Located above a rickety, struggling Ford dealership at the corner of Fifth and K Streets in northwest Washington, it meant visitors had to kick aside cans, newspapers, and the occasional sleeping drunk on the sidewalks just to make it to the building. The stairway to the second floor was barely illuminated, and the railing frighteningly wobbly.

Yet the door at the top was heavy steel, set into a reinforced frame. And inside that door was the most modern photographic analysis facility in the world. The NPIC was truly Art Lundahl's baby: It had been born at the same time as the U2 aircraft became operational, and the reconnaissance plane and the analysts' lab made for a perfect match.

Over the last seven years, Lundahl had installed the most advanced equipment and assembled the most skilled staff available. And they had only gotten better with experience. Teamwork was stressed, and the personnel included both military and civilian. Over time, they had learned to glean incredibly detailed bits of information from the seemingly most innocuous details taken by an aerial photographer.

The rest of the staff had been notified of a high-priority job, and the men had all assembled by 6 a.m. An analyst from the CIA and another from the Air Force took charge of the pictures that Heyser's U2 had taken over San Cristobal, and throughout the morning they began to spot crucial details.

"These are SAM sites, here," the CIA man, Gene Lydon, pointed out when Lundahl came over to check on their progress. "Looks like they're fully operational now, but on the last round of pictures, from August, they'd just started construction. Somebody's been very busy down there. You can see they've installed the launchers in the same six-pointed star shape that they use in Mother Russia herself, which usually means they're protecting something in the middle of that circle."

"In the homeland, that's how they post them around airfields, army bases, and strategic rocket sites," Lundahl remembered.

"But here, this—this is the interesting part," interjected Jim Homes, of Air Force Intelligence. He pointed to a blurry area in the middle of a circle of the SAM launchers. "You see these six trailers, here? They're pretty damned long. I think we have us some missiles—missiles that are a helluva lot bigger than the SA-2."

Within minutes, other analysts were pulling out voluminous books containing data on Soviet missiles, while the first two men carefully took measurements from the photos, using the known scale to determine the exact length of the trailers and their pencil-shaped cargoes. The men at NPIC had distilled a great deal of intelligence about Soviet missiles systems, from sources as varied as public displays such as the May Day parades, where the missiles were shown to the masses—and to visiting dignitaries and intelligence agents—to aerial reconnaissance of Russia. Some of the data almost certainly came from spies, since it contained detailed reports of the equipment needed for each type of missile, as well as the procedures for fueling, aiming, and firing the rockets.

The technicians used delicate calipers to measure the exact length of the objects in the photos and compared those lengths to the catalogue. By mid afternoon, the conclusion was obvious.

"We have an installation of SS4 Sandals," Homes reported grimly. "medium-range ballistic missiles. They can only have come from the USSR."

"All right," Lundahl acknowledged. He'd come to the same conclusion himself but had held his suspicions private in order to avoid influencing his analysts. It was nearly 5 p.m. "Fellows," he announced. "Call your wives and tell 'em you won't be home for dinner tonight. I think we have an all-nighter in front of us."

At 5:30, Lundahl put a call through to the Deputy Director of Intelligence at CIA, Ray Cline. He summarized his findings in flat, emotionless terms.

"Okay, we're going to need to move fast," Cline replied. "I'm going to call McGeorge Bundy at the White House to give him the heads up and see how he wants to proceed. I think it's safe to say we won't be sitting around on this."

"I thought not," Lundahl agreed, knowing that the National Security Advisor would take great interest in, and feel a great deal of alarm about, these pictures.

"You're going to need to prep some briefing boards," the DDI said. "Can you have them over here at 7:30 tomorrow."

"I'm working on them right now," Lundahl replied. "They'll be ready."

"Good," Cline answered. "Get an hour or two of sleep if you can. I have a feeling you'll be taking those boards to the White House sometime tomorrow."

16 October 1962
0245 (Tuesday very early morning)
Sleepee Time Motel
Fayetteville, North Carolina

"Did anyone ever tell you, darlin', that you have really gorgeous tits?" Greg Hartley asked the pretty blond who was perched, somewhat unsteadily, on the side of his bed.

He meant every word of it, too. Those breasts had been the first things he'd noticed about the young waitress who'd served him a burger and French fries at the diner near Fort Bragg, just about eight hours ago. Her name was Misty something, he'd learned, and she was free after her shift ended at 8. And she was a girl, she let on, who liked to have fun.

"I may have heard that somewhere before," she admitted, giving her chest a little shake. Hartley had found it hard not to stare while he was in the restaurant—though he'd given it a game try—but now those breasts were naked, not more than a foot from his nose. It was downright impossible not to look.

Even through the haze of alcohol and a very long night, he felt a rush of pleasure. The 82nd Airborne Division, where he was a platoon commander, seemed very far away, now that he was nearing the end of a three-day leave. The uniform, with its prized paratroopers badge, meant something to Hartley: it meant an opportunity to meet girls, impress them, and, as often as not, get them into bed. Of course, his prized blue Thunderbird, parked right outside this room, helped a lot in that department as well.

All in all, life wasn't too bad for this Texas boy. He was an oilman's son, and despite his lazy approach to studies and a C average, his father's money had gotten him into college.

An ROTC course have given him the rank of second lieutenant, and all in all everything seemed to be working out pretty well.

"Come on," Misty said, giving him an intimate squeeze as he lay on the bed beside her. "Let's do it again."

"All right, sugar," he said agreeably. "If you can get me ready, I'll try and finish the job."

"I want some more champagne, first," she said slyly. "You should open the last bottle."

"We still have one?" he asked in surprise. His head felt foggy, and his tongue seemed swollen in his mouth.

"You bought four, we only drank three." She reminded him, pointing to the fresh bottle, leaning slightly in a small cooler of ice, on the narrow counter.

Hartley looked at the bedside clock: 2:50 a.m. He concentrated on the math problem, realizing he had three hours and ten minutes until his leave was up and he had to report back to the 82nd Airborne at Fort Bragg. He factored in the rest of the data: Fort Bragg was about 20 minutes away from here. He'd drop Misty off at the restaurant, where she'd left her car, which was more or less on the way back to base.

"I'm just not sure, darling'. I really need to get a little rest," he admitted.

"Come on," she pleaded. She got up and brought him the unopened bottle, then knelt on the edge of the bed. "I'll make it worth your while." Her head dropped down to his lap and she started to go to work on him.

He arched his back and thrust upward reflexively. Damn, it *was* worth it!

"All right, baby," he said, as he struggled to open the bottle without sitting up or dislodging Misty. "Ready or not, here we go again."

0915 hours (Tuesday morning)
Lincoln Bedroom, The White House
Washington, D.C.

"That lying son of a bitch!" cursed the President of the United States.

National Security Advisor McGeorge Bundy was seated beside the President's bed, where JFK was propped up by several pillows while he'd been reading the morning paper. Bundy could only nod solemnly, sharing the President's opnion of Nikita Khrushchev. He'd just finished briefing his boss with a summarized version of the conclusions reached by the team of analysts at NPIC.

"You seem pretty certain about this," Kennedy said, almost accusingly.

"Sir, Art Lundahl's certain, and that's usually worth money."

"Dammit! Ambassador Dobrynin assured us in plain words that they had no intention of using Cuba for offensive weapons. And Khrushchev's said the same thing in God knows how many speeches! For Christ's sake, he's acting more like a gangster than a head of state! We can't trust a goddam word he says!"

The President clenched his jaw and punched a fist into his bed, then made a visible effort to calm down. "All right," he said, leaning back against the pillows and closing his eyes. "We can't take this public, not yet. How soon can the principals get here? And you'll need to clear my schedule sometime today for at least a few hours. But we can't afford to arouse any suspicions, to let the press know that anything's up. I want to have a plan in place before this makes the evening news! We need to talk about our options."

"Wally Schirra is bringing his family by this morning, and the photographers are looking forward to that, so I don't think you should cancel."

"I agree," JFK said. Schirra was one of America's original seven astronauts, and one of Kennedy's favorite heroes. He had just returned from orbiting the earth on the Sigma-7 mission, America's longest space flight to date.

"I think I can clear your schedule by noon without raising any eyebrows," the NSA replied.

"That's when we'll do it, then," the President replied. "We'll meet in the cabinet room. You know who to bring."

"Yes sir, Mr. President. Noon it is."

Bundy left the bedroom for his office, leaving Kennedy to breakfast with Jackie and his two children. A few hours later he welcomed Schirra, and the two families mingled. Caroline was pleased to show off her pony, Macaroni, on the White House lawn, and the assembled photographers snapped countless adorable pictures.

In the meantime, the National Security Advisor was making calls. He'd already seen the briefing boards prepared by Lundahl and had informed the NPIC director about the noon meeting. Lundahl, too, spent a busy morning at the White House, preparing Bobby Kennedy and several other officials with a preview of the news. Bundy ended up moving a few of JFK's appointments from the early afternoon hours. By 11:45, most of the invitees had trickled into the White House, arriving at separate entrances, sometimes two or three to a car, in order to prevent any rumors from starting.

The men made their way to the cabinet room, where they found the President chatting with five-year-old Caroline. Jack Kennedy escorted his daughter from the room, returned, and locked the door behind him. He took a seat at the middle of the table and looked around. No one saw his hand slide under the table and push the button to activate the tape recorder that would make a record of this conversation.

John F. Kennedy had made it a point to surround himself with men he considered "the best and the brightest" that the nation had to offer. Now these men would make up the group that would determine the future course of American policy, and very possibly the future course of the world. Among them were General Maxwell Taylor, Chairman of the Joint Chiefs of Staff and a personal friend of the President; Defense Secretary Robert McNamara, the former president of Ford Motor Company who was renowned for his quick, almost computer-like, brain; and the professorial Secretary of State Dean Rusk. Former ambassador to Moscow, Llewellyn (Tommy) Thompson, one of the few Americans with face-to-face knowledge of the Soviet leadership, had been invited because of his unique perspective. Others, such as Vice President Johnson, the secretary of the Treasury, and various CIA and NSA officials, were also present, some eighteen men in all for this first strategy meeting.

McGeorge Bundy took a seat at the head of the table. "This is a meeting of the Executive Committee of the National Security Council," he said. He waved Art Lundahl forward, and the director of the NPIC put a bulletin board onto an easel. The board displayed several large black-and-white photographs, with accompanying text and arrows indicating certain features on the pictures.

"These pictures are the result of a U2 flight over western Cuba. They were made two days ago, Sunday, October 14. Yesterday two more U2 missions were conducted over other parts of the island. That film is being processed as we speak.

"However, even from this initial mission, it has become clear that Soviet ballistic missiles have been brought to Cuba, and launching sites are being prepared for them."

He paused to let the expressions of outrage, universal among these men, resonate through the room. They all knew that Khrushchev and his lackeys had pledged, publicly and privately, that the USSR had no interest in turning Cuba into a base for offensive warfare. The sense of betrayal was real and raw; anger ran deep around the full circle of the group.

Lundahl went on to explain the capacities of the missiles, pointing out that Washington D.C. was well within their range. "This battery has four launchers, which is only one half or one third of a missile regiment. It seems likely there are more. We should have additional information on that tomorrow, after the more recent pictures are developed."

"How long would it take, following launch, for one of these missiles to reach this city?" the President interjected.

"About ten minutes, Mr. President," Lundahl replied.

"Why would they do this?" Rusk demanded. "It doesn't make sense!"

"They must feel the same way about our Jupiter missiles in Turkey, and elsewhere," McNamara retorted. "More important is, what are we going to do about them?"

"Exactly," JFK declared. "General Taylor, what can we do?"

"The most direct response, and I think one that would have the full backing of the armed services, is a surprise airstrike with as many USAF and Navy assets as can be brought to bear. We'll need more recon to make a full target assessment, but we can hit them very, very hard."

"With conventional weapons, not our own nukes?" Kennedy followed up. "A surprise attack?"

"Yes, Mr. President. Napalm, wing-mounted rockets, and a whole lot of conventional gravity bombs. The element of surprise is crucial: it would give us the chance to catch them in the open and inflict the greatest possible damage.

"But could we be sure to destroy all the missiles?" Bobby Kennedy wanted to know.

Taylor took a moment, then shook his head. "No, Sir. I'm afraid there is no way to guarantee that every target would be destroyed. In fact, I'd have to say it's very unlikely that the first strike could accomplish that."

"So we'd go to war against them—with a surprise attack, like our own version of Pearl Harbor—and we'd kill lots of Cubans, and probably Russians, too." He turned to Lundahl. "Would there be Russian personnel at these sites?"

"Almost certainly, Sir. For one thing, the Soviets are very closely guarded with their nuclear technology. Also, it's complicated stuff; I doubt Cuban crews would have the technical expertise to use them."

"So a surprise attack would leave both Russia and Cuba scarred and angry, with at least a few ballistic missiles capable of reaching our nation's capital," JFK summarized succinctly and bitterly. "This does not sound like a satisfactory plan. Any other options, gentlemen?"

"We can file a diplomatic objection in the United Nations," Rusk noted. "Try to get the rest of world opinion on our side."

"Khrushchev doesn't give a plugged nickel for world opinion," McNamara argued, while Taylor, Bundy, and many of the others nodded in emphatic agreement. "And there's no guarantee that he would launch a missile against us if we attack. We still have a huge intercontinental arsenal pointed at his country."

"And he has nuclear assets of his own," the President pointed out. "No, gentlemen, we need to keep this situation from escalating to the point of a nuclear exchange."

The meeting continued as the men wrangled around the edges of the airstrike idea. All agreed they needed more information, and at the President's insistence they acknowledged that, during these discussions, they would rule nothing out.

"We'll meet again this evening, seven o'clock," Bundy finally declared, when the discussions had become circular and he knew that the President needed to be elsewhere, if eyebrows were not to be raised in the public and, in particular, the press. "Remember to arrive discreetly, travel together when you can, and let's keep the lid on this thing for as long as we can."

Three: ExComm

"Somebody's got to keep them from doing the goddamn thing piecemeal!"

General David Shoup, Commandant, USMC
Meeting of the Joint Chiefs of Staff, 19 October 1962

17 October 1962
0830 hours (Wednesday morning)
Cabinet Room, The White House
Washington, D.C.

The director of the CIA, John McCone, strode into the imposing and historic building on Wednesday morning as a man whose controversial opinion had been vindicated, but one who could take very little pleasure from the fact that he'd been proved right. Even if he had been inclined to gloat, he was further burdened by the reality that he'd had to fly back to Washington from California under a somber cloud—he'd been called urgently to return from the West Coast, where he'd been to attend the funeral of his daughter's husband, who had died suddenly just a few days earlier.

Thus, it was a weary and discouraged DCIA who carried the envelope containing the latest intelligence data, which had crystallized overnight with the analysis of vast reams of photo evidence,. New pictures were coming in a steady stream, from multiple and extensive U2 flights over Cuba every day. The film was arriving in Washington almost faster than NPIC could keep up—in fact, Lundahl's lab had never before had to work so hard, and the staff had gone to a 24-hour-a-day schedule to keep up with the flow of film.

Most of the members of the President's advisory group, which had come to be known as ExComm—short for "Executive Committee on National Security"—were present for the DCIA's briefing, though President Kennedy did not attend. Bundy called the meeting to order, and the men listened attentively as DCIA McCone spoke for several minutes.

"We've now identified five separate ballistic-missile sites on the island. Three of them are in the west, around San Cristobal, while two are closer to the middle of the country, an area around the medium-sized city of Sagua la Grande. Those sites, and the entire coastline of Cuba, are protected by a ring of at least 23 SAM batteries, though we suspect there are even more of those to be discovered.

"Most of the SAMs look to be completely operational, though a few remain under construction—and even at those, steady progress has been made on preparations at all the unfinished sites. The Cubans and their Soviet helpers have clearly made major strides in improving their air defenses in the last eight weeks." If McCone was bitter because his advice on maintaining the U2 flights over that interval had been ignored, he gave no clue to the men of ExComm.

"Even the completed sites have not been activated for operations yet, but from the looks of the launchers and the installations, it might be as simple as flipping a switch. The SAM search radar is called 'spoon rest,' and once that's turned on, we'll be able to detect the emanations, but they'll be able to follow our aircraft and shoot."

"How certain can we be about this?" asked RFK.

"We have a ship, the *Oxford*, that has been patrolling off the north coast of Cuba for several months, now. It's carrying some of the most highly developed electronic analysis equipment in the world. We're fairly certain that if a search radar gets turned on anywhere on the island, *Oxford's* crew will immediately be aware of the fact."

"How far along are the ballistic-missile sites?" asked Max Taylor. The chairman of the JCS looked grim.

"It seems likely that at least some of them will be ready to go into action this coming weekend. Others should be ready to fire by early to middle of next week," McCone replied bluntly.

"Are all of these strategic missiles the SS4 Sandals, the medium-range ballistic rockets?" asked McGeorge Bundy.

McCone shook his head. "More bad news, I'm afraid. The indications are that at least two of the sites are being made ready for the SS5 Shyster. It has twice the range of the Sandal. However, those sites are in the early stages of preparation. There's no sign that the missiles or launchers have actually been delivered to the location, or even to Cuba at all."

"What are we doing about this?" Bundy followed up.

"We continue to step up the aerial surveillance. You may know that the 4080th SRW has transferred operations from Texas and California to McCoy AFB in central Florida. Additional pilots have been brought in so that Majors Heyser and Anderson—our most experienced U2 pilots—can get enough rest to stay fresh.

"A total of six missions are scheduled for today, but it will be Friday morning before we'll be able to have any conclusive results from those pictures. Still, it's fair to say that our picture of Soviet missile operations in Cuba is becoming more tightly focused every day."

"Do we have enough targeting information to begin launching airstrikes?" Defense Secretary McNamara asked.

"I would say 'no,'" the CIA director replied. "At this moment, that option presents too many risks to issue a 'go' order."

"I'm inclined to agree with John," General Taylor said. As the only military man present, his opinion carried a great deal of weight on this question. "As we discussed yesterday evening, our own vulnerabilities in Turkey and Berlin mitigate against an immediate act of war. And we still don't have a complete picture of the target situation. A premature strike could trigger a response from units we don't even know about yet."

"Has there been any interference with the U2 flights?" Bundy asked. "Cuba MiGs coming up after them or anything?"

"Not so far," McCone responded. "They have to know we're up there, but for whatever reason, they've not chosen to react."

"Well, we're not just going to sit here, are we?" demanded Bobby Kennedy. "We know that the Soviets respect strength and determination, and very little else!"

"Agreed," McCone said. "But any airstrike is going to kill an awful lot of Russians and Cubans, and pressure the Kremlin to make some kind of equal response. A gradual imposition of some kind of sanction—such as a naval blockade of Cuba—would demonstrate strength, and give both sides time to evaluate before lives start to be lost."

"I think we need to consider that option a little more carefully," Tommy Thompson agreed, with Dean Rusk seconding the idea. "Khrushchev is volatile and hot-tempered, but he's also shrewd. When given a chance, he'll take the long view—although he doesn't always think things through. Still, I think it's crucial we figure out a way to give him some time to prepare a response, rather than do something that's going to cause him to fly off the handle and react out of anger."

Once again, no clear path was determined, but by the time McCone left the meeting at 9:30 to brief the President, ExComm at least had two clear options on the table. Most of the men present still favored launching massive airstrikes against the missile installations as soon as the target list could be completed. Some favored following up the air attacks with an invasion of Cuba, as soon as it could be mounted.

But a few, including Bobby Kennedy, McCone, and Thompson, among their influential advocates, were beginning to seriously discuss the more patient option of some kind of naval blockade.

1345 hours (Wednesday afternoon)
"The Tank"
Joint Chiefs of Staff Meeting Room
The Pentagon, Washington, D.C.

"What's the hold up?" Curtis LeMay demanded, as soon as the five chiefs had settled into their places around the flight-deck-sized conference table. "Why haven't we been given the order to start bombing? We've known about these damned missiles for two days now!"

His belligerent challenge was directed to the chairman, General Maxwell Taylor, who held up a hand in a useless gesture intended to calm the volatile Air Force leader. They knew that the chairman had the ear of the President, and also that he'd been present at the White House strategy meetings. For now, he presented a convenient target for their frustrations.

"Don't tell me we're going to let the bastards get away with this?" the Air Force Chief spluttered. "That's a goddam outrage!"

The Air Force Chief of Staff may have been the most vocal, but the other four service commanders clearly agreed.

"The Navy has 4,000 Marines aboard ship right now in the Caribbean, in a fleet of nearly fifty ships," Admiral George Anderson, Chief of Staff of the United States Navy, pointed out. "They're embarked on a landing exercise, planning to go ashore at Puerto Rice—Vieques Island, to be precise. We've been working on this through the summer. The men are thoroughly trained, and I think they're ready for the real thing."

The others nodded. The training exercise, dubbed Operation ORTSAC in a not-too-subtle reference to the Cuban dictator, was the largest such action attempted in the last few years. As if sharing the same thought, the other men looked to General Shoup, commandant of the Marine Corps. The bellicose officer had won the Medal of Honor at Tarawa, during WW2, and though he was not a full member of the JCS, his opinions on matters relating to the Marines were valued.

"I think we should cancel the exercise and turn those ships around so that the Marines can make a start at the real thing," Shoup proposed. "We'd need to provision for live action of course, but the troops and their equipment are assembled."

"We need to take steps to get ready, at the very least," General Earle Wheeler of the Army suggested. "This might be the best excuse we'll ever get to go after Castro with world opinion at least partly on our side."

The other officers digested that thought without disagreement. In fact, over the last several months, they had tossed around several ideas to justify an invasion of Cuba, including such schemes as blowing up an American ship in Guantanamo Bay, sponsoring acts of terrorism in Miami or Washington, or downing a civilian airliner—with each triggering event being falsely portrayed as the act of one of Castro's agents.

"Why doesn't Kennedy let us go ahead with the airstrikes?" LeMay persisted. "We could remove those missiles in the first hour of the campaign! Then the Marines and Army could move in and mop the place up."

"He's got to look at the big picture," Taylor argued. "An attack against Russian installations seems very likely to provoke Russian retaliation."

"Bullshit!" the Air Force general barked. "If we go in there fast enough, with enough force, Khrushchev'll take the message that he can't get away with this kind of crap. He'll have no choice!"

"And once the missiles are destroyed, we'd proceed with the invasion," Shoup added. "With respect to the admiral, I think we could be ready to put two Marine divisions ashore with no more than a week of notice."

"And the Army could attack at short notice with the 82nd and 101st airborne," General Wheeler agreed. "We could follow up with a heavy formation, like the 1st Armored Division, as soon as we had a secure port to land the tanks. There's little to no risk of the USSR becoming involved, and we could overrun the entire island in a matter of days. Afterward, our analysis suggests one infantry division would be enough to hold the whole country until they can get a stable government up and running."

"I think you might be underestimating just a bit there, Earle," said the Marine general. "The Corps has done a lot of analysis—we've had boots on that island quite a bit over the last seventy-five years. Cuba is over 44,000 square miles in size, with a population near seven million. Our expectation is that three divisions will be needed over the course of a few years before the place is pacified."

"At the very least, let us start the mobilization," Wheeler said, again addressing Max Taylor. "That way, if—when—we're needed, we're ready. We've had the plans drawn up for years now, just this past summer revised into OPLAN 314 and OPLAN 316." These two plans represented schemes to attack Cuba with airstrikes followed by an invasion, the first with an interval of only two days notice, the second being a stronger attack that theoretically required four days to set up.

"I know," Taylor stated with a bit of an edge to his voice. "Get your staffs reviewing all aspects of the OPLANs. Make the preliminary preparations so that if and when the President gives the order, you're ready to go in the requisite time frame."

"Well, that's something. At least we'll have units in position," the Army Chief of Staff acknowledged.

"I've already got Sweeney down at Tactical Air Command in Virginia moving his strike aircraft to our bases in Florida. We'll be ready to go," LeMay pledged.

"All right," the Chairman agreed. "Start the call ups, cancel leaves, that sort of thing. Continue moving units, ordnance, and supplies into position, both for a bombing campaign—which might have to begin on just a few minutes notice—and for an invasion."

18 October 1962
0900 hours (Thursday morning)
82nd Airborne Division
Fort Bragg, North Carolina

"What do you see here, Hartley? Can you tell me that much?" Captain Martin's voice was a growl, not unlike the aggressive noise made by one of the bulldogs that he so closely resembled. He thumped his fist on his desk.

Second Lieutenant Greg Hartley had been standing rigidly at attention, eyes fixed on the wall—and the photo of airborne hero General Matthew Ridgway—behind his commanding officer's desk. At Martin's gesture, however, Hartley forced himself to look down, while managing to avoid meeting the angry captain's eyes.

He saw a black-and-white picture of a crumpled hood, a twisted bumper, and shattered windshield, and he recognized the image at once. "That is my car, Sir. My blue '56 Thunderbird, to be precise."

"Your car, huh?" Martin replied, spinning the photo so that he could mockingly examine it. "That's funny. It looks like a piece of junk to me. Scrap metal, I'd call it."

Hartley sighed inaudibly but didn't think an answer was called for. And indeed, his commanding officer proceeded as if his subordinate couldn't possibly have anything to say. "The MPs tell me this—'car,' you called it—was found wrapped around a tree, about two miles outside the gate to this very fine military installation. They found it yesterday morning. Coincidentally, you were reported entering the fort through that gate on foot, at approximately 0800 hours that morning. Let's see: if my math is correct, that is approximately two hours after your leave was over. Is my math correct, Lieutenant?"

"Yes, Sir, it is." Hartley braced himself. His hangover had faded by yesterday evening, but he felt sick to his stomach as he thought about the crash that had cost him his most prized possession. His bandaged forehead still ached from the impact.

"You have identified this piece of scrap metal as your car. And you returned to the fort on foot. The gate guards reported that you had some blood on your forehead as well. Can I deduce, Lieutenant, that you have some knowledge of how this former automobile came to be wrapped around a tree outside the front gate of Fort Bragg."

"I'm afraid I drove it there, Sir. I—er—it was an accident."

Martin changed tacks almost faster than Hartley could follow. "Did you or did you not volunteer for this unit, Lieutenant?" demanded the captain, knowing full well that the 82nd was an all-volunteer unit.

"Volunteered, Sir. I am proud to be an All American."

"Do you know this history of this unit? Do you know about the heroic American paratroopers who landed behind the Nazi front line at Normandy? Who paved the way for the defeat of Adolf Hitler? Do you understand the meaning of the word 'elite'?" continued Martin, the sarcasm growing even thicker—if that was possible.

"Sir! Yes, Sir."

"Well, Hartley, if it was up to me, I'd cashier you out of this unit so fast you'd have to slow down just so your underwear could keep up with you. You'd be out of the airborne, and shipped off to whatever godforsaken backwater they could come up with. Probably filling out supply requisitions to buy seal blubber from the eskimos! And I'd be happy to be rid of you! Do you read me, Lieutenant?"

"Loud and clear, Sir. I would like to offer my apol—"

"Shut up about that! It wouldn't make any difference. But it so happens that it is not up to me, that I can't, at least of this moment, ship you out of here! And do you know why, Lieutenant?"

"No, Sir, I do not," Hartley replied honestly.

"It's because we need your worthless ass in that uniform, in command of your platoon—and we need it there right now! As of this morning, the entire 82nd Airborne Division, including F Company and its ineptly commanded Second Platoon, is being activated and ordered to prepare to move out. We are to be ready to move on one hour's notice. So you will march out of here, Hartley, and you will make sure your men are ready to go. And when I order you to move, you will move when and where I tell you to go! Do I make myself understood?"

"Absolutely, Captain." Sensing—at least hoping for—dismissal, Hartley snapped a crisp salute, right hand tight against his bandaged forehead. When Martin didn't say anything further, the lieutenant took his chances and did an about face, then marched stiffly out of his CO's door.

1012 hours (Thursday morning)
Harry S. Truman Annex
Key West Naval Air Station
Key West, Florida

"Well, Sullivan, now they've decided to go ahead and send us that Hawk battery," Commander Alex Widener told his chief petty office, tossing the latest coded message from Washington onto a steadily growing stack of paper. "The thing is, they're not sending me any more acreage!"

"I see, Sir," the non-commissioned officer replied, knowing as well as his commander that the small naval air station was already packed to capacity. "Hawks are antiaircraft missiles, our most modern. I suppose this means they're worried about an air attack against Key West. From Cuba, obviously."

"Well, that's the only reason I can think of for them to deploy an antiaircraft missile battery here. We'll have to find some place to put them—and if the Commies come north, I guess we'll be glad we have it here."

"What about the Marines, Sir? Any word about them?"

"Not yet," Widener said with a groan. "But I've been told we might be getting a whole Marine Air Group. That'd be strike aircraft and fighter support. If that happens, I've got them earmarked for the south apron. The planes and most of the equipment will have to stay outside."

"What about the men, Sir? How would we house them?"

"I don't know what the hell I'm going to do," Widener said. "It'll probably come down to buying up every hotel room in town."

"One good thing, then," Sullivan said, looking for a silver lining. "Key West has a helluva lot of hotels."

1245 hours (Thursday midday)
Atlas F Missile Silo
310th Bombardment Wing
Schilling AFB, Kansas

First Lieutenant William Bodden, USAF, took a few seconds to reread the communication that his dedicated teletype machine had just spit forth. He knew what the message meant, and he'd been trained to react with all haste to just these words. But he wouldn't have been comfortable with God, or his conscience, if he hadn't taken the time to make sure. He read it again slowly, and then he was sure.

He took the microphone from its stand on his desk, clicking the button to make sure it was active. "This is

Bodden," he began. "We are going to mobilization status. Prepare to fuel the rocket."

His team of six men didn't hesitate. The Atlas F was the most modern version of that venerable program, the USA's oldest ICBM design, but the new model had done away with many of the flaws of the earlier Atlas. The "F" variant was the first to be stored vertically, in an underground, hardened silo, which greatly enhanced the missile's chance of surviving a Soviet first strike.

More significantly, the Atlas F operated on an advanced fuel compound. Unlike the earliest versions, which relied upon liquid oxygen that could not be pumped into the rocket until immediately before launch, the F variant began the countdown phase with a very stable kerosene liquid fuel. Two of Bodden's men were already attaching the fueling lines, beginning the process.

Once fueled, the rocket could remain underground, protected in its silo. Once the launch order was received, the kerosene would be replaced by liquid oxygen in a matter of minutes, before an elevator lifted the ICBM up to the surface. Bodden and his men knew that once the initial preparation had been completed, they could have a devastating nuclear payload launched into the sky in a matter of about ten minutes after receiving the "launch" order.

1701 hours (Thursday evening)
Oval Office, The White House
Washington D.C.

President Kennedy found it hard to conceal his anger at the two men who had just been seated on the couch in his Presidential office. Soviet Ambassador Anatoly Dobrynin was known to him, and even more well known to his brother, who stood just behind JFK's seat in his desk chair. Jack had made a point of asking for Bobby's attendance at this meeting.

Over the past summer and early fall, Dobrynin had been most ardent in denying that the Soviets would ever install offensive weapons in Cuba. Bobby Kennedy, in particular, had taken his assurances to heart. Now both Kennedys felt personally betrayed, and angry.

Foreign Minister Gromyko was more of a cipher. His visit to the U.S. was the occasion for this meeting, which had been scheduled for many weeks. It was one of several face-to-face encounters, supposedly intended to improve the often balky communication between the two great powers. To prepare for the meeting, the President had ordered a series of photographs prepared, proving the existence of the missile sites in Cuba. Those photos were in a folder in the top drawer of his desk. In the event JFK could maneuver Gromyko into an obvious lie, he intended to produce the pictures and watch his adversary squirm.

As soon as the pleasantries were out of the way, however, the Soviet foreign minister went on the attack. "My government must protest, again, your nation's continued interference in the affairs of our erstwhile ally, Cuba," he declared stiffly. "American influence is being projected beyond your borders in ways that are intolerable, and dangerous to the world. There have been reports of sabotage missions too numerous to recount, and these saboteurs—all of whom have been arrested by Cuban security personnel—are clearly carrying equipment provided to them by your CIA."

The Russian didn't give Kennedy a chance to respond before he turned the focus to Berlin, accusing the Americans of fomenting the division in that walled city by inciting "good, honest citizens" into fleeing their homeland for the West. All the while, Ambassador Dobrynin sat in silence. The President thought the ambassador seemed puzzled by his boss's harangue but didn't dare contradict him or steer the conversation in a more constructive direction.

"Cuba is in our sphere of influence," JFK stated, when he finally got a chance to get a word in. "And, by historical precedent and practical reality, we will take a great influence on happenings there. This does not mean we are committed to destroying Castro's regime. But if, for example, your country was to place strategic offensive weapons there, we would clearly be required to take some action."

He left the implied accusation hanging, but Gromyko didn't rise to the bait. "Berlin is in our sphere!" he barked. "How do you think it feels to have American and other NATO troops there—an enemy garrison in the midst of our friendly territory? It would be like asking you to tolerate a Soviet Army Base in the middle of Texas!"

The President could only shake his head at the ridiculous analogy. "To continue," he said. "We are hoping to establish a more direct dialogue with your government—so that we can discuss important matters, before they reach the crisis stage," he concluded ominously.

Gromyko merely moved on to a litany of complaints about Turkish patrolling of the border that NATO ally shared with the USSR—as if Turkey was a threat to the Soviet Union! He complained about economic activity in West Germany, designed, he said, "To exploit the labors of the dedicated workers of East Germany."

The meeting became little more than an illogical harangue. Gromyko did all of the talking for the Soviets, employing every faulty debate trick out of the high school handbook: circular reasoning, "straw man" arguments, and imaginary facts. He fell back on doctrine and ideology, pressing the verbal offensive so vigorously that there was no chance to bring up any substantive issue. By the time the pair of Russians rose to leave—after about forty minutes—JFK was glad to see them go.

He spoke to his brother privately, as soon as the office door was shut. "They're going to wait until the missiles are operational before they admit they're there," he said bitterly. "They want a *fait accompli*."

"Then you've got to make sure that doesn't happen," RFK replied. "Whatever we do, time is running out."

"I know. Tell me, what did you think about Dobrynin?" Jack asked, since Bobby knew the man better than he did.

"I get the feeling he really doesn't know about the missiles."

"You know what? I do too. He's just one more pawn in their game. But it makes me wonder: how many others in the Soviet hierarchy either don't know about the missiles, or don't approve of what's going on?"

"That is a very good question. But we have to assume that both Castro and Khrushchev are in full support of the plan. And if they're for it, it doesn't really matter what anyone else on that side of the wall thinks, does it?"

"No, it matters what we think, though," the President noted. "And the more I think about it, the more reluctant I am to start a war over this. I want ExComm to come to some sort of consensus. As for me, I'm leaning toward starting with a blockade of Soviet shipping, and letting things develop from there."

"All right," Bobby agreed. "Are you still going on that campaign swing this weekend? You're scheduled to leave tomorrow for Ohio, then Saturday in Chicago with Mayer Daley."

"How could I pass that up?" Jack said, with a wry shake of his head. "I think you'd better hammer the point home to the committee while I'm gone. I want to have a plan in place by the end of the weekend."

1824 hours (Thursday evening)
Apartment 5-B
4571 Dupont Circle
Washington, D.C.

Stella had stripped off her work dress and stood in her bathroom in just her bra and panties as she applied a new layer of lipstick and carefully brushed her blond hair. She realized she was humming a little-remembered dance tune from her high school years. The music was so captivating to her imagination that she almost didn't hear the phone ringing in her living room.

Racing in her bare feet, she picked it up on the seventh or eighth ring. "Hello?"

"Stella!" She recognized Bob Morris's voice. "I'm glad I caught you."

"I'm not ready yet," she replied, chiding and flirting at the same time. "You said you've be here at seven."

"Yes, I know." She heard the apology coming, and she was surprised by how deep her disappointment cut. "Listen, I am so very sorry, but I'm afraid I won't be able to make it tonight. Something has come up with, well, work."

Immediately her whole being transformed from a starry-eyed young woman to a veteran reporter. "Really? What's going on?"

"Well, of course, I can't say. But I'm going to have to work tonight. Probably every night for the rest of the week," Bob said. "I'm really sorry—I can't tell you how much this aggravates me! Running into you the other night, making this date...well, it was just great."

"Well, I thought it had the potential to be rather great, too," she said, deciding to play hardball. "But if you're going to break our date—with a half hour's notice, no less!—you'll have to give me a little more explanation." She tried to sound stern, while she listened carefully to any kind of clue in his voice. She knew instinctively that something big was going on.

Stella could sense Bob's hesitation, but she waited, projecting patience she in truth did not possess.

"All right. The thing is, there's kind of a crisis going on. The President's schedule is really up in the air, and they've increased the roster of agents on duty. People are coming and going—well, I really can't say any more."

"You mean, there's some kind of plot against him?" she asked, feigning horror even as she was fairly certain that wasn't the case.

"No, no," he confirmed. Apparently he decided that the least he could do was ease her fears about the President's immediate safety. "It's a political—really, an international thing. Honestly, I'm sorry. But I'm not allowed to talk about it. I hope you understand."

"Apology accepted," she said, graciously enough. "Please keep our President safe," she added, as if in jest but in fact very sincerely.

"I will do my best," Morris said. "Can I...would it be all right if I called you when this is over?"

"Please do," she said. She hung up the phone and leaned against the kitchen wall. There was only one explanation she could think of, and she couldn't help but put the conclusion into her father's and her brother's words:

The shit in Cuba was about to hit the fan.

19 October 1962
0545 hours (Friday early morning)
Chairman Khrushchev's Apartment
Kremlin, Moscow

As Operation *Anadyr* approached completion, it became the focus of Nikita's Khrushchev's full attention. He was becoming increasingly aware that he had thrown the dice on a major gamble, and those dice were still rolling.

Most of the time, he felt confident that the Soviet plan would prove triumphant. When the Americans awakened to the fact that they had a lethal strategic arsenal parked virtually on their doorstep, they would have little choice but to accept that state of the affairs—as the entirety of the Communist world had been forced to accept the reality of American missiles targeting them.

But sometimes, a tiny voice of doubt would begin to whisper in the corners of his mind. What if the missiles were discovered before they were operational? The installations were terribly vulnerable, he knew, and the feeble Cuban air force—and even the relatively small portion of the Soviet military present on the island—would be powerless against American air power. The bases could be destroyed by bombing, which would be a tremendous humiliation to the chairman personally, and to the cause of world communism.

Even in his darkest, weakest moments, he didn't give much thought to the dangers of an American invasion. There, he was convinced, the Soviet ground forces present in Cuba would prevail. They had an array of battlefield nuclear weapons, such that they could probably wipe out an imperialist invasion fleet even before the first troops landed on the shore. The Americans would be foolish to try and attack into the face of such a defense, and whatever the Americans were, Khrushchev knew they were not fools.

His agitation was such that, last night, he had decided to stay in the small apartment maintained for his use in the Kremlin, disdaining the drive out to his residence and a night at home with Raisa. He was not one to work late into the evening—that brought back too many memories of the Stalin era, those eternal sessions where the previous chairman had insisted his subordinates, including Khrushchev, get drunk on vodka. Often he had endured Stalin's fierce glare, knowing of the paranoia, and the utter ruthlessness, behind the man's cunning mind. No, those days were over, and Khrushchev would not subject himself, nor his own subordinates, to that treatment.

Even so, he had been too restless to go home. He retired early, with a KGB man standing guard outside the apartment, but tossed and turned all night, never able even to get comfortable. Finally, near dawn, he did slumber—only to be awakened by a knock on the outer door of the apartment.

He looked at the clock, alarmed to see the time, realizing that it would take a good reason for someone to knock at the door of the Chairman's apartment at this hour.

Khrushchev was sitting up in bed when the KGB man on guard duty tentatively tapped at the bedroom door.

"Come!" he declared curtly.

"I am sorry to disturb you so early, Comrade Chairman, but this cable arrived from our embassy in Washington. They have just decoded it and felt it should be brought to you immediately."

"Very good," Khrushchev said. "Give it to me and leave me to my privacy."

He picked up the piece of paper as soon as the man had left, annoyed to see that his hand was shaking. It was a message from Foreign Minister Gromyko, and the chairman felt a chill as he read the few lines:

Met with President Kennedy as scheduled 18/10/62. No overt acknowledgement of ANADYR, *but suspicions raised. Concerns on operational security increasing. JFK issued warning against installing "offensive weapon systems" in Cuba, said USA would not tolerate presence of such weapons.*

Khrushchev felt a shiver of panic. Had the weapons been discovered? Surely not—the Americans would certainly do something if they knew about the missiles! No, Gromyko, damn him, was just worried, like the old woman he was! The operation remained on course, and now they were close, so close, to being ready. It was too late for anything to go wrong!

Despite his most resolute reassurances, however, he was not able to go back to sleep.

0945 hours (Friday morning)
Cabinet Room, the White House
Washington D.C.

The five Joint Chiefs of Staff came into the cabinet room like they were marching to war. At least, that's how it looked to the young President, though at least the Chairman, Max Taylor, was a friendly presence. The other four: LeMay of the Air Force, Anderson of the Navy, Wheeler from the Army, and Shoup of the USMC, could barely muster a polite greeting to their Commander in Chief.

Taylor started out by reporting on the briefing the JCS had just received at the Pentagon. "The latest round of pictures show conclusively that there are at least two sites in preparation for the SS5 Skean, the intermediate-range missiles that would be able to reach virtually the entire continental US. Those missiles themselves have not been seen in Cuba yet. The SS4 Sandals, however, are probably going to be operational sometime this weekend."

"That's my understanding, as well," the President replied. He looked around the circle of stern, military faces. "What do you gentlemen think should be done?"

LeMay, not surprisingly, was the first to speak. "We need to go in there with air power, Mr. President, and flatten those missile sites into the ground! All this talk about a blockade, well, that's just dilly-dallying around. We need to take them out! And we'll neutralize their airfields while we're at it. As for an invasion, well, I guess the jury's still out on that one. But we have to attack!"

"The problem with attacking, General, is that Comrade Khrushchev might be inclined to attack back. He's made enough noise about Berlin that I'm certain the Soviets would take over that city in the blink of an eye, if we give them an excuse."

"They wouldn't dare!" LeMay countered.

"I think they would dare. And if they do, the only option left to us is to fire nuclear weapons—which is a hell of an alternative."

The Air Force Chief drew a deep breath, visibly trying to maintain his self control. "Sir, you don't understand. It's if we don't do something that they'll know they can take Berlin. A blockade, to them, will look like weakness—like appeasement." LeMay blinked, then blurted it out: "It would be as bad as Chamberlain at Munich!"

The President stiffened, angry. All these men remembered Munich, the benchmark of craven leadership in the face of dictatorial threat. More personally, JFK's father, Joseph Kennedy, had been the American ambassador to London at the time and had supported Prime Minister Chamberlain's acquiescence to Hitler's demands. Ambassador Kennedy had finally been recalled by President Roosevelt when the elder Kennedy voiced public skepticism of Britain's chances of survival in the face of Nazi military superiority. His mistaken assessment of Hitler had ended Joe Kennedy's political career, but now it seemed that his son was picking up right where the father had left off.

President Kennedy remained silent, his eyes boring into the Air Force Chief's. If he was waiting for an apology for the audacious remark, it was not forthcoming. Instead, LeMay pressed on. "You're in a pretty bad fix!"

The President snorted, a sarcastic bark of laughter. "Well, you're in it with me. Personally!"

LeMay blinked, and the other generals chuckled slightly, the tension broken. When it became clear that Kennedy was determined to pursue the blockade option, the JCS began to discuss, earnestly, how that blockade could be implemented.

"If you do opt for the airstrike option," LeMay said, "You should know we could be ready to go by Sunday morning, 21 October. Although we would have more assets on hand by Tuesday, the 23rd."

The conversation was suspended for a moment when Bundy came into the room. "Sir," he said to the President, "It's time to leave for your campaign trip."

"Thanks, George," JFK replied, standing. "And thanks for your input, gentlemen. I'm going to step out, but you can continue your conversation if you wish."

In the hallway, Kennedy told Bundy they'd make a small detour. He stopped at the private recording studio, where Ron Pickett was dutifully watching the tape recorders. The technician looked up, a little startled at the intrusion, but quickly returned to studying his dials and reels.

"Can you put that onto a speaker?" JFK asked.

"Certainly, Sir." His hand trembled slightly, but Pickett flipped a switch. Moments later the voices of the JCS, angry and frustrated, came crackling into the room.

"You were really screwed, there," someone said.

"It had to be said," LeMay's flat Midwestern voice proclaimed. "Let him fire me if he wants to. We're giving Castro and Khrushchev a green light!"

"Don't I know it, Curt," said Marine Corps Commandant General David Shoup. "It's like you said: we have the Russian bear by the balls. We should cut off his legs, and take his balls while we're at it! Use your bombers to take out these bases, and then send in my marines to clear the commie bastards right off of that goddamn island?"

"Damn straight. But he won't listen to reason. Shit! He's every bit as bad as his father," LeMay growled.

"Turn it off," JFK ordered. "I've heard enough."

He turned to Bundy as he started down the hallway to the elevator. "You know, the problem with LeMay and these blowhards is if we do what they want us to do, and they're wrong, there won't be anyone left to tell them so!"

1015 hours (Friday morning)
Battery 2, 539th Missile Regiment
San Cristobal, Cuba

Tukov had taken to starting his morning routine an hour early, so that he would be finished with his initial patrol by the time Che Guevera made his almost daily stop at the missile base.

"I have an idea," the Argentinian said without preamble, when he was ushered into Tukov's tent.

"Go on," the Russian said politely.

"As we've discussed, your missiles are vulnerable to American air attack. Even with the SAM protection, there is a chance that a surprise attack could knock them out of service before they could be used."

"Yes, that is true," Tukov agreed. It was one of the hazards of this position, and he had taken it for granted.

"Standard doctrine would call for you to have a reserve position, would it not? In case this installation becomes compromised?" Che noted suggestively.

"Yes, it would. But a lot of standard doctrine has been set aside in light of the circumstances. For example, we need a solid concrete pad to base the launchers on, and we're just now getting the last of those installed. We don't have any more available to create a reserve position," Tukov pointed out.

"Hence, my idea," Guevera said, cheerfully undeterred. "Did you know about the quarry?"

"I don't understand," the Soviet colonel replied, annoyed at the feeling he was being toyed with.

"It's very near here, an old pit where limestone was excavated. One side has been bulldozed away—there's a nice flat ramp leading down to the bottom. And that bottom is smooth, hard limestone. It's as solid and flat as any concrete pad."

"Really?" Tukov replied, intrigued in spite of himself. Indeed, the lack of a reserve position was something that had bothered him, though it had been too far down on his list of concerns while he was still trying to bring his unit to operational status. But it was something he would like to address. "Can you show me this place?"

"It would be my honor," Che Guevera replied with obvious sincerity. "I know you are busy here," he added—acknowledging the fact for the first time, Tukov thought. "Tell me when you have a couple of free hours, and we will go there."

"All right," the colonel agreed. "How about we make it first thing tomorrow morning?"

20 October 1962
0900 hours (Saturday morning)
Cabinet Room, the White House
Washington D.C.

The Saturday morning ExComm meeting began while the President was campaigning with Mayor Daley and the Democratic party in Chicago. When most of the other members were present, however, DCIA McCone got right to the point.

"Our latest evidence, from yesterday, indicates that the SS4 sites in central Cuba, Sagua la Grande to be precise, are operational. Those in the west, around San Cristobal, are only a couple days away from completion. Our time is running out."

The news, having been anticipated by progress reports over the last few days, came as no great shock. By now, the consensus had moved away from the surprise air attack option. Pearl Harbor had been invoked too many times for these men, all of whom had vivid memories of that stark betrayal—and the vengeful spirit it had roused in the American people—to order a similar action from this government.

"Can I conclude we're leaning toward the option of some kind of blockade, then?" Bundy asked as they moved to a decision point. A murmur of agreement rumbled around the table, though Max Taylor shook his head grimly. The Chairman of the JCS, it was known, still favored some kind of military action.

"We need to get the President back here," Bobby said. "I don't think we can proceed to the next step without him."

They called in Pierre Salinger, the Press Secretary. Salinger had intentionally been kept out of the ExComm in order to avoid putting him into an awkward situation with the reporters he needed to interact with on a daily basis. Even now, he was told only the minimum: "We need to get my brother back here today. There's an urgent matter that needs his attention, but we don't want to set off any alarms, or cause any undue publicity."

"Daley's not going to be happy about it," Salinger noted.

"He'll have to get over it," Bobby replied. "The point is, how can we get it done?"

"The tried-and-true method is probably the best," replied the veteran at press relations. "We'll announce that President Kennedy has a cold and needs to cut short his campaign trip to protect his health."

1955 hours (Saturday evening)
Apartment 5-B
4571 Dupont Circle
Washington D.C.

Stella had been working the phone and pounding the D.C. pavement for several days, and had gathered enough confirmation that, together with her hunches, allowed her to put together a blockbuster story. She was convinced that the Soviets were actively installing nuclear rockets in Cuba, and that the United States knew about it and, apparently, was doing nothing to prevent it from happening.

Her pieces assembled, she had come home from work tonight with the intention of writing the whole story by the end of the day on Sunday. She sat at her kitchen table and pounded away at her Royal typewriter, feeling the story come together with a natural flow. It was powerful, compelling, and accurate. She had a few more loose ends to tie together, but she expected to have it to be a prominent feature of the Monday evening news program.

When the phone rang, she hoped it would be one of her contacts—perhaps the petty officer who worked for the Navy department at the Pentagon—calling back with some necessary confirmation. She snatched up the receiver with a breathless "Hello," almost as if she'd been running a footrace.

"Stella! This is Bob—I'm glad I caught you."

"Hi, Bob. Are they giving you some time off work tonight?" she replied lightly.

"Well, yes. Um, that's why I'm calling. It's late notice, but I just found out. We were supposed to be campaigning in the Midwest through Sunday, but we came back early."

"Yes, I heard about that. The President has a cold, they said. I hope he's not terribly ill?" She made the last statement into a question.

Morris couldn't resist the baited trap. "Oh, no. That was just a—that is, he didn't seem like he was suffering too much on Air Force One. I think he'll be okay, with some time in his own bed."

"What a relief," she replied.

"Listen, again, I know it's not much warning. But is there any chance you'd be free for dinner tonight? Or have you already eaten?"

"No, I haven't yet. And I'd like to see you, but I'm sorry, I can't, not tonight. You see, I have a story to write. I'm working."

"Oh, of course. Listen, I'm sorry—"

"Don't be sorry. I'm glad you called. And like you said when you called me Thursday, when all this is over, let's take some time to get caught up. Please, call me again."

After she hung up the phone, she went back to her typewriter. This story was practically writing itself. Now that the President had returned to the White House, she sensed that the ending was coming, not too far down the line.

21 October 1962
1130 hours (Sunday morning)
Oval Office, the White House
Washington D.C.

Defense Secretary McNamara introduced the man who accompanied him into the office. "Mister President, this is General Sweeney, the head of Tactical Air Command at Langley."

"Yes, General—thank you for coming," said Kennedy with an affable handshake. He led the two new arrivals to the couches and chairs arranged for comfortable conversation, and indicated the other three men already waiting there.

"Perhaps you know my brother, the Attorney General, and Director McCone of the CIA. I know you're familiar with General Taylor."

Introductions out of the way, the President sat in an armchair with the other men seated to face him, and got right to the point. "General Sweeney, I know you've been preparing plans for a series of airstrikes on military targets in Cuba. I'd like to ask you a few questions about those plans."

"Certainly, Mr. President."

"First, how close to readiness are you, if the order comes to make this series of air attacks?"

"I can safely say, Sir, that by the time I issue the order, we will have planes in the air within an hour. We're ready to go."

"Very good. Now, how would these strikes be conducted? With what kind of weaponry—I presume that would vary by target?"

"Yes, sir." Sweeney went on to outline the types of attacks the Air Force was prepared to make. Napalm, the incendiary jelly that had been developed late in the Second World War, would play a primary role, as it would devastate a large swath of the target area. Gravity bombs would also play in important part, as would aircraft-mounted rockets and even machinegun fire. Sweeney had enough assets to hit every identified strategic target in the first strike, with followup attacks used to "clean up" tactical sites, troop concentrations, and supply and ammunition stockpiles.

"We anticipate some vigorous air defense by the enemy," the general said. "But our aircraft superiority, both in numbers and in the capabilities of individual types, gives me a high degree of confidence in predicting that Cuban and Soviet fighter assets will quickly be degraded."

"An important question, then," the President followed up. "Can you be certain of destroying each strategic missile site on the island of Cuba."

Sweeney hesitated, then shook his head in a frank gesture. "I can't be certain, Sir. First, air strikes—while devastating—cannot deliver guaranteed results. Secondly, can we rule out the fact that there might be other sites, strategic missiles bases, that have not yet been discovered?"

"No," JFK said. "We can't rule that out."

"And we have to consider the overall morality, and the historic record," Bobby Kennedy added. "There are too many parallels to Pearl Harbor for me to be comfortable with this. I realize, if we warn them that we will attack if they don't remove the missiles, that we give them time for countermeasures. But if we attack without warning—well, how are we different from Tojo?"

"I agree with the attorney general," DCIA McCone said bluntly. "We're taking too big of a risk if we bring the bombers out of the blue. Although I need to stress, Sir, that we have to keep this airstrike option on the table, make sure General Sweeney and his people are ready at a moment's notice."

"I agree," said the President. "General Sweeney?"

"We'll be ready, Mr President. It's your call, but rest assured that if you send my men in, they will do their very best to get the job done."

The Air Force general departed, and the other men, the heart of ExComm, settled on their plan: They would use the United States Navy to block the approach routes to Cuba, stopping any ships that were suspected of carrying offensive weapons.

"A 'blockade' is generally regarded as an act of war," Secretary McNamara said. "What if we call it something else. Say, a 'quarantine'?"

"Good," JFK agreed. "Now, what else do we need to get ready?"

"The press is starting to get on this story," Bobby said. "I think you need to make some kind of statement to the public, very soon. Until then, we should try to keep a lid on the story."

"Right. I'll have Pierre get me time on the networks, say at 7:00 p.m. Monday."

"What about our allies?" McNamara asked. "And I hate to say it, but perhaps some of the Congressional leadership should be brought on board."

"You're right, Bob," the President said with a wry chuckle. "Let's get our ducks in a row. Tomorrow night, before this story breaks outside of our control."

22 October 1962
1700 hours (Monday evening)
Presidium Chamber
Kremlin, Moscow

"What do you mean, 'He's going to make a speech?'" The Chairman demanded of the messenger who'd just interrupted the meeting of the Presidium.

"Just that, Comrade Chairman. It is a news story that has just been broadcast in America, and Ambassador Dobrynin wasted no time in passing the information to us. President Kennedy has demanded time on all of the American television networks. He intends to address the people of his country tonight—" The messenger checked the piece of paper in his hand so that he could quote accurately: "On a matter of the utmost urgency."

"Why?" Khrushchev asked, looking around at the implacable faces of the Soviet leadership. He fixed his eyes on Defense Minister Malinovsky. "Why would he do this?"

"I can think of only one reason, Comrade Chairman. And that is that our missile deployment in Cuba, Operation *Anadyr*, has been discovered by the Americans."

1100 hours (Monday morning)
NBC News Washington Bureau
Tenleytown, Washington D.C.

"You're killing my story?" Stella asked in disbelief. She had just handed the copy to Bill Tuchman, her bureau chief, a few minutes before. When he called her into his office, she had expected—hoped for, anyway—some enthusiastic praise. She had prepared herself for a request to rewrite, to do some more digging....

But this?

Tuchman shook his balding head in a mixture of regret and resolve. "I'm sorry, Stella. Pressure from the White House. The President is going to speak tonight, and they've practically ordered all news outlets to keep a lid on the story until he's off the air. It's pretty clear he's going to talk about the same thing you wrote about."

"They can't do that!" she said. "He can't do that!"

"Technically, you're right—they can't do it legally. But they can put a lot of pressure on us. And they implied pretty strongly that the President's authority, and his message, will be weakened if these details start to leak out ahead of time."

Stella slumped in her desk chair. Tuchman was right: her story would reveal the presence of Soviet nuclear missiles in Cuba and charge the President with failing to act—except that now, it seemed, he was acting. She could quickly imagine the national outcry if her story was broadcast before the speech.

"The Republicans would eat him alive," she acknowledged morosely. "When he does go on the air, he'd appear to be reacting to a political crisis, not a military one."

She felt a sudden urge to cry, quickly tamping it down with a wry smile. "Dammit, Bill—that piece was going to win me a Pulitzer!"

"I read it," he said, "And it may well have done that. For now, I know you've got a jump on everyone else in town on this story. I'm going to need your best stuff while this thing is played out."

"That," she agreed, "you can count on. Just as soon as I hear that damned speech."

Four: Countdown to Quarantine

"Now, in the thermonuclear age, any misjudgment on either side about the intentions of the other could rain more devastation in several hours than has been wrought in all the wars of human history."

President Kennedy
Address during the Berlin crisis
25 July, 1961

22 October 1962
2100 hours (Monday night)
Publisher's Office, *Revolucion* Newspaper
Havana, Cuba

Carlos Franqui had been a member of *Movimiento 26 de Julio* since the very beginning. When Fidel Castro and his revolution, which had come to be known as the "26th of July Movement," prevailed and forced dictator Juan Batista to flee the island, Franqui had been placed in charge of the most influential newspaper in revolutionary Cuba. His publication was granted a fair degree of autonomy by the authoritarian regime, because he could be counted on to support the goals of both the revolution, and of *El Máximo Lider*.

As recently as this morning, the paper's front page had trumpeted a warning under the broad headline: "Preparations for Yankee Aggression." The story had proceeded to describe, in slightly exaggerated detail, the gathering in Florida of American military forces. Even before JFK's Monday night speech, Fidel had approved the alarmist approach. After all, though many Cubans were not enthusiastic supporters of the now openly communist revolutionaries, they were even more fearful of *yanqui* aggression.

So it was that, after listening to the American President on the radio, Fidel ordered his driver to take him directly to the newspaper's office. Franqui had immediately assigned a technician to record an audio tape of their leader, and several stenographers busily took notes as Castro, smoking cigar in hand, strode back and forth between the journalists' desks and dictated the story that would appear on Tuesday morning's front page. If the Americans had expected any contrition or hesitation in their Cuban antagonist's attitude, they were to be sorely disappointed:

"The nation has awakened on a war footing, ready to repulse any attack!" Castro proclaimed. He spoke without notes, and at such a speed that the stenographers frantically scribbled to keep up. "Every weapon is in its place, and beside each weapon are the heroic defenders of the Revolution, and the Motherland.

"And the Revolutionary leaders, the entire government, stand ready to die next to the people. From the length and breadth of the island resounds like thunder, from millions of voices, with more fervor and reason than ever before, the historic and glorious cry: *Patria o Muerte!* Homeland or death!"

Castro kept up the barrage of words for an hour, reinforcing his determination to defeat the Americans, underlining the courage and patriotism of his people, highlighting the arrogance and imperialist ambitions of the neighbor to the north. He denounced the incursions of American spyplanes, accused the enemy of sabotage and espionage against the sovereign state of Cuba, and promised to "blast them to oblivion" if they so much as dared to approach the shores of his island.

He went on to warn of extensive beach defenses, fortified landing zones, and thousands upon thousands of armed, trained revolutionaries who were committed and skilled, and who would turn the battle into a bloodbath for the imperialist invaders. One fact he didn't waste any time developing, because to him it seemed too obvious even to mention. He believed it to the very core of his soul:

The American invasion was coming, and it was coming soon.

23 October 1962
0800 hours (Tuesday morning)
Headquarters, USN Atlantic Fleet (CINCLANT)
Naval Station Norfolk, Virginia

Admiral Robert Dennison had a lot of responsibilities under his command, which under normal circumstances covered the entire Atlantic Ocean. In the last few days, however, his focus had narrowed considerably—specifically, to the island of Cuba, its sea approaches, and the vast military force the United States was gathering for potential action against that Caribbean outpost of the Communist world.

The Department of Defense and the Joint Chiefs of Staff had agreed that any offensive activities required against Cuba would be launched under the United States Navy's auspices. The Commander in Chief, Atlantic Fleet, was to be the summit of the chain of operational command, not just for the Navy and Marine forces, but for the Air Force and Army assets, as well.

Under his immediate control, Dennison had overall command of two large carrier task forces, including a large number of destroyers and support ships, two smaller carrier groups with a special focus on ASW (antisubmarine-warfare) duties, land-based naval air units on Key West, Guantanamo Bay, Puerto Rico, and other airfields. He had dozens of destroyers and a smaller number of cruisers; many ships of both classes were very modern, equipped with guided missiles for antiaircraft or antiship combat. Most ships carried at least one helicopter aboard, while the ASW aircraft carriers *Essex* and *Randolph* had dozens of choppers, since the "rotary wing aircraft" had proven to be especially adept at sub hunting.

General Sweeney of TAC would still coordinate the strikes made by the United States Air Force tactical attack squadrons from many bases in the southeastern part of the country, but Dennison would be in charge of the timing, and would coordinate the target selections, of those attacks as well. Ground forces gathering under his umbrella included two full Marine divisions, one of which was currently en route from the Pacific, due to traverse the Panama Canal in a matter of days, as well as two airborne divisions, and the heavy punch of the follow-up force, the 1st Armored Division, now in transit from its base in Texas to ports along the Gulf Coast. Naturally, Dennison's command also included the ships needed to transport all of these units and their supply services to Cuba, as well.

He'd already accomplished his first important task, even before the end of the previous day, when all of the civilian noncombatants at the Guantanamo Bay Naval Base had been evacuated. The operation had gone very smoothly: Word had gone out late morning on Monday that the noncombatants were to pack up one suitcase apiece and gather outside their residences. They had been given one hour of warning, and that had proved to be adequate. Pets were to be leashed and tied up outside the houses, where they would be retrieved and cared for by military personnel until the family members were allowed to return.

At the allotted time, buses had gone around the base to collect the wives and children of the Navy and Marine servicemen and carry them to the airfield or port, where they embarked onto ships or airplanes. By 5 p.m. that day, every one of them had been pulled out of the naval base. Today, another battalion of Marines, with a full Marine Air Group, was landing on the American installation to increase its defense capabilities. In the event of war, Guantanamo—which lay on the south coast near the east end of Cuba—was expected to defend itself, while offensive operations against the Cubans began on the north coast at the other end of the island.

On this morning, barely fourteen hours after the President's speech, Dennison's headquarters was a beehive of activity. He'd had a large conference room dedicated to this mission, with a huge map of the action area spread on several tables. Teletypes chattered along one wall, continuously spitting out updated order-of-battle and location information. Enlisted personnel deployed and moved counters indicating American assets, and suspected Soviet and Cuban forces, on the land and sea spaces of the giant map. Dennison was considering the deployment of the forces along the quarantine line when his aide called him back into his office.

"Urgent message from Admiral Anderson at the Pentagon, Sir."

Dennison took the sheet of paper and tried to keep his pulse from pounding as his job just got significantly more complex and dangerous:

Unconfirmed reports Soviet submarines, FOXTROT class, moving into Western Atlantic. As many as four submarines may be present. Best estimates suggest could reach Cuban waters within one week. Take extra care to prevent or anticipate surprise attacks from submarines. Use all available intelligence, deceptive tactics, and evasion to counter.

Soviet submarines, if located, should be warned with practice depth charges and forced to surface.

Merchant ships approaching quarantine line should be stopped with radio communications, backed up by shot across the bow. Boarding parties should be prepared to inspect cargoes.

The halting and boarding operations had been established and reviewed during conferences with Admiral Anderson and Defense Secretary McNamara over the weekend. At least one Russian-speaking officer had been dispatched to each of the dozen or so destroyers in the picket line. With no Soviet surface warships in the vicinity, Dennison didn't anticipate trouble, even against an armed merchantman.

It was the submarines that now caused the admiral the most unease. Clearly, they had been dispatched weeks earlier, to have reached the positions they currently occupied. Dennison had an idea as to how they had been tracked, for he knew about a top-secret system of undersea microphones called SOSUS—an abbreviation of Sound Surveillance System. These sensitive devices had been installed across much of the Atlantic sea floor during the preceding decade, with an emphasis on choke points, such as the passages between Greenland, Iceland, and Scotland. The reports from SOSUS had undoubtedly allowed Navy Intelligence to determine the class and general location of the Soviet subs. But it was not nearly detailed enough to allow ships or ASW planes to actually find, much less engage, the undersea craft.

At 1105 today, Tuesday, solid confirmation came in the form of another report. An observer aboard a P5M Marlin, a twin-engine piston-powered amphibious patrol plane operating out of Bermuda, spotted a churning on the surface of the ocean that was almost certainly caused by the snorkel of a submerged submarine. Before the spotting could be confirmed, the submarine had disappeared, no doubt going deeper. But it was enough for Dennison, who had ASW aircraft operating from Iceland, eastern Canada and the United States mainland, Bermuda, Puerto Rico, and Guantanamo Bay.

"We have a probable submarine contact, Soviet, 500 miles south of Bermuda," he reported to his ships at sea, after checking the disposition on the map of his own assets. "Aircraft Carrier *Randolph* and support group should make for the location at flank speed. Use all air and surface units, including helicopters, to prosecute the search. Aircraft Carrier *Essex* and support group should stand by, ready to act against further contacts."

He had no doubt but that the *Randolph* group would be able to locate the submarine. As to what happened after that, God only knew.

1030 hours (Tuesday morning)
Battery 2, 539th Missile Regiment
San Cristobal, Cuba

By Sunday night, the last of the concrete pads for Tukov's battery had been measured, leveled, and laid. The launchers were now mounted on stable platforms. The missiles were nearby, in their tents, and all of the fueling and targeting equipment required to launch the SS4s was ready, tested, and waiting for orders. Monday the men had rehearsed the launch procedures, without actually fueling the rockets, and the colonel was pleased to see that they could complete the entire process for each launcher in less than four hours.

Of course, the warheads, each of which had a yield of one megaton, or about seventy times the force of the Hiroshima bomb, were not on site yet. Pliyev was keeping them secure in their bunker, but Tukov had measured the distance from the bunker, which was near Havana, to the battery. He estimated that the warheads could be brought to his battery within a matter of two or three hours, as soon as they were released by high command.

Also on Monday, Tukov and the other regiment and battery commanders had been summoned to El Chico for a meeting of the Soviet Military Council. There, he had listened with his colleagues to the American President's speech, broadcast in both English and Spanish, so he had been able to follow the Spanish version. He had been pestered for details by many of his monolingual fellow officers, and so Tukov had provided a running translation as best he could.

General Pliyev had returned to the Soviet headquarters after the speech, which he had listened to with Fidel Castro up at Casa Una. He was pale and sweaty—though all Russians were sweaty in Cuba—and the palsied shaking of his hands suggested something serious was wrong with his health. Even so, he had spoken to his officers resolutely, telling them of the blockade, then ordering them back to their units with specific orders to be prepared for an American paratroop attack at any time.

Tukov understood that the crisis was approaching a climax. He wasn't particularly worried about the blockade, since everything needed to employ the SS4s was already present, in Cuba. But he realized that the potential for combat between the North Americans and the Cubans and

Soviets was much closer than it had been before now. And he had never considered the possibility of a paratroop attack. Now, as he thought about it, he realized that his unit would be fairly vulnerable to a unit of elite infantrymen, if those soldiers could come down from the sky, rather than having to fight their way through the 134th motorized rifle division that was some 15 kilometers north of the battery.

The normally two-hour drive from El Chico back to his battery had ended up taking more than four, since in the hour following Kennedy's speech, the highway was crowded with cars, trucks, and buses transporting huge numbers of Cuban reservists to their units. Checkpoints lined the road, seemingly one every twenty or thirty kilometers. The traffic jams at each roadblock were aggravating, but once his Soviet Army command car was recognized, he and his driver were waved through—often with shouts of *"Viva la Union Sovietica!"*

By the time they reached San Cristobal, it was nearly dawn, yet he knew there was an important task he would need to take care of that morning. He entered his tent for one hour of sleep, then rose and immediately ordered Private Smirnovich to bring his scout car around. He sent word for his targeting and engineering officers, Captains Kutuzov and Dubovik, to join him. He also called for the lieutenant who was in charge of the battery's infantry company, the 100 or so soldiers tasked with defending the unit against direct enemy ground attack.

"General Pliyev says we're to be alert for attack by enemy paratroops," Tukov told the young officer, who looked barely old enough to shave. "I want you to have your men plot out defensive fire positions on all sides of the battery. Plan where you will set your machineguns. Dig some prepared positions, and be sure to consider attack from any quarter. You and your men must be able to react at a moment's notice."

"Absolutely, Comrade Colonel!" declared the lieutenant, eyes wide. "It shall be done at once!"

"Good man." By that time the two captains had arrived. They took the back seat in the scout car, and Smirnovich drove the three officers out onto the highway toward San Cristobal. After four kilometers, Tukov had him turn onto a wide, but slightly overgrown, road leading off of the highway. Che Guervara had shown him this place on Saturday morning, as he had promised to do, and Tukov had been intrigued by the possibility it presented. Now, today, he had brought two of his smartest and most knowledgeable SS4 officers to see if they shared his opinion.

"I want you to consider the problems involved in moving one of our launchers here," Tukov told his captains. "In the event we need to move some of the battery to a reserve position, this might be our best option."

"The approach road is wide," Dubovik noted. "It must have been cleared for heavy trucks at some time in the past. And the ground is solid stone, under a little clay. Not much danger of mud."

"I agree," Tukov said. The car came around a shallow bend in the road, and the large open pit of the quarry came into view. "Turn left here, and follow the ramp down into the pit."

The driver followed his instructions, and they all took note of the fact that the car didn't lurch or bump much—the terrain was easy to drive over. Smirnovich did have to veer around a couple of large boulders, but the engineering officer assured them those could easily be bulldozed out of the way.

The ramp down into the quarry was wide and gently graded. Obviously, it had once been employed by large stone-

or gravel-hauling trucks carrying heavy loads out of the pit, so it was relatively easy to negotiate.

At the bottom, the three officers got out and kicked through the dust lining the limestone bedrock. "It is smooth," Dubovik noted. "If I put some men on it with grinders, we could level it sufficiently to base a launcher."

"I doubt we would have time to establish the exact coordinates," cautioned Kutuzov, the targeting officer. "We will lose considerable accuracy if we are forced to launch from here."

"Ah, but you have coordinates from our current site, correct?" Tukov countered. "Given that, we could establish an exact distance and direction from that site to this, and make an educated guess as to the difference in elevation, I think an adequate shooting solution could be established. Don't you?"

"Yes, Comrade Colonel, if precise accuracy is not required."

"I don't think it is," Tukov replied. They all knew what he meant: a one-megaton warhead would obliterate an area quite a few miles across, so if the missile detonated on the outskirts of a target city as opposed to directly over the downtown center, the damage would still be catastrophic.

"One other thing, Sir," the engineering officer pointed out. "I am certain we could get one of the trucks and trailers down this ramp and close enough to transfer the missile to a launcher." He gestured to the high walls rising on all sides, except where the ramp descended. "However, I'm not at all certain there will be room to turn the truck around to get it out again."

"I had thought of that too, Anatoly Alexandrovich," Tukov said, with a weary shake of his head. "However, if things reach the point where we are moving a missile to a reserve position, I think we will consider this our last stand. It won't be necessary to move any farther."

1041 hours (Tuesday morning)
USS DDG 507 *Conning,*
Quarantine Line, 500 miles NE of Cuba

Seaman George Duncan had finished United States Navy basic training just six weeks before. After a leave that he had spent back on the farm in Wisconsin, he'd been assigned to the crew of the fast, modern destroyer, *Conning.* He'd learned that it was named after some Navy hero of the War of 1812 or something, though he wasn't exactly clear on the details. In any event, he had settled into his job as cook's assistant with enthusiasm, since he liked to cook and he quickly had learned that he liked to be on the ocean.

But he had never expected things to get as exciting as they had in the last few days. Five days earlier *Conning* had been pulled from a routine training exercise off the coast of Massachusetts, racing south at high speed to join up with a bunch of other destroyers and some larger ships. Chief Petty Officer Weber, who had sort of taken the young sailor under his wing, had pointed out a guided-missile cruiser and an antisubmarine-aircraft carrier, and once they'd even glimpsed the massive fleet carrier *Enterprise,* which Weber had claimed was the largest ship in the world. Gaping in awe at the massive flattop, Duncan hadn't been inclined to argue.

When he wasn't working or sleeping, Duncan spent all the time he could on deck, just watching the water, the wake of the fast ship, the sky, and any other vessels that happened to be in view. That's what he'd done today, after breakfast had been served and the cleanup completed. Chief Weber found him near the stern of the ship, watching the churning white wake expanding in a broad "V" behind the destroyer.

"Duncan," the chief said. "Come with me. You've got boarding party duty."

"Sure, Chief," he said, falling into step behind the broad-shouldered NCO. Weber was all of twenty-five years old, but he seemed to Duncan like he'd had about 100 years of experience in the Navy.

"Uh, what's boarding party duty?" he asked, as the chief led him through a hatch and down a ladder into a part of the ship Duncan had never seen before. He didn't think "boarding parties" had been covered in basic training, as far as he could remember.

Weber didn't answer. Instead, the chief unlocked a large metal hatch and pulled it open to reveal racks loaded with rifles, shotguns, and other weapons. Weber reached to a high rack and pulled down a submachine gun. He took three stick magazines from another shelf and closed the hatch behind him.

"Do you know what this is, Duncan?"

"I think that's a Tommy gun, chief. Isn't it?"

"Good job, kid—thought technically it's a 'Thompson submachine gun.' Still, you get the gold star." He tossed the weapon, barrel sideways, to the sailor, who caught it reflexively.

"For now, it's your security blanket. You'll sleep with it, you'll cook with it—well, I don't mean you'll use it to cook, but you'll damn well wear it on your back while you're stirring soup and peeling potatoes. You keep it with you when you use the head and when you eat. You get the picture?"

"Sure, Chief."

"Have you ever shot a Tommy gun before?"

"Uh, no, I haven't."

"Well, that's why I got the extra ammo. Let's go back to the rail." Weber led the young sailor back to the position he'd occupied when he had been watching the ship's wake. The chief showed him how to snap the stick magazine in place on the underside of the gun, just in front of the trigger guard.

"This is the safety. You keep that clicked 'On,' unless someone like me tells you otherwise, got it?"

"Sure." Duncan clicked the safety on and off a few times. Next, the chief showed him how to set the gun on fully automatic and semi-automatic firing patterns.

"There are twenty rounds in that stick. Try it on semi-auto, and squeeze off five quick shots. Aim for the horizon."

Duncan did as he was told, trying not to wince at the loud reports from each shot. He wished he had a target to aim at, but the chief told him not to worry. "Now try it on full auto. Again, aim at the horizon."

This time the gun chattered loudly, blasting out the remaining fifteen rounds in a matter of a few seconds.

"Are you still aimed at the horizon?"

Duncan was chagrined to note that the barrel was pointed steeply up in the air. "Uh, sorry, no, Chief."

"It happens to everyone. That thing climbs like a bitch. Now, I don't think you're going to have to shoot anyone, but shoot off another magazine just so you get the feel of it."

Duncan followed the instructions, and managed to do a better job of holding the barrel down, though it took a lot of effort and concentration. "You just checked out on the Tommy gun," Weber said proudly, handing him the third magazine. "This one's for you to keep. But put the safety back on first."

"So what's this about boarding parties?" Duncan asked, doing what he'd been told. There was a broad leather strap on the gun, and he slung it over his shoulder, getting used to the weight against his back.

"We're going to look for some Russian ships and try to pull 'em over like we're traffic cops," Weber told him. "When they stop, *Conning* will lower a boat, and Lieutenant Decker, some other officer from Naval Intelligence who I guess speaks Russian, me, and six sailors, are going to go over and have a look around on that Russian ship. You, Seaman George Duncan, get to be one of those six sailors!"

"Okay, Chief. You got it."

"I knew I could count on you," the NCO said, clapping him on the shoulder and strolling away.

That's the Navy for you, George reflected, not at all displeased by the new assignment. Never a dull moment.

1055 hours (Tuesday morning)
Recording Room
The White House, Washington D.C.

They were talking about ships coming toward Cuba this morning, how many there were, and what they might be carrying. Ron Pickett could hear every word through the big earphones he wore on his head, but, as usual, he wasn't paying any attention to those unimportant details. He had his own crucial responsibilities, and they required his undivided attention.

Tape rolled on the dual recorders as the conversation in the Cabinet Room continued. Pickett was vaguely aware that "Big Things" were going on these days, that history was being made in this building and was being recorded on his tapes. But the significance of that history meant only one thing to the recording technician: It was absolutely crucial that these tapes be perfect.

His eyes widened in alarm as he saw that one reel was within a minute of the end of its tape. He'd almost missed it! The shock was great enough that his hands were shaking as he quickly opened a fresh reel. He stared at the ending tape, and as soon as the tail ran through the machine, he pulled the full reel off the sprocket, replaced it with an empty one, and simultaneously fed in the start of the fresh tape.

Only when he had the new tape secured, slowly spiraling onto the reel, did he mount the second reel, heavy with its load of blank tape, onto the feeder sprocket. When all was rolling smoothly, he let out a deep breath, unaware that he'd been holding it for nearly a minute. Nervously, he glanced over his shoulder, half-afraid that someone had seen his almost-mistake. It was just a reflex, of course—no one watched him in here. The door stayed closed at all times, except when Ron—or, rarely, someone else like Bob Morris or the President—passed through.

It was a pleasure, in fact, to be able to do his work in such unsupervised solitude. Such a change from the way he'd grown up, when She had watched his every move, looking for reasons to criticize, to rebuke, to strike him. She had enjoyed punishing him, as She had enjoyed punishing the men who came and went from their lives. Even now, though She was dead, he could feel Her watching him, and he instinctively flinched away from Her displeasure.

He found that his hands were shaking too much to properly label the tape, so he waited for a few minutes, thinking pleasant thoughts about vacuum tubes, about the reliability of microphones and speakers. Finally he was calm enough to label the just-completed tape in his clean, block print. He opened the cabinet and placed the reel on the shelf next to the others, realizing with surprise that he had recorded an unprecedented amount of tape in the last week. If this kept up, another crate of tapes would have to be transferred to long-range storage. He didn't like doing that, sending them away where he couldn't keep an eye on them, but it had to be done. There was only so much space in this small room.

But it was his space, in his room, and that made it fine.

1101 hours (Tuesday morning)
Harry S. Truman Annex
Key West Naval Air Station
Key West, Florida

"Operation Blue Moon" they were calling it, and it seemed like as good a name as any. Commander Widener strolled along the flight line of the RF8 Crusaders, eight of which were fueled and ready for the first flight of what might prove to be a very significant mission. He came up to the unit flight leader, Commander William Ecker, who was watching ground crews load film into his aircraft's six cameras.

"Obviously, we're taking the gloves off," the base commander said. "It takes a lot of guts to do what you guys are going to do."

"All in a day's work," Ecker replied. "Plus, at low altitude and the speed we'll be flying at, we'll be past before they even know we're there. And given what we heard last night, I think it's high time we get some close-ups of that place."

The veteran pilot had projected a breezy confidence since his unit had been deployed here a couple of weeks earlier, and Widener could see why his men were ready and eager to follow their commanding officer into harm's way. Ecker had taken the time to show Widener the ins and outs of their aircraft, which were equipped very differently from the F8 Crusader that had been a workhorse fighter and light bomber for the Navy for some years now.

The RF8 was an unarmed aircraft, strictly dedicated to the low-altitude photo reconnaissance mission. The main camera shot a forward view, four frames per second—or one frame about every 200 feet traveled by the speeding aircraft—and exposed six-inch by six-inch negatives. Other cameras took side shots, a straight down view, and images to the rear, trailing out to the horizon. Unlike the U2, The RF8 was designed to get close to its subject, using speed and surprise to avoid taking antiaircraft fire. The quality of pictures obtained could reveal far more in the way of detail than the U2 cameras, which shot from many miles in the air.

On this mission, the Crusaders would split into pairs, with each pair assigned a different reconnaissance zone in western Cuba. They would cross the Florida Strait at wavetop height to avoid enemy radar, then pop up to about 1000 feet for their photo runs. After shooting for a few minutes, they would have exhausted their film and would head north again, flying all the way to Jacksonville, Florida, to land. The film would be removed for transport to NPIC in Washington, and the planes would return to Key West to be prepared for another round of scouting tomorrow.

Widener stood outside of his command building as the Crusaders took off, in pairs. They veered south and traveled very fast, almost Mach 1. At their low altitude, it was only a minute or so before each plane was out of sight of the base.

As soon as the Blue Moon flight was gone, Widener was back at his desk. He ordered fuel trucks to line up and ground crews to be ready. Next up was a flight of Marine fighters and light bombers. The first planes were due in an hour or so, and by this time tomorrow, the full MAG would have passed through. They would stop in to refuel and get any last-minute trouble spots checked out. After an hour or two on the ground, they'd be off again, destined for Guantanamo Bay.

His paperwork cleared for the moment, Widener thought of Derek, out at sea on *Enterprise*. The massive fleet carrier would be involved in this operation, the commander knew, which meant that his son would be in the thick of it. Pride vied with concern as he considered that fact.

Then his thoughts turned to his daughter. A reporter in Washington…she, too, would be have a lot of work to do in the current crisis. He thought of the rockets the President had described as being present in Cuba, and for the first time a chilling awareness hit him. In this war, his daughter might be in an even more dangerous combat zone than either his son or himself.

1804 hours (Tuesday evening)
Outside the Pentagon
Washington D.C.

Stella sat in the back of the news van, brushed her hair quickly, and checked her handheld mirror to make sure that her lipstick hadn't smeared and that her makeup was still intact. Everything checked out adequately, and today "adequate" would have to be good enough.

"You're on in one, Stel," said her director, Pat Seghers, sticking his head through the van's open doors.

"All right, thanks," she replied, sliding out, taking a few steps on the parking lot so that the cameraman could get her in the shot, with the five-sided military headquarters—

famous as the largest office building in the world—as a dramatic backdrop. She checked her notes one last time, then let them drop so that she could fix the camera with a dramatic, serious, and focused expression.

Seghers held up his hand with fingers outspread, listening to a feed on his headphones. "Five, four, three…" he said, ticking off the last two seconds silently.

"Good evening." Stella addressed the camera squarely, maintaining a serious, stern expression. "This is Stella Widener, reporting from the Pentagon, twenty-three hours after President Kennedy's dramatic announcement regarding Soviet strategic missiles in Cuba. The blockade, or quarantine, of that country is set to become active at 10 a.m. Eastern time, tomorrow—Wednesday. At that point, Soviet ships will be stopped, and those carrying offensive weapons will be, at the very least, turned back. The President made it clear that normal civilian goods, such as food, clothing, and presumably even manufacturing materials and supplies, would be allowed to proceed to Cuban ports.

"As of tonight, we can report the following: Virtually all of the United States military forces, including the Army, Navy, Air Force, and Marines, have been placed on a status of heightened alert. All leaves have been canceled, and a large movement of forces into Florida and the Gulf Coast region has commenced. Reports out of California suggest that at least two regiments of Marines based at Camp Pendleton have been embarked on ships, destined for the Panama Canal and the Caribbean Sea."

She paused and drew a breath, gesturing to the building behind her. "Officials at the Pentagon remain tight-lipped about the actual deployment of our naval forces at sea, but given the President's stern warning, it can be expected that the US Navy is moving surface ships to form some kind of barrier along the quarantine boundary, reportedly about 500 miles east of the easternmost terminus of the island of Cuba itself.

"In the meantime, we have been gathering reports from anti-Castro Cuban exiles, who as you probably know have been fleeing the communist regime in large numbers—averaging nearly a hundred people a day over the last year. Most of these exiles have landed in Florida and are establishing a large expat community in Miami. I send you now back to David Brinkley in the studio, for information on what we've been able to learn from these Cubans, some of whom arrived in Florida as recently as yesterday. David?"

She didn't have an earphone attached, so she couldn't hear the anchorman's reply, but she saw Seghers give the throat slash gesture telling her she was off the air. "Good job," he told her.

"Thanks," she replied. "But I think it was kind of thin. I wish to hell someone in that building would give us more than a 'no comment' once in a while."

"You made the most of what you had—that's one of the things I like about you. Now let's get back to the studio and start collecting news for tomorrow's report."

The cameraman was already loading his gear into the van. Pat climbed in the back with him while Stella, in deference to her skirt and stockings, climbed into the front seat to sit next to the driver. A moment later he put the van in gear, merging into the D.C. rush hour, slowly working his way toward the nearest bridge over the Potomac, and the city streets back to Tenleytown.

2211 hours (Tuesday night)
Presidium Chamber
Kremlin, Moscow

Khrushchev had ordered all members of the Presidium to stay in the Kremlin for as long as the crisis lasted, so even at this late hour there were a dozen Soviet bureaucrats gathered for discussion after their hearty dinner. Many of them were drinking, and some of them were drunk, though the chairman himself was having his usual evening beverage of tea sweetened with lemon. But even that usually soothing beverage couldn't calm his churning stomach. He beckoned to Defense Minister Malinovsky and Foreign Minister Gromyko, who were discussing something privately, and they came over to sit beside him.

"What are we going to do about this imperialist threat?" Nikita Khrushchev demanded of both men. "The Americans intend to commence their unlawful and piratical blockade tomorrow morning! Would they dare to stop our ships?"

"They would, and they will, in my estimation," Malinovsky said dourly. "And they have the naval power to do it."

"We should have sent the Baltic Fleet to escort the freighters!" the chairman declared.

"It would have been hard to maintain the *maskirovka* with warships steaming along beside our missiles," the defense minister said, reminding him of the strategic deception that had concealed the plan almost long enough.

"True enough" Khrushchev conceded. "But now what is the status of shipping for Operation *Anadyr?* Those vessels that are still at sea?"

"One important vessel, *Alexandrovsk*, is already past the line of demarcation for their blockade," Malinovsky said, as if seeking a silver lining. "This ship is carrying all of the warheads, 28 of them, for the SS5 missiles. It is within 400 miles of eastern Cuba right now."

"Then we should order it make for a port, a Cuban port, with all possible speed, before the Americans change their minds and move the blockade in closer," the chairman declared decisively. But then he remembered some additional details from the many briefings he'd been given on the Cuban operations. "But the missiles themselves, they are still at sea, are they not? Farther away from Cuba."

"Unfortunately, yes, Comrade Chairman," the minister replied. "The ships carrying the SS5 missiles, as well as much of the fueling equipment and launchers, have yet to reach the quarantine line declared by the Americans."

"What about the submarines? Is there any way they can neutralize the American fleet?"

"It would seem unlikely, Comrade Chairman. Within the whole area of operations our submarines will be vastly outnumbered by the ships of the American navy." Malinovsky was obliged to report.

"But the submarines can stay hidden, can they not? When they are underwater the number of American ships might be neutralized!" Khrushchev realized he was clutching at straws.

"Submarines can hide, but freighters cannot. If a submarine struck at their surface ships, I have no doubt but that they would sink our cargo ships." The defense minister turned to address Gromyko. "In fact, we received a communication from their embassy regarding the submarines, did we not?"

"Indeed, Comrade Minister, Comrade Chairman," the foreign minister said with obvious reluctance. "They claim to be aware of our four submarines approaching Cuban waters, and have warned us that they will be taking steps to make sure those boats do not interfere with American naval operations."

"What? How can they know about the submarines? And what steps can they take?" Khrushchev demanded. He was beginning to feel terribly trapped in a noose of some diabolical design. He was fiercely resentful of these fools. Why had they not mentioned some of these complications before it was too late?

"We do not know how they found the Foxtrots," Malinovsky responded with a shrug. "But they fact that they claim we have four, and we do have four, would make it seem that their intelligence information is accurate. Unfortunately, the Americans possess rather robust antisubmarine forces. You will recall, in the Great Patriotic War, they fought a long battle against Nazi submarines, and this allowed them to hone their tactics and skill to a very high level."

Khrushchev waved away that reminder. Like most Russians, he didn't feel as though the West had exerted any great effort to defeat the Nazis. The credit for that victory belonged to the Red Army, and to the people of the Soviet Union.

"What was in this message from their embassy, besides a warning?" the chairman wanted to know.

"They included some audacious instructions. The American navy intends to use simulated depth charges against our Foxtrots when they are located. These are intended as a warning, a command for our submarines to surface. They request that we inform the submarine commanders of this tactic, in order to avoid a misunderstanding."

"Bah!" Khrushchev snapped, insulted. "Who do they think they are, to give us orders! Our submarine captains have their orders, from the Soviet government. We will leave it to them to follow those orders!"

"I agree, Comrade Chairman," Malinovsky said, hesitantly. "But there are some admirals in the Undersea command who feel that we should at least give our submariners advance warning of the tactic the Americans claim they will use—"

"I told you, we will take no orders from the Americans!" the chairman shouted, his eyes bulging. "Let them take their chances with our ships!"

"And what about the missiles? The weapons of mass destruction? Do you want to clarify our instructions in any way?"

Khrushchev thought about that. "Yes. Send an order to Pliyev. He is not to employ those weapons, under any circumstances, without explicit orders from the Kremlin.

"It shall be done," Malinovsky promised. "What about the rest of the ships, the ones still approaching the blockade line?" he asked, changing tacks.

"I will need to think about this," the supreme leader replied, brooding. "We have until tomorrow morning before the blockade goes into effect. I will decide by then what we are going to do. In the meantime, make sure the Alexandrovsk gets word. I want those warheads in Cuba, not floating on the open sea!"

24 October 1962
0940 hours (Wednesday morning)
Cabinet Meeting Room, the White House
Washington D.C.

The tension in the ExComm thrummed like a steel wire stretched taut. With twenty minutes to go until the quarantine went into effect, there had still been no direct response from Moscow. The latest reports, from the dawn surveillance flights, indicated that all Communist Bloc ships bound for Cuba were still making headway. Though only about a quarter of the ships were under direct observation, they were still enough to convince the American leaders in the White House that the matter had not yet been decided.

The President and his brother were in attendance, as well as DCIA McCone, NSA Bundy, former ambassador Thompson, Secretary of State Dean Rusk, and Defense Secretary McNamara—though the latter planned to drive over to the Pentagon soon to confer with Admiral Anderson in the Navy Flag Headquarters. He wanted to be directly on scene with the admiral when the first potential confrontations occurred.

As usual, the meeting began with a report from McCone—"Saying Grace," Bobby had dubbed this part of the routine, in a nod to the Catholicism the Kennedys shared with the director, as well as his rather flat, droning delivery. "We have confirmation of twenty-two Soviet-controlled merchant ships, including ships flying other flags that are carrying cargoes embarked from Soviet ports. Two of these, the *Kimovsk* and the *Yuri Gagarin*, are drawing very near to the quarantine line. There's been a lot of chatter on the radio waves, mostly signals coming from Moscow, but the ships aren't replying—probably trying to observe radio silence. Still, they've clearly been getting instructions.

"The former is of particular interest," McCone continued. "She's Finnish built, designed for hauling timber. But she's got deck hatches nearly a hundred feet long, practically tailor-made for loading and unloading missiles."

"What are we planning to do about those ships?" the President asked.

"The Navy is sending a destroyer to stop the *Kimovsk*, first," McNamara interjected. But we've also located two of the Soviet subs. One was spotted refueling from a Russian tanker—it dived as soon as the plane was observed, but our men got a good look at it. The second was tracked on sonar, and it seems to be right between those two freighters."

"Dammit!" snapped JFK. "I don't want a sub to screw up our first intercept!"

Before anyone could reply, a knock drew their attention to the door. At the President's call, Secret Service Agent Morris looked in. "Excuse the interruption, Mr. President, but there's a Navy courier here, from the Pentagon."

"Send him in!"

The uniformed officer, a lieutenant commander, almost jogged into the room. He was out of a breath, and as he nervously snapped a quick salute—unnecessary, since he was indoors, in addition to the fact that none of the men in the room was a uniformed superior officer. Obviously, he could barely stand still.

"What is it, man?" snapped the Secretary of Defense.

"Word from our reconnaissance aircraft, out of Bermuda and Puerto Rico, Sir. They have eyes-on contact with five Soviet or Bloc vessels approaching the quarantine line. Sir, two of those ships have stopped dead in the water. A third has turned around 180 degrees and seems to be heading back toward Europe."

A brief, elated cheer broke out from the men at the cabinet table. "You did it, Jack!" Bobby said, slapping his brother on the back.

The President held up his hands. "That's good news, officer. But what about the other two?"

"One is a tanker, another a Greek freighter contracted to the Soviets, out of Odessa. They are continuing toward Cuba."

"All right. I'm guessing the ones continuing on are carrying civilian cargos. I think we should let them through."

"I agree, Mr. President," McNamara said. "The worst thing we could do is disable some freighter, and then find out it's carrying a load of baby food or something."

"But I'm still worried about that submarine," JFK brooded.

McNamara replied with a reminder of the procedure that had been established, with "practice depth charges" used to signal the sub to surface. "I think the Navy has a good handle on that possibility, Sir. And we've signaled the Soviets on our hailing procedures. The submarine captains should know we're not trying to sink them, just force them to the surface."

Kennedy did not look convinced, but he waved at McCone. "Do you have anything more for us, John?"

"Yes, Mr. President. We've gotten some low-level pictures from Operation Blue Moon," McCone reported. "They increase our detailed understanding of the missile sites significantly. If it comes to an air attack, we'll have a much better idea of our targeting priorities, too."

"That's good," JFK acknowledged. "Those fliers must have some balls, to fly over those places at 1,000 feet!"

"They're good men, veterans and experienced," McNamara said. "The commander of the squadron at Key West, Ecker, is the best the Navy has. Admiral Anderson had him fly up to Washington yesterday, after his recon mission. He reported directly to the Chiefs while his film was being developed over at NPIC. I gather that they fly over so fast that the troops on the ground are caught with their pants down—literally, in one case. It seems that Russian latrines don't always have roofs on them."

That remark provoked a round of nervous laughter, and a solid chuckle from the president, before the director continued. "And speaking of that, there have been some disturbing elements in these new pictures," McCone noted, quickly bringing the mood back down to earth. "We're still working on the analysis, but it looks like there are more Soviet ground troops in Cuba than we had expected to find. So far, we've got pretty good evidence of two motorized rifle divisions, one each in the vicinity of San Cristobal and Sagua la Grande."

McNamara nodded. "These are formidable combat units, sir, roughly equivalent to an Army brigade. A little more emphasis on combined arms and armor than an American unit of similar size. Very self-sufficient, with modern tanks, heavy artillery, fully mechanized ground troops."

"Damnit! Khrushchev's really going all in on this, isn't he?" Kennedy snapped.

"And thank God we found out before they finished the job," Bobby chimed in.

"Also," noted the Secretary of Defense, "It would appear that all of the SAM sites are fully completed. They have transporters present and launchers installed. I think we have to assume that the transporters are loaded with missiles, so it's just a question of when they decide to use them."

"Well, they haven't so far…that's an encouraging thing," JFK mused.

"I agree," McNamara said. "But the chiefs have asked for a contingency, and I think it makes sense. The Air Force has a squadron of light bombers at MacDill AFB, Florida. They want to arm those with a mixture of ground-attack ordnance, napalm, and fragmentation bombs, and keep them on standby. Their request is that, if one of our planes gets shot down by a SAM, this squadron be launched immediately to make a reprisal raid against that battery."

The President exhaled, leaning back in his chair and closing his eyes. "I hope to hell it doesn't come to that, Bob," he said, finally, sitting up and regarding the Secretary with a level gaze. "But it might. I think it makes sense, and it's a good, measured response—if they take down one of our planes, we take out the battery that did it. But we go no further without discussion and authorization. Can you make that clear to the Chiefs?"

"Yes, Sir, I'm sure that I can."

"All right," the President summarized. "We will assume those two ships that are still inbound are carrying goods that we will allow to pass. We made it a point to specify only offensive weapons would be turned back, so for now, it looks like the plan is working."

"That would seem to be the case," Dean Rusk agreed, wiping his bald head with a handkerchief.

"Thanks for this news," JFK said to the courier. "But we know there are a lot more ships out there—twenty or so by last count. Please make sure that Admiral Anderson keeps up the effort to locate them, and bring us more information as soon as you have anything to report."

"Aye aye, Mr. President—I certainly will!" With another salute, this one tinged with elation, the Navy officer left the room, while at the same time another courier came in and handed a note to the Secretary of Defense. Bob Morris remained at the door until he could close it behind the second departing messenger.

"Here's another news flash, Sir," said Secretary McNamara, reading the note. "General LeMay has just ordered the Strategic Air Command to go to DEFCON 2— that is, one step short of war."

"Nice of him to let us know," JFK said curtly, sarcasm dripping from his words. "That wasn't part of the plan, was it?"

"Actually, Sir, we left it to the discretion of the Air Force."

"Bob, you'd better keep a tight leash on that cowboy. He's too eager to launch his bombers. That guy always gave me the creeps, talking about burning cities and nuclear exchanges...'acceptable casualities.' How the hell can he think we'd have won a war where twenty million Americans get killed? I tell you, he's starting to scare me even more than he did before."

Five: DEFCON 2

"We were eyeball to eyeball and the other fellow just blinked."

Secretary of State Dean Rusk
24 October 1962

24 October 1962
1100 hours (Wednesday morning)
Headquarters, Strategic Air Command
Offutt Air Force Base
Omaha, Nebraska

General Thomas Power had been the hand-picked replacement as the Commander in Chief of SAC, when the previous—and founding—commander of the unit, General Curtis LeMay, had been promoted to Chief of Staff of the Air Force. Like LeMay, Power was a dedicated anticommunist, and a veteran of the strategic bombing campaign against Japan during World War II. And like LeMay, he chafed over the restraints placed upon his hugely powerful force by the realities of politics and, especially, politicians.

Together, they had turned the Strategic Air Command into an organization unlike any other in history. It was an empire, with first LeMay and now Power, as emperor. It could carry more destructive power in the payload of a single bomber than had ever been unleashed in all the wars ever fought. It sucked massive amounts of money from the federal government because, in the era of the Cold War, any politician who was not willing to grant SAC everything it wanted would be called "soft on communism." And because of the single-minded determination of both of its leaders, SAC exerted an incredibly strong pull on American military planning and operations, such that traditional forces like the Army's ground units and the Navy's surface fleet had to fight for every crumb they could get.

In point of fact, and the President's misapprehension notwithstanding, it was Power, not LeMay, who had authorized the increase in SAC readiness to DEFCON 2—one step short of war. But the CINC-SAC wasn't done yet. As he made his way to his command post, three floors underground in Building 500, he was formulating a plan that he expected would drive icy knives of fear into the hearts of the Soviet military commanders. That was a prospect that gave him a great deal of satisfaction.

The general took long strides as he descended, following a spiraling ramp through the first two underground levels. At each passage, a heavy steel blast door rolled open to let him through, then rolled back into its standard locked position. When the doors were closed, as they almost always were, the command post was hermitically sealed from the outside world. Many layers of filters scrubbed all the air that was forced down here by massive fans.

Even three floors underground, behind a triple barrier of blast doors, Power knew that his command post was not proof against Soviet nuclear attack—and he, and everyone who worked for him down here, knew that this base, and even this particular building, would be important targets for any enemy strategic missile attack. To this end, the general had made sure that command responsibilities would not be neglected in the event of his, and his command post's, obliteration.

Somewhere over the United States, at every moment of every day, an EC-135 aircraft—a military version of the Boeing 707—was in the air on the "Looking Glass" mission. The airborne command post always carried an Air Force general and was equipped with the most advanced mobile communications facilities in the world. In the event that SAC HQ was destroyed, control of the strategic bomber and missiles forces would automatically pass to the Looking Glass flight, and the prosecution of strategic nuclear war would theoretically continue uninterrupted.

Once he reached his control room, General Power studied the strategic situation as it was displayed on an impressive array of television screens and maps. Clocks recorded the time in Omaha and Washington, but also in several Soviet cities—including Moscow—that were prominently featured on the target list. Around the nation, three B-52 Stratofortresses, each armed with four thermonuclear bombs, took off every hour.

The massive bombers, affectionately called Big Ugly Fat Fuckers, or BUFFs, by their crews, were the most powerful and deadly aircraft in history. With the DEFCON 2 order, many of these bombers had begun to move north, gathering over Canada and the Artic Ocean. There they circled, ready, waiting for orders either to stand down or to continue on to pre-designated targets in the Communist bloc.

More than 400 refueling tankers were available to SAC, and many of these were also airborne. With virtually unlimited fuel available, it was not unusual for a BUFF and its crew to remain aloft for twenty-four hours; the crews even included an additional, third, pilot so that the men flying the plane could get some rest.

At the same time, missile complexes in the central United States also went to full alert, with strategic rockets fueled and crews standing by. The brand new Minuteman missile, of which only ten were currently in service—and those activated only in the last month—could be launched at literally a moment's notice, since they were fired directly from their silos. But even the solidly reliable Atlas and Titan rockets needed only about a ten-minute warning, since the missiles needed to be lifted up to the surface by gigantic elevators. As soon as they had fully emerged, however, they too would be ready for launch.

Farther out across the globe, on bases as far-flung as Italy, Morocco, Spain, and Scotland, older B-47 bombers stood on stand-by, awaiting orders to take off and fly toward targets in the Communist Bloc. They had shorter ranges than the B-52 but could also carry immensely powerful payloads. Crews slept in their flight suits, and the planes were fueled and armed, ready to take off on Power's command.

As of now, within an hour of the order to go to DEFCON 2, Power had more than 900 bombers and 130 intercontinental ballistic missiles ready for action at a moment's notice, with more coming online at all times. The attacks, when they began, would initially target more than 200 high priority sites, called "Task 1 Targets." Many of these were remote airbases and military complexes where much of the Soviet nuclear arsenal could be found. But at least a few were important headquarters and communication networks, which were invariably located in large cities. One of the primary targets designated for immediate destruction—by at least four one megaton bombs—was the Kremlin, in the heart of Moscow, Russia's largest city.

On the general's desk, below the vast arc of televised displays, were two telephones, a gold one that linked SAC directly to the JCS in the Pentagon and, if necessary, to the President in the White House; and a red telephone that connected him to a huge network of subordinate commanders at SAC bases around the world. Now General Power picked up the red telephone, which immediately broadcast a signal to those subordinate commanders, ordering them to be ready to take a message from their CIC. Power watched the illuminated map, bright with white lights to mark every SAC asset around the world. As the commanders in those distant bases answered their phones, the white lights for each thus-connected base blinked out.

Finally, the map was dark, the network activated. Power knew that his message would travel around the world on powerful radio waves. Yet, when his coding officer asked if he wanted to encrypt his message, he curtly shook his head "no." This warning would be broadcast in the clear, understandable to anyonewith a scanner and working radio—including countless KGB and Soviet Military Intelligence outposts.

The SAC commander had his eye on Moscow as he spoke into the phone. "This is General Power," he began. "I want you all to know that we have taken Strategic Air Command to a level of alert unprecedented in our glorious history. We now stand at DEFCON 2. I cannot understate the seriousness of the situation facing you. It is important to realize that our entire Strategic Attack Force could be ordered to war at a moment's notice. I repeat, we could go to war at a moment's notice."

He set down the phone and leaned back with a smug, satisfied smile. He had no doubt that the message had been received, by exactly the people he wanted to hear it, loud and clear.

1130 hours (Wednesday midday)
USS DDG 507 Conning
Quarantine Line, 500 miles NE of Cuba

Seaman Duncan stood on the fantail of the fast destroyer. Her battery of guided missiles, twin rockets perched on a swiveling launcher, loomed over him. He tried to squint, to see into the distance toward the east and north, half-believing he could make out the gray shape of a Soviet merchant ship. In truth, it was his imagination.

But he knew they were out there, and not just because Chief Weber had told him so. In fact, the captain himself had come over the loudspeaker several times in the last day, explaining that *Conning* was part of a destroyer screen waiting to intercept communist ships carrying unauthorized weapons to Cuba. Duncan felt the unusual weight of the Thompson submachine gun on his back as a reminder. Per Weber's order, he had slept with the gun at his side and had been carrying it since he got up that morning. The gun, on a leather strap, was heavy, but it was a good weight. It felt kind of odd to stir a pot of oatmeal with the gun strapped to his back, but it was a "good odd."

He felt the deck lurch slightly underfoot and braced his hands on the railing as *Conning* started a sharp turn away from her previous course. The sun, nearly overhead, didn't give much clue as to their bearing, but he saw from the wake that the fast ship had turned some ninety degrees toward the north. He could feel the thrum of her powerful engines in the deck under his feet, and sense that the guided-missile destroyer was accelerating to flank speed.

Chief Petty Officer Weber approached, and Duncan called out to him, pointing eastward. "Hey, Chief—I though the Russians were coming from over there. What gives?"

"What, are you a navigator now?" the chief asked.

Weber had a canvas sack in his hands, and he pulled a belt out of it as he came up to Duncan. "New plan, Georgie. We're off to hunt a Russian sub. And you get to help!" He held out one of the belts, and the seaman noticed a half dozen heavy objects, about the size of a can of fruit, hanging from the strap.

"What are these?" he wondered, taking the proffered belt.

"Those are practice depth charges, like hand grenades. When you get an order, you drop one of them over the side. If you're lucky, you'll hit a Russian sub and force it up to the surface. You got that?"

"Well, sure, Chief, I think so." Duncan looked at the "cans" and remembered basic training, where he'd learned how to throw a hand grenade. "I guess I pull this pin here, huh?"

"Yep. Pull it, and drop it over the side, and wait for the 'boom.'"

"Aye aye, Chief. Am I supposed to bag a submarine all by myself?" he couldn't help asking.

"Don't be a smart aleck. No, we've got some help." The chief pointed to the north, and Duncan was surprised to see a large ship, now clearly visible a mile or two away. The flat deck, broken only by the tower of a single island, marked it as an aircraft carrier, though it wasn't as big as the huge fleet carrier, *Enterprise*, that *Conning* had passed on the way out to the quarantine line.

"That's *Randolph*," the chief explained. "Back in WW2 she was as good a carrier as there was. Now, she's a hangar for helicopters and search planes—dedicated to ASW work. So it's her job to find the subs, and our job to bring them to the surface."

"All right." Duncan tried not to keep the skepticism out of his voice, though the plan sounded crazy to him.

"Good. Now, take that Tommy Gun back to the weapons locker. Chief Denning will check it in; you won't need it for this job. Then get back here and wait for orders."

"Got it, Chief. They find 'em, we bring 'em up," he clarified as Weber walked away. Under his breath he muttered the final detail, the one he still couldn't really believe:

"With a hand grenade."

2130 hours (Wednesday night)
Virginia Highway Patrol Weigh Station
Leesburg, Virginia

The CB radio in Captain Jake Miller's closed jeep crackled. The device was set to the 6th Battalion's channel, but he couldn't be sure it wasn't some civilian. After all, they were just thirty miles or so west of Washington D.C. There were a lot of people living around here. Nevertheless, he reached for the microphone and pressed the "speak" button.

"Miller, here," he said.

"Uh, Captain. This is Sergeant Snelling, in truck one. You'd better get back here—we have a problem. We're in the weigh station."

"Hold tight, I'll be right there—I'm only five minutes away," the captain replied. "Miller out."

He turned his driver. "Turn around—back to the weigh station."

A few minutes later the jeep pulled in to find a convoy of trucks, the entire battalion, lined up in front of the truck scale. The lead truck was on the scale, and a highway patrolman had been standing below the driver's door. When Miller got out, the trooper turned to face him.

"Captain," he declared, clearly unimpressed by Miller's silver bars of rank. "This truck is too heavy. I can't let it through. And those other trucks behind, if they're the same as this one, they won't pass either."

"Dammit, Trooper—we're on orders from the Department of Defense. We have to take those trucks from Maryland to Key West Florida, and we have to have them there yesterday!"

"I'm sorry, Sir. You'll just have to find some way to do it that doesn't involve driving on the roads of the Commonwealth of Virginia."

"You've heard about the crisis with Cuba?" Miller said sarcastically. "These are antiaircraft missiles intended for the airbase at Key West! If that base is attacked by communist aircraft, these missiles will be needed to shoot them down!"

"Good luck with that mission, sir. But I haven't received any notice to make an exception. You'll have to turn back."

"I don't believe this shit!" the captain fumed, nearly exploding.

"Sir, you will keep a respectful tongue in your mouth, or I'll have to arrest you."

"By God, I think you mean it!" Miller declared, drawing a deep breath. He looked at the well-lighted office beyond the scale. "Do you have a phone I can use?"

The trooper pointed to the ditch next to the road. "There's a pay phone down there."

Miller clapped his hands to his helmet. He wasn't even sure who he could call, what he could do. In fact, there was only one thing to do.

The 6th Hawk Battalion, 65th Artillery Regiment—the modern antiaircraft missiles intended to defend Key West Naval Air Station against enemy air attack—on the move from its base at Fort Meade, turned around and the whole convoy headed north, back into Maryland.

25 October 1962
0340 hours (Thursday early morning)
Submarine *B-59*, on the surface
Approximately 650 miles NE of Cuba

Foxtrot *B-59* had cruised on the surface for almost four hours, which was a nice break for the men, since each crew member had gotten two full half-hour stints on the deck, breathing fresh air under the open, starlit sky. But Captain Savitsky, in the watchpost on top of the sail, was growing increasingly displeased. For about the tenth time, he reached for the speaking tube and called down to the command center.

"Has there been any broadcast from Moscow? Any communication with information or orders?"

"I'm sorry, Comrade Captain," the radioman replied. "There has been nothing directed at us, not since we surfaced before midnight."

"Damn," he muttered, straightening up. The sky was moonless, but the stars were bright enough that the whole ocean seemed to glow with a silver phosphorescence. He knew, in an abstract way, that it was beautiful. But he couldn't think of anything except how alone they were, how far from the *rodina*, and how many questions he had about what was going on in the world outside of this submarine.

The hatch opened, and Commander Arkhipov climbed up the ladder to join the captain and the two lookouts. There was room enough, barely, for the four men and the hatch leading downward.

"Look at it as good news," Arkhipov suggested cheerfully. "If anything had gone wrong, they'd have to send us a message. As it is, things must be proceeding exactly according to plan."

"But we don't even know what the plan is!" the captain snapped, then shook his head. "I'm sorry, Vasily Andreivich. You're right. We've made it this far without—"

As if he'd cursed their luck with his own words, an alarm klaxon suddenly brayed a warning. The men on the fore and after decks sprinted for the hatches leading down into the hull, as did the two watchmen on top of the sail. Savitsky snatched up the end of the speaking tube. "What is it? What's going on?"

"An American ship, Captain," the radar operator came back. "About twenty kilometers away, and closing on us fast. By the speed and size of the radar image, I suspect it's a destroyer. And she has us painted on her own radar."

"Damn!" spat the captain. He gestured to Arkhipov, wordlessly sending his exec down the hatch after the two lookouts. A glance fore and aft confirmed that the last of his crew had dropped out of sight, vanishing into the dubious safety if the submarine's hull.

"All right, take her down—crash dive!" Savitsky, the last man outside the boat, ordered.

Immediately he felt the lurch as seawater poured over the bow, roaring back to churn around the base of the sail, appearing to climb quickly as the sub angled sharply into the sea. Savitsky dropped through the hatch and quickly spun the lock shut behind him. He slid down the ladder into the command center, allowed a crewman to close off the secondary hatch block access to the sail.

He realized that the diving officer was looking at him expectantly. With a ship, potentially an enemy ship, bearing down on them, he didn't want to take a chance on running at snorkel depth—a keen radar man on the destroyer could potentially pick up the sub's location just from the snorkel and the turbulence it raised on the surface.

"Take her down to 100 meters," he said, then picked up the tube that connected to the engine room. "Switch over to batteries. Rig for silent running."

Immediately a shroud of quiet seemed to blanket the submarine as the three powerful diesel engines shut down. The sub glided, almost like a giant fish, deeper beneath the surface.

Arkhipov was eyeing him, nodding in approval. "We won't stay down that deep all day," the captain explained. "But I want to shake this pesky destroyer before we start up the engines again."

* * *

Far to the rear, the diving fins contorted the submarine's hull ever so slightly from the force of the sudden maneuver. That force was enough to twist and stretch the tiny crack that had appeared in the hull two days earlier. The crack extended several centimeters farther, and the dripping of water through the opening, almost unnoticeable before, became a steady trickle.

Propeller shaft number three passed through the hull where the tiny crack had just expanded. For now, the flaw wasn't enough to impeded the rotation of that steel rod, which spun steadily, cradled in its roller bearings. But, very slightly, enough play entered into the opening so that the shaft started to vibrate, just a bit.

It was subtle, still—so subtle that no one in the submarine noticed that anything was wrong.

1012 hours (Thursday morning)
Presidium Chamber
Kremlin, Moscow

"Comrade Malinovsky, would you report on the readiness of our military forces?" Khrushchev asked from his position at the front of the room. He was pleased that he kept his voice steady, and he imagined that he now projected a sense of cool control.

His manner was a far cry from the almost paralyzing dash of terror he'd felt the previous evening, when KGB and military intelligence sources had both reported that the United States Strategic Air Command had advanced its readiness to DEFCON 2. Upon hearing the news, the chairman had retired to his apartment to collect himself, a process that had required more than an hour. When he had emerged, he still felt rattled, and he sensed that these dour bureaucrats could sense his fear. He had ordered Malinovsky to advance the state of readiness of the Soviet armed forces, then claimed that he was tired and needed to go to bed.

In fact, he hadn't slept much at all, and in his darkest moments had more or less taken it for granted that he, and the Kremlin, and all of Moscow, were going to be incinerated by a thermonuclear explosion sometime during the night. As a consequence, when he woke up to find the sun shining, a beautiful autumn day commencing, and no ominous mushroom clouds rising from any point on the horizon, he had decided that, once again, the Americans were bluffing.

"All branches of the Soviet Military have moved to standby alert," Malinovsky intoned, reading from a briefing sheet. "Leaves have been canceled. Weapons have been prepared for use and tested, and our aircraft have been dispersed to advance bases. Our strategic bomber forces have been fueled, with bombs loaded aboard. The strategic rockets have yet to be fueled, but fueling stations are ready, and crews are standing by."

"Excellent," the chairman said cheerfully, rubbing his hands together.

It was a hollow cheer for all that. He, and Malinovsky, if not every man here, knew that the Soviet strategic bomber force was a minimal threat to the American mainland. Even from bases on the very far east of Siberia, the Kamchatka peninsula, the farthest those bombers could range against the USA would be the northwestern cities of Seattle and, possibly, San Francisco. And the Soviet Air Force lacked the in-air refueling capabilities of the Americans, so any bombers that made it as far as northern California would run out of fuel within a hundred miles or so of dropping their bombs.

The Soviet chairman had reached another realization during the previous night's long hours of terror. He had come to understand that he would have to pull the rockets out of Cuba. To continue like this was madness. It would be different, he had argued to himself, if the missiles had been made operational before they had been discovered. As it was, however, the SS5—the rockets with the range to reach most of the American homeland—would not be ready ever, because too many important components had not yet reached Cuba. And now, with the blockade, they could not make it to their intended ports of destination.

Of course, he could conceivably unleash a devastating blow against the southeastern quarter or third of the enemy nation, but that would leave far too much of American territory unaffected. Furthermore, it would enrage the Americans to the point where a devastating counterstrike would be inevitable. Khrushchev was an emotional man, but he entertained no illusions about his country's ability to withstand a full-strength thermonuclear attack from the world's only other superpower.

In fact, Khrushchev was a veteran of the most brutal war ever to wrack Russia, and the world. He had lost his first son, Leonid, to Nazi aircraft. He had stood in the rubble of Stalingrad, watching the city die around him as the heroic soldiers of the Red Army prevailed in what to him would always be the most important battle in the history of the world. Yet all that death and ruination would be dwarfed the moment a single thermonuclear device—let alone hundreds of them!—detonated over a Soviet city.

So, how could he tell the members of the Presidium what he had concluded, and still save face—his own, and his country's? A natural politician and survivor, he knew that what he had to do was present the truth in such a way that it did not look as though the USSR was losing.

"We have succeeded in drawing all of the world's attention to the plight of our bold ally in Cuba," he began. "Now, it is time to negotiate, time to be flexible and reasonable, so that all we have gained is not lost in the fires of a man-made holocaust…"

The idea was starting to sound good, even to himself.

1530 hours (Thursday afternoon)
82nd Airborne Division
Fort Bragg, North Carolina

"Hey, LT. Is this thing, this whole Cuba war for real, or not?" asked Corporal Skilling, the junior NCO in the platoon. The men were ranged about the grass in front of the barracks, with knapsacks, ammo belts, and weapons scattered haphazardly around them.

"How the hell should I know?" Hartley replied, practically snarling. He ignored the barely suppressed snickers of his men as much as he could, even as he felt the shame of knowing he really was a lousy officer.

But he hadn't signed on for a war! Dammit, the Army was his way to meet girls, to wear a flashy uniform. For a time it was nice to have an organization that fed and housed him, did his laundry, and paid him to boss other, less-educated men around. But now that he might have to take those less-educated men into battle, he wasn't sure he was up to the task. In fact, he was pretty certain that he wasn't capable of doing the job.

Of course, he'd figured that out just a little bit too late. The men of Company F, 2nd battalion, 82nd Airborne Division were gathered outside their barracks, sorting knapsacks, cleaning rifles, collecting and securing ammunition. These were tasks they'd done several times over the last few days, but Captain Martin had ordered the men to go through the procedures again.

It would escape the notice of no one that, while the First and Third Platoons of Company F had completed their repacking in a crisp and timely fashion, the men of the Second Platoon were still at it. Several privates were bickering about who was going to carry some extra grenades—though they quickly settled the issue when they spotted Sergeant Hiemstra approaching. Indeed, as the veteran NCO moved down the line, with his face locked into a thunderhead of displeasure, the men of the platoon speedily arranged their gear, packed their knapsacks, and, one by one, stood at ease to signify their readiness to move.

"Second Platoon ready to move out, Lieutenant," reported Hiemstra, coming up to Hartley. The lieutenant, with some effort, had secured his own kit—he'd been afraid he'd be humiliated by failing to complete the task that his soldiers were doing, even though their commanding officer carried significant less gear in the way of extra weaponry and ammunition.

"Very good, Sergeant. Release the men to the mess hall. Let them get dinner a little early."

"Okay, Sir," Hiemstra said, turning to stroll back to the knot of men that had now gathered in the shade of a giant evergreen. Hartley looked around, noticing that the men of the other two platoons had already been excused for dinner, and realized that "early" would be perceived as a fairly relative term by his own soldiers.

Hiemstra, having designated the dismissal task to Corporal Skilling, headed back over to the lieutenant as the men made for the mess hall. Hartley respected the big Dutchman, and was also a little bit intimidated by him, though he tried to cover up the latter fact with an inordinate amount of bluster. These last few days, however—since the wreck of his T-bird and his chewing out by Martin, followed by the President's speech—he'd found his bluster to be in fairly short supply.

"Sir, might I have a word?" asked the sergeant.

Only then did Hartley realize that the two men were alone on the patch of ground in front of the barracks. The platoon had scattered, and the rest of the company was nowhere in sight.

"Of course, Sergeant. What's on your mind?"

"You are, Lieutenant. You, and these men."

Hartley felt a queasy sensation in his stomach. He didn't like the way this conversation had begun, but he felt powerless to steer it onto a different course. He wasn't physically afraid of Hiemstra—sure, the man was bigger and burlier than the officer, and a legendary brawler to boot, but he wasn't about to get physical with his lieutenant. At least, Hartley was pretty sure that he wasn't.

"You see, Sir. I can't help but remember when I was their age—well, as old as the younger ones anyway. I was eighteen, and we were in England, getting ready to head for France as part of Overlord."

Hartley, and everyone else in the unit, knew that Hiemstra was one of the Old Timers, veterans of the great battles of the Second World War, but now, confronted by the blunt statement, the officer found himself surprised. Maybe it's because he'd never before imagined him as a young soldier, preparing for his first battle.

"Well, Lieutenant. I sat there in the dark, those early days of June, knowing we'd be going into battle in a matter of days. And you know what: I just about shit my pants thinking about it. Now, I had a platoon sergeant—he'd fought with the division in Africa and Sicily, and he told me I was going to do okay.

"And we had us a platoon lieutenant, well, he was fresh from the States. Never heard a shot fired in anger, as they say. But damn, he was gung ho. He made me believe he'd charge through a wall to get to a kraut machinegun nest, he wanted to kill those bastards that bad. And I believed him, and I didn't shit my drawers, and I lived to see the end of the war. I believed in him, but more to the point, Sir—I knew that he believed in me."

Hartley drew a breath. He was touched and shamed by the sergeants words, and he didn't know what to say.

"Now I suggest you forget what these men think of you. That's not the point. But I have ask you a blunt question, Sir: Do you believe in them? And if you do, do you think they know you believe in them? Because the answer to that question just might make all the difference on whether a lot of those boys live, or get killed."

"I...I do believe in them," Hartley said, the words sounding lame even as he spoke. "Truth is, I think they're really good men. Sometimes I don't feel like I deserve them, and I think they know that." Sometimes—hell, I never feel like I deserve them, he realized with a flush of embarrassed resentment.

"Like I suggested, Sir. Forget about what they think of you—that's really not important. But you need to let them know that you believe in them."

"I...thank you, Sergeant. I appreciate that," Hartley said.

"You're welcome, Sir." Hiemstra gave him a salute, which the officer suddenly realized the NCO hadn't been doing for quite some time. "Um, Sergeant—Rick? Your sergeant, and your lieutenant...how did they do, when you landed in Normandy."

Hiemstra shook his head. "I never got a chance to find out, Sir. Our stick overshot the LZ, and there was a pond, a deep pond, just past it. Both of 'em drowned before they could even kick their boots off."

2215 hours (Thursday night)
The Press Club Lounge
Washington, D.C.

"I'm glad you could get away," Bob Morris said, bringing a glass of wine to Stella at their table in a darkened corner of the bar. He had a mug of beer for himself. "It's been pretty crazy in this town this past week. At the White House, of course, but I imagine for you, too."

"Yes, it has," Stella agreed, taking a small sip. She'd been exhausted from an intense week of work when she got home, less than an hour ago, to find her phone ringing. But when Morris had asked her to meet, her fatigue had vanished in a rather amazing fashion. She couldn't help but smile when he'd walked through the door and shyly looked around—he almost seemed surprised to see her, though she'd readily agreed to meet him.

"How...I don't want you to think I'm prying for information—but how is the President?" she asked, feeling some vague combination of professional curiosity and genuine concern.

"I've never seen him better, or stronger," Morris said bluntly. "It's like this showdown with Khrushchev, well, it's really given him something to sink his teeth into. His usual problems, the things that act up all the time, they don't seem to be bothering him."

"What kind of 'usual things' do you mean," she followed up, unconsciously going into 100 percent reporter mode. "I understand he's had some issues with back pain—is that it?"

Morris seemed relieved that she added some detail. Kennedy's health issues were not generally a matter of public knowledge, and certainly not something that was reported by the media. In truth, her awareness of his chronic pain had come from personal experience, something she'd observed—and JFK had confirmed—in the approximately three hours that they had spent together.

"He has a lot of trouble with that, usually," the Secret Service agent was saying. "But I haven't noticed it bothering him these last few days." He blinked, as if remembering where—or more likely who—he was. "Listen, I'm really not supposed to talk about, well, my job. I feel like I can trust you, though. Can we keep this between us, for old times' sake? What would you call it? 'Off the record?'"

Stella leaned back in her chair and arched her eyebrows, thinking about what he was saying. "So, you do remember I'm a reporter, right?"

"Oh, yes. In fact, I saw you on TV the other night, in front of the Pentagon. I used to watch Cronkite but, well, since I met you again, I've switched to NBC." He seemed embarrassed to admit it.

And she was flattered, in spite of herself. "Well, it's a slow way to expand my viewership, but I'll take it. Listen, Bob, I like you, and I like the President—I voted for him! I'm not about to go public with anything that will make him, or you, look bad. And I know how to keep a conversation off the record. So if you think you can have a friendly conversation with an old friend who's a reporter, I'd like to keep talking to you."

"Me too," he admitted sheepishly. He took a sip and looked at her over his mug. "But 'an old friend?' Couldn't you think of me as 'an old boyfriend?' Old, or current, I guess I'd let you pick. Maybe both." His expression tightened into one of alarm. "That is, I mean, I know you're not married, but are you seeing someone?"

She laughed. "You mean, are you treading on some other guy's turf? No, you're not. But I never realized that you thought of me as your girlfriend. I mean, we had that night at homecoming, and went to a few movies I guess, now that I think about it…"

"Well, you were a lot more social than I was," he admitted. "You seemed to go out with plenty of guys. I didn't date much—I was more of a loner. So I have to admit, you weren't really my girlfriend. It's more that I wanted you to be."

She winced, not sure if she'd been insulted or not. What kind of reputation did he think she had, anyway? "Well, you could have said something!"

"No, I couldn't have," he replied frankly. "Not then, anyway. I guess I was too shy, or polite, or something." He reached across the table and put his hand over hers. "But I'd like to see you again, more than once. If you'd like—you know, when things settle down."

"If they settle down," Stella retorted. "I think I'd like that too. But who knows what the hell is going to happen? Do you think it's possible that there will be a war?"

"I think it is possible," Morris said. He looked away, then turned back to meet her eyes frankly. "I've told my parents to get out of Alexandria for a while, to take a week or two at their cabin up on Blue Ridge. And I wonder, Stella...I mean, what about you? You should really think about getting out of town. Maybe go see your parents, or something..."

His solicitous concern for her made her angry. "My mother died three years ago. My father is the CO at Key West Naval Air Station. I hardly thinks he wants family there now, or that it would be a safe place to go. And my brother is a pilot on the *Enterprise*, somewhere in the Caribbean," she responded more sharply than she'd intended. "And dammit, Bob, I have a job to do in this town just as you do. So I'm not going anywhere!"

"Okay, of course—sorry I asked. I was out of line." He gestured at their glasses, which were both empty. "Would you like to stay for another?"

She would have liked another, honestly. But now she felt unsettled, more frightened than she did before—and acutely conscious that she did have a job to do, one that would require all of her alertness in the morning.

"I'm sorry, Bob. I can't, not tonight. But...I am glad you caught me at home when you called. And you should call me again." She rose to leave and he stood too. Quickly, maybe rashly, she leaned forward and gave him a peck on the cheek. "I'll talk to you soon," she said, before passing out through the door.

The night, she was surprised to discover, had grown surprisingly cold.

26 October 1962
1200 hours (Friday midday)
Oval Office, the White House
Washington D.C.

Bob Morris poked his head in the door after the President responded to his knock. "Secretary of State Rusk, and Directors McCone and Lundahl to see you, sir."

"Thanks, Bob—send them in."

The three men joined JFK and his brother in a more casual setting than the usual ExComm meeting, but the topics were no less serious. Arthur Lundahl went to set up his briefing board across from the President's desk, while the Secretary of State began his report.

"I got some unusual news from Ambassador Kohler, in Moscow," Rusk stated. "It seems he got a visit over there from William Knox, president of Westinghouse. Knox is over in Russia to try and set up some manufacturing deals.

Anyway, Khrushchev knew about his visit and invited Knox to come and see him at the Kremlin. The chairman was pleasant enough, according to Knox, but he clearly wanted to pass a message back to Washington. Khrushchev wanted him to let us know that the Soviets intend to stand firm on the matter of the missiles."

"But they've already backed off from the quarantine line," JFK objected. "That doesn't make any sense."

"Apparently they met two days ago," Rusk continued. "It's possible Khrushchev hadn't made up his mind yet, depending on the exact timing. You know they're about eight hours ahead of us over there. But that wasn't the thing Knox thought was most important."

"Go on," said Kennedy impatiently.

"Well, even though he was cheerful, Khrushchev made a threat. He did explain that the missiles would stay under Soviet control, says he knows that the Cubans are, quote, a 'volatile' people, and he wouldn't release nuclear weapons to them. But he also said that if we started an invasion, the Guantanamo Naval Base would, again quote, 'disappear on the first day.'"

"That's one hell of a threat," the President agreed. "Does he mean he would target it with a strategic missile? Wouldn't that be a bit of overkill?"

"Quite possibly," Rusk agreed. "Let's hear what Art has to say about that."

By then the director of NPIC had his easel and display boards arranged, and the other men gave him their full attention. "You'll see here additional evidence of the Soviet ground troops in Cuba," Lundahl said. He indicated a row of what clearly were tanks, lined up and apparently ready for action. Many trucks, armored personnel carriers, and other vehicles were ranked in orderly rows behind the tanks.

"We have confirmation of four motorized rifle regiments on the ground, now, Sir. One of them is in the east, clearly a threat to Guantanamo Naval Base. It's deployed to block any move by our men to advance out of there, though it could conceivably attack as well. A second is in central Cuba, positioned to defend the Sagua la Grande missile sites; a third is doing the same for the San Cristobal sites; and the fourth seems like it could be used to defend Havana, or move out as a reserve."

"All right," JFK said. "That's a lot of troops. But one regiment isn't going to make Guantanamo 'disappear,' is it?"

It was McCone who replied. "Not conventionally, no sir. With recent reinforcements, we have three times as many Marines there as are men in that regiment. And our men are dug in, and that position has been prepared for some sixty years. But show him what you have, there, Art."

"These, Mr. President, are the problem," Lundahl resumed smoothly. He gestured to a pair of tracked vehicles, the size of tanks. Instead of turrets, each one had a cylindrical object, missile-shaped, resting on the hull. "We're pretty sure these are FROG launchers. That is, 'free rocket over ground.' The Russians call this type the Luna, and it is capable of carrying a nuclear warhead. A small one, about a two-kiloton yield."

"You mean that they might have battlefield nukes, as well as strategic bombs, in there?" Bobby Kennedy demanded.

"'Might' is the operative word, Sir," McCone said. "We still haven't had any luck finding where they're storing their warheads. The FROGs could be conventional high-explosive rockets. But we have to consider the possibility."

"It's looking more and more like it could get nasty, isn't it?" JFK concluded, as Lundahl started to collect his displays.

"Yes, sir," McCone replied. "That's some very evil stuff they have on the ground over there."

1315 hours (Friday afternoon)
USS CVN *Enterprise*
120 miles East of Cuba
Windward Passage

Derek Widener had flown CAP missions the last two days, and would no doubt be scheduled again tomorrow, Saturday. But for today, he wasn't on the duty flight list. He decided to take advantage of the free time by seeing what he could learn about the strategic situation. His second-seat man, Ensign King, came with him as they entered the pilot's briefing room.

"Looks like we've come around to the east end of Cuba," King observed, looking at the ship's position as it was plotted on the map. For the last week the carrier task force had been cruising to the south of the island, so this was an interesting development to both pilots.

The long chain of the Bahamas stretched from the southeast to the northwest, screening *Enterprise* and her task force from the Atlantic Ocean. The nearest of that chain were the Turks and Caicos Islands, but there were deep water passages to both sides of that archipelago that would allow easy ship access to the open sea.

"You don't suppose we're leaving Cuba behind, do you?" King asked.

"I doubt it," Derek replied. He gestured to another American task force, some 300 miles northeast of them, already in the ocean. "They've got a carrier out there already—looks like *Randolph*. She's been converted to ASW now, hasn't she?"

"I think you're right," the ensign replied. "Do you suppose she's on a hunt?"

They knew that any suspected Russian subs would not be displayed on the pilot's chart. Information on sub tracking was highly classified, and really none of their business. Still, it was easy enough to put two and two together.

"Well, at least we're close enough to help, if something happens out there," Widener remarked. But he looked to the left, where the tip of Cuba was still very close, and the naval base at Guantanamo not that much farther away.

"Still, if trouble comes," he concluded, "I'd expect us to find it on Castro's tropical paradise."

2134 hours (Friday night)
Battery 2, 539th Missile Regiment
San Cristobal, Cuba

Lieutenant Colonel Tukov kept the lamp burning brightly in his tent, going over readiness reports. His men had drilled and tested, proving that they were able to fuel the rockets and hoist them on their launchers to the ready position in fifteen minutes or less.

He had taken the precaution of moving several trucks, as well as one of the reserve missiles, into a grove of trees on the outskirts of the battery site. He had another truck tractor nearby. All of the vehicles had been heavily camouflaged. In the event of an emergency—and only if Tukov gave the order to fall back—his men had been instructed to hook one launcher to the truck tractor and make for the quarry position with all speed.

Finally, he concluded that all was in readiness. The only thing lacking was access to the missile warheads, and he expected them to be released on General Pliyev's order within a day or two.

The battery's communication network was connected to El Chico by an old telephone line, since radio silence remained a primary requirement. Tukov had ordered an officer to remain at all times within a few steps of that phone connection, and now the young lieutenant who was in charge of the switchboard came into the tent. The colonel looked up expectantly.

"A message from General Pliyev, Sir," the communications officer said, handing a typed note to the battery commander. Tukov needed only a moment to digest the brief contents:

Warheads for SS4 rockets released from storage as of 1900 hours 26 October. Anticipate delivery to San Cristobal sites by 2400 hours, 26 October. Warheads are to be stored in a secure location at battery site. Do not install on rockets unless explicitly ordered by Command, Soviet Military Mission, Cuba.

Also note: as of dawn 27 October, SA 2 radars will commence operation. America aircraft incursions over Cuban air space will be resisted with all force.

Tukov took a deep breath and looked at his watch. He knew that the warheads, in their bunker at Bejucal, were only a few hours truck ride away up the main highway. They would arrive by the middle of the night tonight, and maybe sooner.

"All right, Lieutenant," he told the communications officer, who had been standing by in case the colonel intended to make a reply. "Looks like we'll have a long night ahead of us. But by tomorrow, we'll finally be able to make a difference in events. For better or worse."

Almost certainly worse, he thought, but he kept that idea to himself. He was still pondering the possibilities when he heard the rumble of an old jeep approaching his tent. The sound was a familiar one, and besides, only one person would be coming to visit him this late in the evening. He went to the flap of his tent and held it aside as he watched Che Guevera bounce out of his passenger seat and stride over to the colonel. The driver kept the jeep motor running, so Tukov assumed this would be a short visit.

"Comrade Colonel," the revolutionary said without preamble. "I come to warn you: *El Máximo Líder* has determined that the American invasion will almost certainly commence tonight. He has put Cuban forces on full alert and advised, in those cases where we are closely coordinating with our Russian allies, that we share word of his warning with those allies. I consider you to be a very close ally, Comrade, and so I bring you this warning."

"Thank you, comrade," Tukov replied. He thought about telling Che that the warheads were on the way to the battery site but decided against that. He did have something he felt he could reveal, however: "My general has informed me that the SAM radars all around Cuba will be activated at dawn. I think those incursions by American spyplanes are about to come to an end."

Guevera's handsome face broke into a broad smile. "That is excellent news, Comrade—thank you for sharing it!" He strode back to his jeep and hopped in, offering his customary departure: "*Viva la Revolucion!*"

Tukov saluted, casually, as the vehicle roared away.

2210 hours (Friday night)
Submarine *B-59*, submerged
Approximately 400 miles NE of Cuba

The sudden appearance of American warships the previous day had sent the *B-59* deep. For more than twelve hours, she had lurked hundreds of feet below the surface, relying on her the virtually silent power of her big batteries, combined with careful restrictions on crew activities. This so-called "silent running" made a submarine very difficult to find, even with modern detection equipment.

There were two significant problems inherent in operating a submarine on battery power: First, the boat could not move nearly as fast as it could when the three powerful diesel engines were driving the trio of six-bladed propellers. Even submerged, when the snorkel was extended above the surface and the diesels ran at full power, the boat could glide through the ocean at a respectable fifteen knots.

Battery use, however, cut the speed to less than half of that, and even that would drain the cells very quickly—which brought up the second problem. The batteries needed to be recharged frequently, and certainly after a couple of days at depth. To get more than twelve to eighteen hours out of the battery, power had to be used very sparingly, which meant that the speed was reduced to barely two or three knots.

The Foxtrot had been operating to conserve power for more than twelve hours, now, and the batteries were getting dangerously low. The air in the sub, though it wasn't further fouled by the diesels at the moment, still grew increasingly rank merely because of the respiration of the 78 officers and men who made up *B-59*'s crew.

"What's going on up there?" Captain Savitsky demanded in a breathy hiss to no one in particular. The thickness of the air, heavy with carbon dioxide, was clearly fraying his own nerves, maybe even his judgment.

He was angry at the Americans, angry at the navy hierarchy that had sent them on this fool's mission, and irritated with the increasingly erratic performance of his men. Just moments ago, one of the youngest sailors in the crew, groggy from lack of oxygen, had fallen as he made his way through the control room. He hadn't made much noise, but any unusual sound could prove fatal when the American navy was listening for any clue as to the boat's whereabouts. Savitsky's rage had nearly erupted, and he had to bite back a profane outburst that would have been much louder than the young sailor's tumble. Instead, the captain had closed his eyes and forced himself to breathe deeply while the young man had hastily tiptoed out of the control room and back to his station in the forward torpedo room.

The interior of the boat was nearly pitch dark, in order to conserve battery power, and the emergency lighting cast every man's gaunt, sweaty face in an eerie red glow. Commander Arkhipov approached and touched Savitsky on the shoulder, a friendly gesture that nevertheless caused the captain to flinch.

"Comrade Captain," said the executive officer quietly. "Allow me to take the helm for a few hours. Perhaps you can get some rest?"

The suggestion, a perfectly normal one that had occurred multiple times in their years together, almost threw Savitsky into another rage. He recognized the signs of stress, and nodded wearily.

"Let me listen for a moment, and then I'll lie down." He went to the sonar table, where a young sailor sat hunched over, earphones clamped to his head. The man jerked when the captain touched him, then removed and handed over the earphones at the captain's gesture.

"Stay here," he told the lad, who had moved to give his chair to Savitsky. "I just want to hear for myself, a minute."

The sounds in the 'phones were faint, but definite. First he heard the crackling growl that told him propellors, of more than one ship, were churning the water overhead. The searching ships were not directly overhead, but they were not too many miles away. Every few seconds he heard the ping of an active sonar array, seeking to locate the sub by the echo that the sound would return if it was accurately directed at a metal hull.

Nodding, the officer handed the earphones back to the sailor, and turned to Arkhipov. "They're still there, but not close, Vasily Andreivich," he whispered. "I will try and get some sleep—but wake me if there's any change in status."

"Aye aye, Sir," replied the loyal first officer.

At least I can leave my boat in good hands, thought the captain, as he weaved his way unsteadily—almost as if he was drunk—toward the illusory comfort of his cabin.

2344 hours (Friday night)
FKR Cruise Missile Battery
Vilorio Village, Cuba

The *frontovaya krylataya raketa* (FKR) cruise missile was an ungainly looking weapon, but it was one of the most lethal in all the vast arsenal the Soviet Union had dispatched to Cuba.

Two regiments had been sent to the tropical island. One was deployed to defend the beaches around Havana, and the other had been posted in the east, where it could menace the American naval base at Guantanamo Bay.

Colonel Dmitri Maltsev was in command of the easternmost regiment. In the event of war, he had been tasked with the destruction of the deeply resented American military presence at Guantanomo. His unit consisted of eight launchers and a full forty FKR cruise missiles, each of which was equipped with a fourteen-kiloton atomic warhead—almost exactly the yield of the Hiroshima bomb. The cruise missiles were launched by rocket, but a jet engine activated as soon as it was clear of the launcher. The FKR flew under the power of that jet and could be steered by remote control radio. The missile could fly to a range of some twenty miles.

The FKR was, in effect, a pilotless jet fighter, with a single engine, wings, and a tail. When it was over its target, the radio operator would cut the engine, and the missile would fall. Since it was well known that a burst some distance above the ground would inflict much more damage over a larger area than if the bomb was allowed to impact before detonation, the nuclear warhead would activate when it reached a designated altitude, usually some 250 feet above the target.

For two weeks, the men of Maltsev's battery had been cooling their heels near the town of Mayarí, where Raul Castro—who was responsible for command of the eastern third of the island—maintained his headquarters. The rockets were hauled on trailers, but the wings folded back enough that they were not easily recognizable from the air. Because of the large number of missiles, Maltsev needed a lot of space to park his vehicles, but they had been dispersed around the outside of the town. Fortunately, they were smaller and easier to hide than the SS4s. So far as Maltsev could tell, they had escaped notice by American surveillance aircraft.

Two days ago, the colonel finally received his orders to move out, hand delivered by none other than Fidel's brother himself. Maltsev had been instructed to bring his convoy to this advance position, some twenty miles from the target, and to await further orders. The launch position, where he would actually set up his battery to fire, had been designated as the village of Filipinas, about ten miles away, closer to the coast and a mere fifteen miles from the American naval base.

"Remember," Raul Castro had reminded him, "If war breaks out, you are to wipe that excrescence from the face of the earth!"

"I will remember, Comrade—it will be an honor to strike a blow for my Cuban revoltionary allies!" The promise had been sincere: Maltsev was a good soldier, and he viewed America as the mortal enemy of his country.

As soon as he had reached the advance position, Maltsev ordered an advance team to move to Filipinas and prepare the firing position. Flat spots for the eight launchers had been designated, and trees had been bulldozed out of the way to ensure that each of the rocket-assisted missiles would have a smooth flight as it ascended to cruising height.

Now, on the night of the 26th, the order to move out had been delivered to Maltsev by a courier carrying a sealed envelope. It had the authority of both General Pliyev and Raul Castro, and though it was well after dark it was marked "For Immediate Implementation."

He cursed the timing, since the road to Filipinas was rough and narrow and passed through treacherous terrain. But he was a soldier, and he and his men would follow orders. Within an hour, all the men and equipment had boarded their vehicles and the massive convoy, more than

100 vehicles stretched out for more than two kilometers, began to creep toward its launch base.

They traveled with no radios and were not allowed to use headlights, so progress advanced at a crawl. At one point, a huge engineering truck with twenty soldiers riding in the back slipped off the edge of a precipitous road and rolled into a ravine. Three men died in the crash, and precious time was lost restoring order to the convoy. In the end, the wrecked truck was left in the ravine, and the convoy crept onward.

It took more than four hours to traverse the ten miles to the launch site. There, despite the advance party of Russians who'd been working for two days, a Cuban militia unit—charged with defending the perimeter against intrusion—opened fire on the first trucks, and another hour was lost sorting out the confusion. Fortunately, there had been no additional casualties.

By the time dawn started to brighten the sky, the launchers were being hauled into firing position. Camouflage nets were pulled across the missiles and as many of the trucks as could be concealed. Sunlight finally spilled into the clearing, where eight cruise missiles, each tipped with a Hiroshima-equivalent atomic bomb, were pointed at the American base only fifteen miles—and two minutes' flight time for the FKRs—away.

And the Americans had no idea they were there.

Six: *Foxtrot* B-59

"Even little wars are dangerous in this nuclear world."

John F. Kennedy
November 8, 1963

27 October 1962
0300 hours (Saturday early morning)
Soviet Embassy, Vedado Neighborhood
Havana, Cuba

The cobbled streets of the Vedado evoked Cuba in the Spanish era, lined as they were with stately villas, walled compounds shrouded with vines and leafy trees. One two-story mansion, formerly the domicile of a clan that had become wealthy in the sugar trade, had been claimed by the Soviets for their embassy. The ambassador, Alexander Alekseev, had made it his residence and the housing for much of his staff, as well as using it as the official state office building.

Now, despite the early, or more accurately middle-of-the-night, hour, the ambassador and his staff were up and expecting a visitor, having been alerted by a phone call from *El Máximo Líder's* residence nearly an hour before.

The guards at the wrought-iron gate pulled the barrier aside as Castro's jeep raced down the shadowed, otherwise abandoned street. Alekseev himself greeted the Cuban leader as Fidel uncoiled his long frame from the small vehicle's passenger seat and stretched beside it. Naturally, he was smoking a cigar.

"You have a bomb shelter, do you not?" he demanded, bypassing the usual pleasantries of diplomatic greeting.

"Yes, of course," the ambassador replied. He had been in Cuba since shortly after the revolution, and his Spanish was passable. Most importantly, Alekseev was the Russian Castro knew and trusted better than any other.

"Let us go there, at once!" declared the Cuban leader. "Tonight is the night that the Americans will attack— certainly from the air, and perhaps with an invasion as well. We must be ready!"

Alarmed, the Russian led his visitor down a damp stairway and into a stone-walled passage. In moments they had entered a windowless room, and embassy guards pulled a stout wooden door shut behind them. Castro looked around skeptically, but shrugged. "It will have to do."

"Now, tell me how you know this about the invasion, comrade," said Alekseev, trying to sound soothing. "Our sources have said nothing of the sort—though of course, we remain ready for anything." He sat in a wooden chair at a long table and gestured to his guest to have a seat as well.

But Castro was manic. He paced back and forth, filling the room with cigar smoke, ranting. "It is a matter of common sense—the odds are insurmountable that the attack will *not* come. And your General Pliyev, he fails to sense the urgency, the danger in the situation. Why has he not shared more information with us, his trusted—his *only*—allies? Why must I learn details of the blockade from American news broadcasts, when my ally, who is a guest in my country, could share that information with me firsthand?"

"I'm sorry you're upset, Comrade. How can I help?"

"I must send a letter to Comrade Khrushchev in Moscow. I ask your help in drafting this letter."

"By all means. Allow me to bring in some stenographers, and we will begin at once." Alekseev went to the door, barked a command in Russian, and stood back. A moment later two enlisted men bearing notepads and pens came in and took up positions at the table. "These men are both fluent in Spanish. They will record your words and then translate them for the message to Comrade Khrushchev. Now, what is it that you would like to tell our Chairman?"

"Just this: I suspect that the war that begins tonight will be a conventional war at first, but it will very quickly escalate to a nuclear war. He must understand that I, and all of my countrymen, are willing, even happy, to die in the cause of this war. Certainly death is preferable to allowing the *yanquis* to make us their slaves!"

The young scribes were writing furiously, but Castro continued unabated. "We know your troops have powerful weapons, nuclear weapons, on the ground here. We expect— no, we demand—that those weapons be employed to defeat an imperialist invasion!

"Know that I am committed to doing everything in my power, even including sacrificing my life, to further the cause of world socialism. I expect nothing less than that every effort of every party, every person and organization in the Socialist World should be employed in common cause. And I suggest, also, that we—that Comrade Khrushchev—would do well to consider the merits of a preemptive strike. Why wait for our enemies to attack? Why yield initiative, when we can establish the ground rules for this strife?"

He paused just long enough to puff his cigar back into a crimson, glowing coal. He waved it in the air and glared at the Soviet ambassador. "Why don't we take action *before* the Americans preempt our position in this war?"

Alekseev blinked. It was late at night—or very early in the morning—and he wasn't sure he had heard *El Máximo Lider* correctly. "Excuse me, Comrade: are you suggesting that the Soviet Union launch a nuclear first strike against the United States?"

"I am merely asking questions that must be asked," Castro chided. "Do not put words into my mouth!"

"Of course not," the ambassador replied. He touched a hand to his stomach in a subtle but universal gesture, and nodded his head toward the door. "Please continue—I, er, need to step out for a moment but my men will continue to take your dictation."

Castro stalked and spoke as Alekeev slipped out the door. He'd implied he needed a visit to the lavatory, but instead he hastened to the embassy's radio room, where coded transmissions could be dispatched directly to the Kremlin.

"Quickly!" he ordered the radioman, who had been dozing in his chair. "I need to send a message to Moscow—mark it 'Most Urgent!'"

"I am ready, Comrade Ambassador," said the communications man, a veteran agent of the KGB. He snatched up a pad of paper and sat up attentively.

"'Fidel Castro is here, dictating a letter—a long letter—to Comrade Khrushchev. Most important detail: He is requesting that we, the USSR, initiate nuclear hostilities against the United States.' Okay, send it just like that," he told the radioman. "I have to get back to the bunker."

The KGB man, his mouth hanging open, watched in astonishment as the ambassador dashed out the door.

0508 hours (Saturday morning)
Headquarters, Soviet Air Defense for Eastern Cuba
Camaguey, Cuba

Colonel Georgi Voronkov was the division commander for all of the SAM sites on the eastern two thirds of the island of Cuba, all of it except the area from Havana to the western tip. His batteries lined the coasts, protected strategic rocket sites, cities, and military installations. They had been completed for weeks, at least, and some of them for more than a month. They had watched in impotent anger as the American spyplanes had flown overhead, but they had been denied permission to fire.

Finally, however, Voronkov had received the order from General Pliyev, the authorization he'd awaited since his first battery had been set up more than a month earlier. The news had first come via the telephone, yesterday evening, but before sunrise a courier had brought him a printed copy of the orders. At last! The time had come to deny the Cuban skies to the enemy.

It was not yet dawn when he picked up his telephone handset, after the operator had confirmed that the communications channel to each individual SA-2 battery was open.

"By order of General Pliyev," directed Voronkov, speaking to the officers in charge of all of the individual SAM batteries under his control. "Activate all Spoon Rest targeting radars. Track any unidentified aircraft and report their presence directly to headquarters. Confirm receipt of this order."

One by one the communications technicians at each site gave their vocal acknowledgement of the order. By the time the sun started to brighten the eastern horizon, the hitherto dormant air defense system over Cuba was fully active, and totally alert. Twenty-three sites along the length of the island, each with six launchers ready to fire surface-to-air missiles, came alive, radar signals beaming into the atmosphere on all sides, and directly over, the island nation.

"Now," Voronkov said in satisfaction, "Let them try to fly over us."

0900 hours (Saturday morning)
McCoy Air Force Base
Orlando, Florida

Major Rudolf Anderson taxied his spyplane down the tarmac and accelerated into the slight wind out of the west. Bright sunlight dappled his canopy, and the sky was full of puffy white clouds. His U2 lifted off well before the end of the runway, the wing struts falling away as the graceful aircraft rose into the warm, humid sky.

This would be his sixth U2 mission over Castro's isle, all of them performed since the 4080th SRW had been moved east from Texas to its temporary home here in Florida. He and Major Heyser, who'd flown the crucial mission on 13 October that first revealed the missile sites, had become the most experienced U2 pilots in either the USAF or the CIA. The 4080th had established its place in history, and Anderson took pride in knowing that he had played a big part in that.

As he climbed through the clouds, weaving just a bit to stay in clear air as much as possible, he thought of his wife, Jane, back in Del Rio, Texas. That had been the hardest part of this temporary deployment to Florida—he missed her, a lot. But he had long ago learned not to speculate about when an assignment would be over. He had a job to do, and he would do it well.

Orlando was a region of orange groves and trackless swamp, sprawled around a sweltering and unimportant little town. The area fell behind as Anderson banked gently and angled south. His mission was straightforward: he would cross eastern Cuba from north to south, getting some pictures of the garrison town of Camaguey. He would then cruise along the south coast over the major city of Santiago, passing near to the American naval base at Guantanamo, fly to the eastern tip of Cuba, then track northwest for a hundred miles before breaking for home. He was going to photograph some of the SA-2 sites, as well as the Camaguey garrison and a few other installations. It was a mission not unlike the five he had flown in the last ten days.

Except that he didn't know that the SAM sites had activated their Spoon Rest tracking radar. This time, they would see him coming.

Nor did he know that Jane Anderson, back in Del Rio, had just learned that she was pregnant.

1100 hours (Saturday morning)
Headquarters, Soviet Military Mission
El Chico, Cuba

"We have an intruding aircraft, designated Target Number 33, passing over Camaguey and continuing along the southern coast of Cuba," reported the tracking technician, watching the target acquisition radar that had just been turned on at dawn.

He was in the main headquarters building in the former school administration building at El Chico. By turning a dial, he could look in on any of the various remote radar sets at the twenty-three SAM sites on the island, albeit at a several-second delay. Camaguey, ironically enough, was the location of the headquarters for the 27th Air Defense Division, the unit charged with controlling the SA-2 sites in Cuba east of Havana.

"Target displays the flight characteristics of high-altitude spyplane," added the spotter. "The 27th is requesting permission to engage the target."

"Where's General Pliyev?" asked the duty officer, General Stepan Grechko. He looked at his second in command, who was another general, Garbuz. "Should we order it destroyed?"

"Put in a call to the commanding officer," General Garbuz suggested. "After waiting this long, I don't want to be the one to give the order to start shooting."

"He announced last night his intention to take down those damned U2s," Grechko retorted, even as a messenger tried to raise Pliyev on the phone. "And the Americans are supposed to be attacking at any time. Didn't we hear that from him ourselves? How do we know this is not the precursor to a major air raid?"

"We don't," Garbuz replied. "Still, this is just one plane."

"General Pliyev is not answering," the messenger reported, after nearly a minute of listening to the phone ring.

"The general himself believed that the major attack would commence last night or this morning," Grechko recalled, standing to pace anxiously in the headquarters office. "Of course, that hasn't happened yet. But because General Pliyev believed that attack would occur, our orders have been updated to engage the enemy."

"What do we do, then?" Garbuz demanded. Both officers were longtime veterans of the USSR military machine, where unwanted initiative was not only discouraged, but had been known to be lethal to the officer who took matters into his own hands. But the orders had been changed last night, hadn't they?

Garbuz stood also, walking across the room to look over the radar operator's shoulder at the screen and its bright blip. Both generals were high-ranking officers who understood the length and breadth of the Soviet Military Mission's responsibilities. They knew which unit was in what location, and they had more than passing familiarity with the tasks assigned to each unit.

Now, Garbuz saw something alarming on the screen.

"Look, the bastard's just flown over the advance FKR battery near Guantanamo."

"That's top secret!" Grechko replied, feeling a growing sense of panic. "We can't let the Americans find out about it."

"No, we can't. I think we must act, and I suggest we issue an order under both our names," Garbuz declared.

"Very well," his colleague agreed. "Send this message to the 27th Air Defense Division, Camaguey," he directed the telephone operator.

"Destroy Target Number 33."

1120 hours (Saturday morning)
Soviet SA-1 Missile battery
Banes, Cuba

Major Ivan Gerchenov had chafed at the overflights of the American spyplanes since his unit had become operational more than two weeks before. Now, he could hardly believe his eyes: his tracking radar had been turned on for less than eight hours, and a prominent blip—labeled Target Number 33—was approaching from the south. If it held course, it would pass directly over his position.

He looked out of his trailer, through a medium rain that drummed against the ground all across his battery of six missile launchers. His men had spent a miserable night, and those soldiers he could see now plodded around with sodden, heavy rain slickers. Most of the rest, he knew, huddled under tarpaulins, or inside tents or the cabs of the unit's many trucks.

But radar had no trouble penetrating rainclouds, and the blip on the screen continued to show up clearly. The Spoon Rest radar had been tracking it for miles, but now, as it neared the battery, Gerchenov ordered the Fruit Set targeting radar to activate. Immediately that tightly focused beam picked up the unknown aircraft.

"Target at 22,000 meters," read the targeting officer. "Bearing 300 degrees, speed 510 kilometers per hour."

"Contact Division Headquarters," Gerchenov order his switchboard operator. "Ask for instructions—tell them it's urgent."

He picked up a microphone. When he spoke, his words were broadcast over loudspeakers posted throughout the battery site. "This is Combat Alert Number One!" he declared. "I repeat, Combat Alert Number One!"

Outside, through the door of the trailer, he saw men burst from their sodden tents, racing to the launchers. He could only see two of the six from his vantage, but he watched with sublime pride as his well-trained soldiers servicing those two launchers quickly hoisted the SA-2 missiles off the transporters and carried them to the racks that would fire them into the sky. They laid them on the tracks while the launchers were still in a horizontal position, plugging in the electrical cables that would trigger the rockets when it was time to launch.

A minute later, both launchers that he could see—and, he knew, the four that were beyond his line of vision—swiveled into launch position, lifting the rockets so that they pointed into the sky. Each launcher was receiving, over a dedicated cable, the target information from the Fruit Set radar, so the launchers swiveled slowly, keeping the rockets pointed at the unseen aircraft some twenty-two kilometers above them.

He turned to the switchboard operator, hoping to get some response. Instead of the telephone line, however, it was the radio that came to life, spitting out a message through minimal static, despite the inclement weather.

"Destroy Target Number 33."

"Fire one, and fire two!" barked Gerchenov.

He heard the roar of rocket ignition and stepped out of the trailer, ignoring the rain, so that he could see first one, then the next, surface-to-air missile blast upward from its launcher. Each quickly disappeared into the murk overhead, leaving a churning trail of smoke to mark its paths.

The battery commander went back into the trailer and again followed the images on the screen of the Fruit Set target radar. He saw two small blips closing in on the larger dot indicating the position of Target Number 33. In a few seconds, all three blips merged together. For just a moment a larger halo of a signal expanded on the screen.

That explosive blossom quickly faded away to nothing.

1330 hours (Saturday afternoon)
"The Tank" Joint Chiefs of Staff Meeting Room
The Pentagon, Washington

"All right," Curtis LeMay declared bluntly, after a loud, profane, and contentious discussion. As usual, his forceful personality brought the conversation of his peers, and their nominal commander General Taylor, to a close. "We're agreed."

The Air Force Chief of Staff ticked off the conclusions from memory: "We need to hit Cuba with multiple waves of air attacks, and we need to do it soon. Target priorities begin with the SAM sites and the strategic missile sites, as well as air bases and other air-defense locations. The next wave will focus on military and government command centers, both Cuban and Soviet, and then we'll take on fortified locations, especially coastal, and concentrations of ground troops. Armored vehicles will be singled out as targets of opportunity. Ports will be shut down, and key bridges will be knocked out.

"Strikes should begin early in the morning, at first light, and continue throughout the day. Bomb damage assessments will be made before dark, and the second day's sorties will be planned accordingly. The air campaign will continue until the invasion can be mounted, perhaps as soon as four days later. The longest expected delay is one week between first air raid and amphibious—slash—airborne troop landing."

"Good summary," General Shoup said. "The Marines will be ready. But will the White House?"

Perhaps fortuitously, or maybe ominously, Secretary of Defense McNamara chose that moment to walk into the room. The chiefs regarded him suspiciously as he took his seat at one end of the table. McNamara appeared not to notice the scrutiny.

The relationship between the secretary and the military was complicated, even though it had lasted a long time, predating McNamara's place in the administration by decades. Bob McNamara had worked for Curtis LeMay during the Second World War, analyzing the effectiveness of the American strategic bombing campaign against Japan. He had provided data and ideas as LeMay was conceiving his revolutionary plan to use incendiary munitions to incinerate Japanese cities. In fact, McNamara had been heavily involved in the detailed planning of the most horrific bombing attack of that war—which was not, as many people believed, the atomic bombing of Hiroshima or Nagasaki. Instead, the firebombing of Tokyo, five months before the atomic bombs were used, had destroyed more property, devastated a larger area, and killed more people than any other air attack.

Yet, in LeMay's view, McNamara had softened in the years since the war. To LeMay, there was no difference in the morality of bombing a city with 100,000 bombs dropped by a thousand bombers, or destroying that same target with one bomb carried by a missile or single bomber. Yet the Secretary of Defense would not recognize the similarity, and the Air Force chief had grown increasingly disgusted with him.

Now, McNamara seemed to have other things on his mind. "The President is investigating possibilities to bring the stand-off to an end. You all know that our Jupiter missiles in Turkey are obsolete. They're short-ranged, exposed on outdoor launchers. Yet the Turks put a lot of faith in them. The idea is, we could move a nuclear submarine—a vessel that is essentially invulnerable to Soviet interception—into the eastern Mediterranean. From there, its Polaris missiles are every bit as much of a threat to the Russians as the Jupiters. We could tell the Turks—and the Russians—about the sub, and use that as a cover to get those damned MRBs out of there."

"You mean, he's still trying to *deal* with the bastards?" LeMay blurted in obvious disbelief. "I tell you, Khrushchev's only playing for time. You keep talking to him, and he keeps making progress on those missile sites! Dammit, the time to act was yesterday—time is slipping away from us!"

Before LeMay could reply, an Air Force colonel entered the Tank and quickly carried a piece of paper over to the Chief of Staff. LeMay read the note and clenched his jaw around his cigar as he glared at the Secretary of Defense.

"Things are heating up," he said bluntly. He slid the piece of paper across the table. It stopped short, and McNamara had to stand up and lean over the reach it, while LeMay explained for the benefit of the other chiefs. "We have a U2 that's more than thirty minutes overdue back to McCoy. I'm damn sure that means we've just had a U2 shot down over Cuba."

McNamara's face paled as he read the confirmation on the piece of paper he'd finally retrieved. "I've got to take this to the President," he said, rising turning toward the door.

"Wait!" said LeMay. "We've got a squadron of bombers standing by at MacDill Air Force Base. The plan was they would be released if the Communists started firing those SAMs we've been watching. Well, I think we can deduce they've done that. It's time to take out the antiaircraft missiles, at least."

"We don't even know which battery did the firing!" McNamara objected.

"Then we take 'em all out!" the air force chief replied.

"No. You're not to take action until I've spoken with the President!" McNamara left the room at a fast walk.

General LeMay turned to the other officers as soon as the door shut. His expression pained, he asked: "Could it be any goddamn worse if Khrushchev himself was our Secretary of Defense?"

1640 hours (Saturday afternoon)
USS DDG 507 *Conning*,
350 miles NE of Cuba

Seaman Duncan had forgotten all about the submachine gun and his "boarding party responsibility." For the last two day's he'd spent his time, when he wasn't cooking or sleeping, patrolling the destroyer fantail with a belt of practice depth charges in his hand, another over his shoulder, and a third strapped around his waist. Like so many things in the military, there was a lot of standing around and waiting.

But every so often the captain's voice would come over the loudspeaker—"Sonar contact detected. Begin deployment of signal explosives."

Then, the sailor would toss a grenade overboard and hope for the best. He was one of four men on the afterdeck of the destroyer performing the function at any one time. He suspected that a couple more sailors were doing the same thing, closer to the bow. Chief Weber had told them to time their throws to about one every minute, and to continue until the captain gave the order to desist.

Even though the little explosives weren't supposed to do damage, Duncan took care to toss each one as far from the destroyer as he could. A passable baseball player, he guessed he was getting them out at least 150 feet or so. He watched them splash into the water and sink. He listened for the sound of an explosion but heard nothing—though every once in a while a swirl of bubbly turbulence would rise to the surface, presumably as proof of a detonation. But there was never any sign of a submarine.

Certainly, there was plenty activity to see on the surface. No less than four helicopters, based off of *Randolph*, swept back in forth within Duncan's field of view. They hovered 100 feet or so above the water, and each had a long cable dangling from it, dipping into the gentle waves. They were dipping microphones, the sailor knew, seeking audio proof of the sub's location.

Twice he'd seen two or three of the choppers hoist their mikes from the water and hurriedly redeploy to new positions, all four taking up a generally square formation. He deduced that those occasions marked times when one source had gained a solid sonar contact, and the others redeployed to seek further confirmation. Once, *Conning* had heeled sharply and churned forward to join the choppers over a given section of ocean. The second destroyer—he'd heard she was named *Viscount*—patrolled opposite *Conning*, the two of them constantly circling, occasionally responding to contact reports with a surge of engines and a churning froth of wake.

Farther out, twin-engine search planes, Grumman S2F Trackers, flew in lazy circles. Every once in awhile, one of the Trackers would drop something that would splash into the water, and the young sailor knew these were sonobuoys, active sonar devices that would help to establish a perimeter the Soviet sub would not be able to sneak through.

The search routine seemed to follow a pattern. The helicopters were in the middle, circling and bobbing, checking the water, usually not moving very fast. The two destroyers remained outside the area where the helicopters operated, circling slowly. Occasionally the crew of one or the other destroyers would be ordered to deploy the explosive charges.

Outside the circle created by the slowly cruising destroyers, the two Trackers curved through a wide arc. Beyond them all, standing off from the action but close enough for George to see clearly—maybe four miles away—the flattop *Randolph* held position. Many times during the course of the day, helicopters would return to the carrier to be replaced by a new quartet of choppers. Activity was constant everywhere he looked. The noise made by the helicopters competed with the wind, the wash of water breaking away from the destroyer's hull, and the rumble of her engines.

In the last twenty minutes, Seaman Duncan had gone through all three belts worth of practice depth charges, standing at the same post near the starboard stern of his fast guided-missile destroyer. Chief Weber came by to hand him another three belts, each with six grenades.

"Are you sure there's something down there, Chief?" Duncan asked.

The NCO shrugged. "Word from the sonar guys is that they keep getting a faint hit. The sub's gone silent, so it's damned hard to find."

"Well, how long are we supposed to keep doing this?"

"How do I know?" snapped the chief, in a rare display of temper. "Until that fucker comes up to the surface, or until we run out of grenades!" Weber, apparently even more frustrated than Duncan, stomped toward the ship's superstructure.

With nothing to do until the captain ordered another "deployment" of the signals, the young sailor simply looked down, staring, trying to penetrate the depths of the blue ocean. How long, he wondered, could that "fucker" stay submerged?

1650 hours (Saturday afternoon)
Submarine *B-59*, submerged
350 miles NE of Cuba

"What the hell are they trying to do?" demanded Captain Savitsky. The *Foxtrot*'s hull echoed with the resounding booms of underwater explosions, the relentless bombardment seeming like it had lasted for countless hours. The blasts were not as powerful as he would have expected—perhaps the Americans were using defective depth charges?—but the strain stretched captain and crew to the breaking point.

And *B-59* already had plenty of problems brought on simply by the long, grueling voyage—never mind the American harassment. The CO_2 concentration in the air had reached critically dangerous levels. The ventilation unit remained inoperable, and the diesel coolers, encrusted with salt, had all failed. More than half a dozen men were prone in different parts of the boat, overcome by the lack of breathable air. The rest looked haunted and terrified, some of them stumbling around like sleepwalkers, others sitting still and staring, sightlessly, through the murky miasma of the submarine's foul atmosphere.

The three diesels were silent for now and could not be used this far under the surface, but the stink of fuel and burned oil still permeated everywhere within the long cylinder of the hull. The battery reserves had fallen dangerously, and the submarine currently floated at neutral buoyancy, completely stopped at some 200 meters below the surface. The sounds of the American fleet came through the hull as a vague hiss, sometimes louder than others. The ship noise faded periodically, giving rise to hope—which was shattered minutes later when the vessels came steaming back.

The relentless pattern of explosions waxed and waned, while the pinging of active sonar searching for them made a nerve-wracking chorus in the background, like the singing of lethal mechanical crickets. Whenever the explosive charges faded momentarily, the pinging of the sonar seemed to ratchet up to an even higher volume.

Savitksy paced around the small control center, checking the sonar screen, the depth and trim indicators. The helmsman sat at his controls, unable to do anything since the boat wasn't moving. Weapons systems and damage control all languished in this kind of dying stasis—*nobody* could do anything!

"Vasily Andreivich," he said to his executive officer, speaking quietly out of caution. "Stand watch at the helm. I'm going to inspect the boat."

"Aye, Captain," Arkhipov replied.

Savitsky started toward the stern, where the stink and oppressive heat in the engine room nearly knocked him down. The duty engineer looked up, eyes glazed and hollow. The four engineer mates sat listlessly, two of them dozing— or maybe already dead? The other two watched as the captain made his way down the narrow catwalk past the silent engines and through the narrow hatch to the after torpedo room.

The torpedo men there nodded listlessly as the captain stepped slowly along the narrow, gray tubes, pausing to whisper encouragement to them. He was proud of these brave Russian sailors, here in the far stern of the boat. Not a breath of air stirred, yet somehow each man clung to consciousness. They had four torpedo tubes, each loaded with one of the "fish," with four more torpedoes in reserve, ready to be loaded to replace any that were fired.

Moving forward again, he came back through the engine room, clapping a few of the engineer mates on the shoulder as they nodded at him. He looked at the three big diesels, cloaked with oil, slick with condensation. Would they ever come to life again? He shuddered at the fatalistic thought. Of course they would—as soon as this goddamn harassment stopped!

But when would the Americans give up the hunt? He began to feel more strongly that he and his men were doomed, that they would die down here, smothered by the merciless sea. And for what? Had their country gone to war, without them even knowing that fact? He felt more and more certain that the simmering conflict of the Cold War had erupted into full boil. Would they be crushed, drowned by a lethal and murderous enemy, even though they had the power to strike back, to lash out with powerful violence?

His men deserved better than to die like that, unresisting, not even recognizing their danger—the true and warlike state of affairs. That much he could see clearly, even though the rest of his thoughts were becoming increasingly cloudy and confused. Blindly he struck out at a bulkhead, punching it so hard that he bruised his fist. Damn them! Damn the Americans!

Savitsky weaved his way back to the middle of the boat, leaning on the bulkheads or holding onto an overhead pipe for balance. He returned to the command center directly under the center sail, the station where he spent most of his time. The boat's nerve center still seemed to be operating at reasonable efficiency. The passive sonar display revealed the locations of ships on the surface, still cruising on all sides of the submarine. The man watching the screen, though gaunt and sweaty, remained alert and focused.

Just beyond him, however, the sailor at the helm had been overcome by hypoxia and lay on his back on the deck, unmoving except for his chest, which rose up and down like a bellows as he struggled to breathe air that had precious little oxygen to give. Savitsky decided to leave him for now—there was no need to steer a motionless boat.

Grimly, the captain continued his inspection, moving forward now. The galley was empty, since every man remained at general quarters—and cooking, even the boiling of water for tea, was forbidden when the boat was running silent. The clank of a metal pot against the steel grate of a stove could be a telltale clue, revealing the sub's location to the listeners, with their advanced electronic search equipment, lurking above.

In the forward torpedo room, things also seemed nearly normal. The torpedo men sat listlessly near their six tubes, ready to launch on the captain's command. Five of the tubes were loaded with conventionally armed torpedoes. The sixth was empty, ready to receive Feklisov's "baby," should the captain order it armed. None of the crew in here seemed to have lost consciousness, perhaps because this far from the engine room the air was a little better. Lieutenant Commander Feklisov looked up and managed a wan smile as the captain came over to him and his special weapon, the torpedo with the ten-kiloton nuclear warhead.

"How are you holding up, Anatoly Yakovlivich?" Savitsky asked softly.

"As well as anyone," the young engineer answered. He patted his "baby" in its shiny gray tube. "I'm ready to go to work if you need me."

"I hope it won't come to that," the captain replied. "But if it does, I have all confidence in you. Stay ready."

"Aye, Captain," Feklisov replied. "If you give the word, it will be ready to shoot within a minute."

Savitsky returned to the command center, proud of his brave men, but bitterly angry at a situation that seemed to doom them all. He was utterly at a loss as to what he could do next. Were his options really exhausted? Could they only cower here and wait for the inevitable end?

And the pinging, and the booming, and the searching, continued relentlessly from above.

1655 hours (Saturday afternoon)
Flight Deck, CVN *Enterprise*
150 miles East of Cuba

The F4 Phantom, both General Electric turbojets roaring, quivered on the foredeck of *Enterprise*, lined up for take off with the nose wheel hooked into the catapult track. In the pilot's seat, Derek Widener pushed those mighty engines to full power, afterburners blasting blistering heat and rocket-force thrust from the twin exhausts. He watched carefully, saw the flight officer chop his hand down, and immediately felt the powerful compression as the catapult whipped the big jet forward like a child's toy. The explosive force rocked him back in his seat and shot the aircraft the short distance to the forward lip of the flight deck, off the bow of the ship, and into the air.

Under the pilot's control now, jet engines still roaring with that almost unimaginable thrust, the Phantom quickly rocketed up and away from the massive warship, like a bird set free from a huge but constricting cage. A catapult launch was always a thrill, and Widener couldn't help but whoop in exhilaration as the powerful engines carried them higher and higher.

He pulled back on the stick, and the Phantom shot almost straight upward at dizzying speed, finally leveling off at the assigned CAP cruising altitude of 30,000 feet. From there, he banked and turned the Phantom into a lazy arc to the east, gradually bringing it back around in a wide circle.

"Tango Three, assuming patrol position." Behind him, Ensign King reported their status over the radio, then switched to the private channel to read data on their airspeed and altitude to the pilot.

"I've got the other three Tangos on the scope," he went on to report from the back seat. "One and two are twenty miles to the west; four is taking up station off our wing," King explained, noting the locations of the rest of the combat air patrol. "And the Stoof with a Roof is on station down below."

Widener chuckled at the ridiculous name and pictured the ludicrous looking—but very capable—aircraft it described. Based on the S2F, or "Stoof" Tracker, which was a Grumman aircraft used to search for submarines, the E1 Tracer had a large, ungainly looking radar dome atop a stubby fuselage, with twin wing-mounted engines and a broad tail. Once the radome had been recognized for its resemblance to a "roof," the name was virtually inevitable. He was glad it was down there—even though the piston-engine plane couldn't reach the altitude of a modern jet, having radar capabilities perched 15,000 feet in the air gave the fleet and its aircraft a powerful "eye in the sky."

A full circle completed, Widener once again brought his plane onto an easterly bearing. The aqua sea of the shallow waters northeast of the Windward Passage sparkled below. He could see Grand Caicos Island to the east. Beyond lay the deeper blue of the Atlantic. He found himself remembering the plotting map he'd seen yesterday and wondered if, somewhere over there, the United States Navy was in fact tracking a Soviet sub. He was tempted to go over and have a look, but duty would keep him flying these lazy circles over

Enterprise—just in case some Russian or Cuban fighter jet came roaring into the sky, intent on giving the world's first nuclear-powered aircraft carrier a trial by fire.

1710 hours (Saturday afternoon)
Submarine *B-59*, submerged
350 miles NE of Cuba

The sounds of the chasing warships grew louder again as the destroyers closed in on the submarine's location. Now the staccato explosions blasted and crumped, apparently right up against the hull. Each report came as a sharp, violent assault against Captain Savitsky's nerves. Echoes rang back and forth through the metallic tube of the *B-59*. The pressure came so fast, with such crunching force, that it seemed like someone physically pounded on the submarine with a hammer. And they wouldn't let up the relentless pummeling.

The pinging rose to a nightmarish level—surely the Americans closed in for the kill! Savitsky could imagine no other explanation. The emergency lighting flickered and faded, plunging the submarine into complete darkness for several seconds. The captain held his breath, certain that this was the end, that the hull would rupture and the sea rush in to kill them all.

"How do we know what's going on up there?" Savitsky demanded aloud, finding his voice. "We could already be at war! We could be killed, sunk, without even striking a blow in the name of the *rodina*!"

"No—we would know!" cried Arkhipov, the executive officer placing his hand on the captain's arm.

Savitsky turned on him, his face twisted in fury. "We would know *how*, exactly? We've been out of radio contact for thirty-six hours! Don't be a fool—they are attacking! If you'd open your ears, you could *hear* that!"

Another series of booms rattled against the hull, almost like pellets cast against the metallic shell, starting at one end and moving toward the other. The captain realized that Arkhipov *was* a fool—how could he not see the awful, deadly truth? Was it because he was afraid? Afraid of war, afraid to do his duty? That was the only explanation that made any sense to Savitsky. He looked at the man, his loyal fellow officer and friend, with obvious contempt.

"Wait!" the exec pleaded. "You must steady your nerves—you don't have enough air. You're worn out—we're all worn out! Sit down and rest. We can ride this out."

"To rest is to die—can't you see that? The time for that is past. We're worn out, and we're doomed! This is the *end*, don't you understand? You are witnessing how a submarine dies!" He croaked out the words, his mind railing against their fate, to die like meek victims of a powerful, merciless foe. He had seen proof on the sonar screen: no less than three ships pounded them, no doubt with air support as well. The Americans had the most powerful navy in the world, and *B-59* was alone, isolated, terribly far from home.

Only then did his mind focus on an important truth, one that had slipped into the background amid the tumult of his anger and fear. The *Foxtrot* had a powerful weapon of its own, a means to strike back at the tormenting enemy. They did *not* need to die a passive death. They could unleash a terrible blow for themselves, for the Soviet navy, for the motherland!

He snatched the speaking tube. "This is the captain to the forward torpedo room. Feklisov—I want you to arm your weapon! Prepare it for loading! Do you hear me? Confirm!"

"Captain," Arkhipov said, eyes widening in panic. "Think about it! We don't know that war has begun—but you could start it! We *must* learn what is happening in the world beyond our hull!"

Angrily, Savitsky turned his back on the man, his contempt rising like bile in his throat. At that moment a dry voice emerged from the speaking tube—Feklisov! That loyal young officer was alert, and ready to follow orders. "Aye, Captain. Proceeding to arm weapon."

"We can't take the chance of firing without some confirmation!" Arkhipov pleaded.

"How would we find out?" snarled the captain. "Should we rise to radio depth? You think the Americans would not notice our antenna poking through the waves? Or perhaps you'd like us to surface, and shoot at them with our sidearms," he sneered caustically.

More booms sounded, rattling noises right against the command center. For too long the submarine had sat still, unmoving. Surely the Americans had a fix on the boat's location by now! He looked at the battery meters; they had less than twenty-five percent power remaining, but enough remained to alter the terrible stasis that seemed certain to lead them all to doom. A sudden maneuver might just take the enemy by surprise.

"We won't just sit here and let them sink us!" The captain declared, to everyone in the comm center—and to himself, as well. He had reached a decision. Now Savitksy snatched a different speaking tube and barked another order, directed to the engineer and his mates in their stinking hellish compartment just to the rear.

"Captain to engine room. Give me maximum speed on battery power—course dead ahead!"

In the engine room, the chief engineer blinked in surprise. It took his fogged brain a moment to process the order—but then his instincts took over. He pulled the lever of the battery power control arm, pouring a sudden jolt of electric power into the motor, causing all three propeller shafts to instantly start to turn at high speed. He continued the movement, pressing the power control all the way down, pushing the stress of sudden acceleration to the maximum.

At the same moment, another round of explosives popped and thudded at the stern of the boat. The propeller shafts flexed and spun under the instant application of power. The screws bit into the water, churning hard, forcing the submarine forward.

And the worn housing on shaft number three, the collar with the slowly growing crack that had been expanding for five days now, snapped in half. One sharp piece of metal jammed, causing the propeller shaft to bend and twist in place, warping the once-watertight tunnel housing it. The rest of the collar broke away and fell into the depths—leaving a small space, a channel only a couple of centimeters wide, where the interior of the boat lay suddenly open to the sea.

Water—under incredibly high pressure at the depth of 200 meters—immediately shot along the bent propeller shaft, following that twisted steel rod through the gap that had been twisted into the outer and inner hull sections, gushing directly into the engine room. It surged against the heavy block of diesel number three and caromed to the side, so forcefully that the rush of salty brine knocked the engineer to the deck. His skull cracked painfully against the diesel housing.

The sailors on the other side of the compartment stared in horror as the rush of foaming liquid churned through the engine room, up from the well, spewing over the catwalk and rising quickly. Two of the engineer's mates fled to the rear, tumbling through the open hatch into the after torpedo room, while the other two lunged forward, toward the other open hatch leading to the command center.

The engineer officer scrambled to his knees, struggling to follow the sailors into the torpedo room—but, weakened by oxygen deprivation, stunned by the blow to the head, he collapsed in the hatchway, his body blocking the passage as one of the torpedo men tried to push the metal barrier shut.

Another of the torpedo men saw it happen. He lunged for the speaking tube. "Emergency!" he croaked. "We have a breach in the hull—water coming in to the engine room!"

Even as he spoke, the thin stream of water expanded to a gush, as the twisted shaft and the monstrous pressure widened the crack it had made around the hull gasket. Within seconds, the seawater was a foot deep on the deck, and rising fast, filling both of the large compartments in the rear of submarine *B-59*.

An alarm sounded automatically, and Savitsky turned in fury to Arkhipov, who again placed his hand on the captain's shoulder, trying to calm, to placate the senior officer. Angrily the captain shook off the gesture. At the same time, the two engineer mates hurtled themselves into the comm center from the engine room hatch.

"We're flooding!" one of them croaked. "The hull is breached!"

"You see!" the captain cried. "They're trying to sink us! We've been hit! The hull is ruptured!"

Arkhipov put both hands on Savitsky's shoulders, his grip clutching hard, his eyes wild. "No—think what—"

Before the executive officer could say another word the captain punched him in the face and Arkhipov went down, stunned and bleeding. At the same time, an incongruously calm voice came through the speaking tube, addressing the officers in the command center from the forward torpedo room.

"The special weapon is armed, Comrade Captain," the young lieutenant commander reported formally.

"Feklisov! Men of the forward torpedo room," Savitsky barked into the speaking tube. "This is the captain. Load the special weapon into the tube. I'll have targeting information by the time you're done." He dropped the speaking tube and turned to the officers and men in the comm center. All of them except the stunned Arkhiopov stared at him, ready to do his bidding. "The Americans are sinking us—but not before we hit them back."

Most of the crew in the command center had rushed to secure the hatch to the after torpedo room, where water was already sloshing waist deep on the men who struggled toward the center of the boat. The closing hatch doomed them to certain death, but it bought a little time for the rest of the boat.

"We're going down by the stern, Sir," reported the diving officer, even as the deck canted under foot. The bow of the boat seemed to rise, but this was an illusion as the stern settled toward the bottom of the ocean.

"Depth now 240 meters." The diving officer read his gauge and intoned the words in a remarkably calm voice

Arkhipov, bleeding from the mouth, moaned on the deck. Savitsky looked at him in contempt—the coward! He'd almost prevented the doomed submarine from striking a glorious blow for the *rodina*.

The captain stepped to the sonar table and looked at the blips on the screen, standing unsteadily as the angle of the ship steadily increased. He had to hold on to an overhead railing, or he would have fallen to the after end of the command compartment. He pointed to the largest blip on the screen. "There—is that an aircraft carrier?"

"Yes, Sir—I believe so," replied the sonar man. "It has stayed several kilometers outside the ring of destroyers."

Savitsky read the targeting data and was back to the speaking tube in fifteen seconds. "Feklisov?"

"Yes, Captain. The weapon is armed and loaded. I await your order."

"Set it to a range of six kilometers. Target is thirty degrees to starboard of our bearing. Fire to destroy."

"Aye, Captain." There was a brief pause. "I have the fire solution!"

"Fire! Fire now, at once!"

The boat shuddered slightly as the torpedo shot out of the tube that was now angled sharply upward. The onboard gyroscope quickly adjusted the device, steadying it onto its target as it churned through the water.

At the same time, the incredible water pressure completely flooded the engine room and the after torpedo room. The stern dropped even more sharply, and the submarine sank faster, passing 280 meters, 300 meters of depth with no way to reverse the plunge. The men who survived—for now—could no longer stand on the decks, but instead tumbled downward until they smashed into the bulkheads at the rear of each compartment.

And Foxtrot *B-59* continued her final dive, plunging into the crushing depths, surrounded by the dark and lethal sea.

1718 hours (Saturday afternoon)
USS DDG 507 *Conning,*
350 miles NE of Cuba

This business of tossing explosive charges off the stern of the destroyer had been going on for so long that Seaman Duncan was starting to find the once-exciting activity to be rather monotonous. His arm was sore, and the relentless noise of the helicopters, the growling of the ship's engines, the occasional *pop* he heard when a charge went off near the surface had started to seem like a permanent backdrop to his life.

How long would they go on doing this? Was there even a sub down there? He certainly hadn't seen anything that would suggest that there was. He was down to the last grenade on his belt, having gone through God-only-knew how many over the last hour. He raised it up and grasped the pin, ready to pull.

But something caused him to hesitate. He didn't register it at once: It was kind of like a flicker in the whole world. The air itself seemed to shudder.

And then the ocean turned to light, a great flash of brilliance that illuminated the aircraft carrier *Randolph* from below, like a giant flashbulb had popped in the water underneath the venerable warship. In the next instant—or perhaps it happened instantaneously—the huge vessel vanished as the sea erupted all around her. Steam and spray shot into the sky, and just kept going up. Craning his neck, staring in awe, the sailor saw fire churning *inside* the column of ocean that still exploded upward.

He saw a furious, angry cloud swelling with unthinkable speed, clearly the result of some powerful blast. Fingers of spuming brine shot out in a blossom of incredible force and sudden violence. The consuming explosion expanded immensely, instantly, as if hungry for victims, clutching and devouring anything in its path. That destruction began with *Randolph*—the carrier simply vanished, despite Duncan's efforts to spot some trace of the huge ship in the midst of that chaotic force.

Conning's fellow destroyer, *Viscount,* was closer to the carrier, just completing a sharp turn toward her sister ship as it curled around the imagined location of the submarine. A blast of invisible force hit *Viscount,* and she broke in half as the blast took her broadside. The stern of the stricken destroyer vanished, while the bow tumbled to the side, rolling across the ocean's surface, scattering debris and men as it broke into pieces. The blast wave ripped outward from the carrier's location, impossibly fast, sweeping toward *Conning* like a force of nature.

Tiny objects tumbled through the sky, blowing toward, and past, Duncan's ship. He realized they were pieces of the helicopters, and crews, that had been circling around the Soviet sub. One of the twin-engine Tracker aircraft smashed into the water a quarter mile away, breaking into pieces that bounced and skipped over the waves.

And then that blast swept over the young sailor, tearing at his body and everything around him. Somehow, without thinking of it, he'd grabbed the ship's rail, and now he held on frantically as the force lifted his feet from the deck, tried to rip him away. The ship rocked crazily beneath him, and he sensed her going over, capsizing. His world turned sideways, and he wondered if he was plunging straight into Hell.

He gawked upward at a mountain of water, a swelling and solid-looking bulge in the ocean's surface looming higher than any earthen massif he had ever imagined. The ocean continued to rise, a vast, steep slope of liquid bearing *Conning* up, turning her sideways, then tumbling past. Duncan felt that water slam him in the face with enough force to pull his hands from their grip on the rail. He was floating, flying, tumbling all at once—with no connection at all to the ship.

There was only water, moving, smashing ocean, all around. It swallowed him, lifting him up, crushing him down, finally enveloping him in blackness.

1715 hours (Saturday afternoon)
F4 Phantom from *Enterprise*
300 miles East of Cuba

"This is Tango Three," Derek Widener reported over the radio channel, his throat tight. Somehow he croaked out more words: "I've got a bright flash, over the northeast horizon. Not natural." He felt sick to his stomach, and heard Ensign King's gasp of horror from the rear seat

"Reporting a strong signal, electromagnetic pulse, bearing eighty degrees," came the dispassionate voice through Widener's earphones. He knew he was getting a report from the electronic detection systems aboard the Stoof with a Roof, the airborne radar and electronics monitor circling below the CAP.

Another voice, his airgroup commander, came through the headphones. "Tangos Three and Four—investigate. Be careful!"

"Altering course to eighty degrees," Widener replied, striving—and failing—to match his CO's calm vocal demeanor.

Unconsciously, he had already started his turn; the Phantom of his wingman, Tango Four, banked off to the side, mirroring his course correction. Now the pilots kicked in their afterburners, and the two F4s shot through the skies, quickly surpassing Mach 1. To Derek Widener, the fighter suddenly didn't feel like a large aircraft any more. As it hurtled toward the source of the flash it was more like an insect, confronted by the force of something gigantic and terrible.

In a couple of minutes, the Phantoms crossed over Grand Caicos island and continued to streak above the Atlantic. The sea below appeared azure and calm, deceptively peaceful, but it looked like a massive storm brewed in front of them. A vast wall of dark cloud churned and expanded.

He and King watched in horror as the cloud swelled in the middle, rising and twisting, black as Hell. Blossoms of living flame billowed within that cloud, the eeriest, most chilling thing he'd ever seen. It was a pillar of *water and steam*, for Christ's sake! How could it be on *fire*?

"God—that looks…" He heard King's hushed voice from the rear seat, fading away before he could find the words to complete the thought.

And there *were* no words to describe it, at least not clearly. Derek's mouth felt dry, his whole body drained of moisture, vitality, even emotion. He was just a husk of a man, and what was left of his awareness peered straight into the Abyss.

Soon the cloud swelled at the top of a vast column of steam, smoke, and fire. There was no denying what he and King were looking at—they'd seen too many pictures of the explosions that had brought World War Two to an end.

"Oh shit," he whispered, not even aware of his open mic.

"Tango Three—report!" The voice of his squadron commander crackled with authority, and seemed to inject awareness back into the numb pilot's being. "What do you see?"

"This is Tango Three," Derek said into his helmet microphone, trying to hear himself over the tumble of his own raw horror. He swallowed, coaxing some moisture into his mouth.

When he could finally speak, his voice sound flat, disembodied. "We're looking at a mushroom cloud, some 80,000 feet in the air. I think—no, I'm *sure*—someone down on the surface, or underneath, has detonated a nuclear device."

1830 hours (Saturday Afternoon)
Cabinet Meeting Room, the White House
Washington D.C.

The meeting had been proceeding for more than an hour, and the mood in the room was grim and resolute. It was clear by now that a U2 had been lost over Cuba, and it seemed hard to argue with the conclusion that it had been shot down.

"Is there any chance the pilot survived?" the President wanted to know.

"Not likely, Sir—not at that height," the JCS chairman, General Taylor, acknowledged. "He'd had been flying at 70,000 feet. Although, I suppose there's always a chance."

A naval courier came in and whispered to Defense Secretary McNamara, who quickly rose and walked out of the room. In the meantime, Taylor followed up. "I think we should send in those bombers, Mr. President, from MacDill AFB in Florida. They've been on standby for several days now, just in case those SAMs start flying, and they're armed with the ordnance necessary to take out a SAM site."

"We don't even know which site fired the missiles, do we?" JFK demanded. "No, they stay on the ground until we get more information."

The door to the cabinet room opened, and Secretary McNamara came back in. His expression was stricken as he stared mutely at the President, while all conversation in the room trailed off to silence.

"Mr. President," he said without preamble, and then he seemed to stumble, to grope for words. For once, the computer-like brain, the emotionless frame of the Secretary of Defense seemed to waver, as he wrestled with something that seemed beyond his comprehension. Kennedy sat watching him, the color slowly draining from the President's face.

"What is it?" JFK asked finally, his voice a dry rasp.

The question seemed to break the spell, and McNamara blinked a few times and struggled for composure. "We have multiple reports of a nuclear explosion in the middle of one of our ASW task forces—a small fleet that had been circling a Russian submarine."

"My God. How bad...what details do you have?"

"Reports are the aircraft carrier *Randolph* is gone, completely vanished. It looks like two destroyers are lost, as well—at least, they've not been able to raise *Conning* or *Viscount* by radio. Surface assets from the *Enterprise* task group are hurrying to the scene. She already has a couple of fighters in the air overhead. They've reported what looks like one capsized destroyer. There may be survivors."

Kennedy looked around the room. His whole body seemed to sag, and he shook his head, groping for words. He sighed, long and loudly, then suddenly, furiously, banged his fist on the table. The gesture seemed to calm him; he lifted his head and looked slowly around the horrified faces at the conference table.

"Gentlemen," he said finally. "It's not a cold war anymore."

2300 hours (Saturday night)
Presidium, Kremlin
Moscow, Russia

"What's going on?" Khrushchev wanted to know, as a half dozen officers hurried into the room to whisper to Defense Minister Malinovksy, who gasped, his jaw sagging. It seemed to the Chairman as though the old soldier aged ten years right before his eyes.

"Tell me!" he demanded, his voice emerging as a near-hysterical squeak.

Malinovsky's mouth worked soundlessly for a few seconds. "Comrade Chairman," he finally croaked. "The Americans are claiming that some of their ships have been destroyed by an...atomic device."

"Ships? At sea?"

"Yes. It seems they were searching for one of our submarines, one of the Foxtrots. They are broadcasting this news over an open channel, in the clear. They have lost an aircraft carrier and some other ships."

"But how? What happened? Could it be an accident?" Khrushchev bounced to his feet, leaning forward. "It *must* be an accident! Or a mistake? They're lying to us!"

The Defense Minister shook his broad, gray head. "It is possibly a mistake. But I can see no reason why they would want to lie to us on a matter as critical as this. I fear that the submarine captain may have used his....special weapon."

It was the same explanation, the only explanation, that had immediately percolated up through the Chairman's own fearful imagination.

"But—I didn't want this to happen!" declared Khrushchev, feeling sick to his stomach. He slumped back into his chair, suddenly drained of all feeling, all vitality. "It was not part of the plan!"

"No it was not, Comrade Chairman," Malinovsky replied lugubriously. "I didn't want it to happen either." He grunted, the sound a mixture of disgust, despair, and Russian fatalism.

"It seems that it was not our decision to make."

The story will continue in:

Final Failure
Tactical Air Command

Pre-Crisis Timeline

1 January 1959: Fidel Castro's rebel forces enter Havana, Cuba, and sweep the government of dictator Fulgencio "Juan" Batista from power. Fidel has not declared himself a communist, but his brother Raul is known to be a follower of the party, and his famous lieutenant, Ernesto "Che" Guevera, is well-known as a Maoist revolutionary.

17 May 1960: An American U2 spyplane is shot down over the USSR by an SA-2 surface to air missile. Pilot Francis Gary Powers is captured and subsequently revealed as a prisoner by the Soviets after the Americans had denied the existence of the aircraft. A planned summit meeting between Soviet Chairman Nikita Khrushchev and President Eisenhower collapses, as the Russian leader vents his outrage and a frustrated Ike is humiliated in the court of world opinion.

3 January 1961: The United States breaks diplomatic relations with Cuba as Castro's government leans increasingly toward the Communist Bloc. Many Cubans have been executed by the new regime, and thousands more have fled to the United States over the ninety-mile sea passage of the Florida Strait.

20 January 1961: President John F. Kennedy takes the oath of office in Washington D.C. and gives a memorable inauguration speech, declaring: "Ask not what your country can do for you; ask what you can do for your country." Although JFK campaigned on closing the "missile gap" widely perceived to exist between the U.S. and the Soviet Union, he quickly learns that the gap is a fictional product of Khrushchev's boasts. In fact, the U.S. has a much more robust and modern nuclear arsenal than does the USSR.

20 April 1961: A CIA-planned and –controlled invasion of Cuba ends in disaster at the Bay of Pigs, as every one of the exiled Cubans in the landing force is quickly killed or captured by Castro's army. President Kennedy refuses to commit United States naval and air forces to the doomed fight, and accepts responsibility for the debacle.

4 June 1961: An apparently ailing President Kennedy takes a verbal pounding from Chairman Khrushchev at the Vienna Summit as the two sides cannot agree on the status of Berlin, where hundreds of East German citizens are fleeing the Communist world in favor of the thriving economies of the Western democracies. "It's going to be a cold winter," the President warns.

13 August 1961: The Soviets and East Germans, acting without warning in the course of one night, seal the east/west border in the city of Berlin with troops and barbed wire. Over the next months, the Communists build a wall to make that divide permanent, as tensions between both superpowers continue to rise.

4 February 1962: President Kennedy announces a total embargo on Cuban imports; Castro denounces "American aggression."

11 September 1962: The Kremlin warns that any U.S. attack against Cuba would "lead to nuclear war." They assure the world that the only military aid the USSR is providing to Cuba is "purely defensive" in nature.

Author's Note

Historians widely recognize the Cuban Missile Crisis as the most dangerous point of the Cold War—that is, the moment when full-scale nuclear war came closest to erupting. This assessment has represented conventional wisdom for a very long time, since well before the fall of Soviet communism in 1989-90. However, since that fall and the subsequent release of Soviet sources about the confrontation, as well as improved access to American sources as security classifications have eased, a new understanding of the crisis suggests that the situation was even more dangerous than the American public imagined at the time.

Neither Kennedy nor Khrushchev wanted a nuclear war to erupt. Once the two leaders clearly understood the risks, they both took firm steps to back away from the edge. The biggest risk of an initial nuclear detonation, however, was never something that was under the absolute control of the leaders on either side. Both nations had hundreds of nuclear weapons that could be employed under the authority of relatively low-level military officers.

Not only did the Soviets have a nuclear-armed torpedo on each of the four submarines they dispatched to support the Cuban operation, but they also had a whole host of tactical (i.e. "battlefield") nukes on Cuba. There is no reason to expect these weapons would not have been used if the Soviet and Cuban forces on Cuba had been subject to ground attack. And such an attack was very much desired by a great many Americans, military and civilian.

The Americans, meanwhile, had placed such reliance on nuclear weaponry that they even equipped some fighter aircraft with air-to-air missiles equipped with a nuclear warhead. (This is a weapon designed to shoot down a *single* enemy aircraft!) Further, the two generals most tightly woven into the command procedures of Strategic Air Command, General Thomas Power and General Curtis LeMay, were both firm and vocal advocates of an overwhelming U.S. first strike against the USSR.

Though they undoubtedly chafed at the restrictions placed on them by civilian leadership, there is no record of either Air Force general, nor of any other U.S. military commander, seeking to act outside of the chain of command during the crisis. However, if that chain of command had been seriously compromised, the responsibility for the employment of the U.S. nuclear arsenal would, by design, have fallen to LeMay or Power. There is no way to know what would have happened, but there is evidence—in the generals' own words—of what they wanted to do.

Writers, naturally, are free to speculate, and alternate history, by its nature, is speculative storytelling. However, I have tried to base my speculations on things that not only *could* have happened, but, arguably, *almost* happened. To that end, I have consulted as many sources as I could find. My information on the military forces that the Soviets sent to Cuba, as well as the American forces poised to respond, is as accurate as I could make it.

I would like to point to a couple of short cuts I've taken, mainly for the sake of the story and readability. First, although nearly all the ExComm discussions were taped, and in the last decade those recordings have been released to researchers and the public, I did not try to craft my scenes using the actual statements made by each ExComm member during the crisis. Instead, I made an honest attempt to create fast-moving dialogue that represented these men's opinions, even though the words are mine. (Those were very long meetings, and it took a great deal of discussion before any consensus was reached.)

Also, the ExComm meetings often included as many as 18-20 men (every attendee was male, this being 1962) and I streamlined the cast of characters down to a manageable number. Nikita Khrushchev likewise had a larger circle of advisers than the book represents; I combined several historical figures to create the opinions and points of view espoused in this book by Foreign Minister Gromyko and Defense Minister Malinovksy.

When it came to the designations of various items of military equipment, I used the NATO/American designations, even when writing from the Russian perspective. The SS4 "Sandal" rocket, for example, was the R-12 rocket to the Soviets. I have characters from both sides refer to it as the SS4, because I judged that would make it easier for the average reader to keep track of what was what.

Many of the characters in the book were real, historical figures. Others, including the Widener family, Lt. Colonel Tukov, Bob Morris, Second Lieutenant Greg Hartley, and Ron Pickett, are my creations and have been placed where their respective points of view can help tell the story. It is my hope that the resulting tale is compelling and interesting on its own merit, but that it also serves as a cautionary tale of how quickly and catastrophically events can spin beyond the control of even the most powerful of leaders.

For additional details, and updates regarding upcoming books in the *Final Failure* series, please visit douglasniles.com or facebook.com/AuthorDouglasNiles.

Acknowledgements

I have had the pleasure of writing three alternate history military thrillers with my longtime collaborator Michael S. Dobson. Some years ago, we conceived of *Final Failure* together, intending it to be another jointly written book. However, due to the vagaries of the modern publishing industry, that project languished and eventually died. When I had the opportunity to pursue it as the sole author, Michael graciously agreed to let me take the idea and develop it into what has now become a series of novels. Michael and I together came up with many of the fundamental ideas that drive the *Final Failure* narrative. As always, I am grateful for his friendship, generosity, and creativity.

My sister Allison Weber and her colleague, Lourdes Zenea, provided good advice on the correct usage of Cuban Spanish in the parts of the novel where I have used a few short snippets of *Español* to enhance verisimilitude. Their guidance is much appreciated, and any errors that have remained in the text are my responsibility alone.

My good friend and colleague, Lester Smith, has created Popcorn Press as—among other things—a vehicle to help writers get worthwhile projects published and made available to readers. Lester has shown a very heartening belief in this story since he first heard about it, and I am very grateful for the work that he has done in seeing that the book finally gets exposed to the light of day.

Katheryn Smith did a marvelous job putting together the cover design for *Eyeball to Eyeball*. Thank you, Kate, for making this book look as good as it does!

My fellow members of the Alliterates Writing Society (alliterates.com) have, as always, been supportive and encouraging—and constructively critical—of my work on every step of the way. The whole group, which is spread across the U.S., has offered critique and commentary via our online communications. The Alliterates of the Wisconsin chapter have allowed me to read selections from the book at our meetings and have been willing to brainstorm and counsel me about this book and the whole evolving process of book publishing as our industry moves forward into a new era.

Finally, I could never have pulled this book together without the support, both moral and material, of my fantastic wife, Christine. She has been with me for every step of my career, and has given me her love and encouragement even when things looked very bleak. Words cannot convey how much she has meant to me.

Selected Bibliography

A lot has been written about the Cuban Missile Crisis, and I am grateful to the many authors whose work made writing this novel so much easier, and the end result so much more thoroughly grounded in real facts. I employed numerous Internet sources and other articles as well, but the books listed below formed the bedrock of my research.

I would recommend these first two books in particular to any reader who wants to be immersed in the actual history of the crisis. Both provide hour-by-hour (and sometimes minute-by-minute) breakdowns of the key elements of the Cuban Missile Crisis, as well as precise details on the orders of battle of the respective sides, and the capabilities of weapons and equipment:

Dobbs, Michael, *One Minute to Midnight: Kennedy, Khrushchev, and Castro on the Brink of Nuclear War.* New York: Alfred A. Knopf, 2008

Polmar, Norman, and John D. Gresham, *DEFCON – 2: Standing on the Brink of Nuclear War During the Cuban Missile Crisis.* New Jersey: John Wiley and Sons, Inc., 2006

The following books also provided much useful information on the crisis, and on the lives of many of the important people who shaped it.

Anderson, Jon Lee, *Che Guevera: A Revolutionary Life.* New York: Grove Press, 2010

Carlson, Peter, *K Blows Top: A Cold War Interlude Starring Nikita Khrushchev, America's Most Unlikely Tourist.* New York: Public Affairs, 2009

Dallek, Robert, *An Unfinished Life: John F. Kennedy 1917-1963.* Boston: Little, Brown and Company, 2003

Dallek, Robert and Terry Golway, *Let Every Nation Know: John F. Kennedy in his own words.* Naperville IL: Sourcebooks, Inc., 2006

Erikson, Daniel P. *The Cuba Wars: Fidel Castro, The United States, and the Next Revolution.* New York: Bloomsbury Press, 2008

Freedman, Lawrence, *Kennedy's Wars: Berlin, Cuba, Laos and Vietnam.* New York: Oxford University Press, 2000

Fursenko, Aleksandr, and Timothy Naftali, *"One Hell of a Gamble": The Secret History of the Cuban Missile Crisis,* New York: W. W. Norton and Company, 1997

May, Ernest R. and Philip D. Zelikow (editors,) *The Kennedy Tapes: Inside the White House During the Cuban Missile Crisis.* Cambridge, MA: The Belknap Press of Harvard University Press, 1997

Quirk, Robert E., *Fidel Castro.* New York: W. W. Norton and Company, 1993

Stern, Sheldon M., *The Week the World Stood Still: Inside the Secret Cuban Missile Crisis.* Stanford, CA: Stanford University Press, 2005

Taubman, William, *Khrushchev: The Man and his Era.* New York: W.W. Norton and Company, 2003

About the Author

Douglas Niles has written more than forty novels in the areas of alternate history, fantasy, and science fiction. He has written extensively for the shared worlds of TSR Inc, (now Wizards of the Coast), notably in the *Dragonlance* and *Forgotten Realms* series. Niles has created two unique fantasy worlds, *Watershed* and *Seven Circles*, in trilogies published by Ace. Writing with Michael Dobson, he has coauthored three WW2 alternate history novels published by Tor/Forge.

Doug Niles has also written a full-length book and dozens of articles on nonfiction topics, ranging from technology and politics to military history. His expertise in American military history has led to projects analyzing all of America's wars. He is an award-winning strategy game designer, having created more than a hundred role-playing and wargames.

Niles is a former teacher who left that profession only because he had a chance to make a living while playing at his twin hobbies of writing and gaming. He lives in the countryside of Wisconsin with his wife (his two children having grown up and moved out) and two large dogs.

1657130R00140

Made in the USA
San Bernardino, CA
12 January 2013

The **Evolution** of **Me**
From Trial to Triumph Through Breast Cancer

Anastasia R. Stevenson

ISBN 978-1-0980-8225-3 (paperback)
ISBN 978-1-0980-8290-1 (hardcover)
ISBN 978-1-0980-8226-0 (digital)

Christian Faith Publishing, Inc.
832 Park Avenue
Meadville, PA 16335
www.christianfaithpublishing.com

Cover photos by Charisma Photography, Christina Ahlheim

Printed in the United States of America